THE VIKING'S HEART

Jacqueline Navin

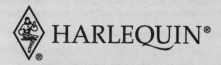

HARLEQUIN®

TORONTO • NEW YORK • LONDON
AMSTERDAM • PARIS • SYDNEY • HAMBURG
STOCKHOLM • ATHENS • TOKYO • MILAN • MADRID
PRAGUE • WARSAW • BUDAPEST • AUCKLAND

ISBN 0-373-29115-9

THE VIKING'S HEART

Visit us at www.eHarlequin.com

Printed in U.S.A.

Available from Harlequin Historicals and
JACQUELINE NAVIN

The Maiden and the Warrior #403
The Flower and the Sword #428
A Rose at Midnight #447
Strathmere's Bride #479
*One Christmas Night #487
The Viking's Heart #515

*In-line Christmas Collection

Please address questions and book requests to:
Harlequin Reader Service
U.S.: 3010 Walden Ave., P.O. Box 1325, Buffalo, NY 14269
Canadian: P.O. Box 609, Fort Erie, Ont. L2A 5X3

This is dedicated to Mick.
Does it ever get old when I keep saying, "Thanks"?

Chapter One

The woman who lay upon the cushions of the gently swaying litter was asleep. Beside her, a slumbering maid snored softly into the still air as if even in sleep she could not stand to be silent. Outside, the steady clatter of horses' hooves, the occasional deep drone of a man's voice, the clang of armaments jostling as their bearers traveled over rough terrain all blended together and filled the air with a busy, hushed din that was somehow soothing. It was this and the rocking motion that had lulled the lovely young woman after three days and nights of anxiety-filled wakefulness.

Her eyes flew open and she sat up.

The dream had come again.

Glancing about, she blinked until sleep released its hold and she recognized where she was. A sigh that was more resignation than relief stole some of her tension as she lay back again and placed a limp wrist over her forehead to push the wisps of golden curls away.

As horrid as her sleep had been, the world unchanged upon waking was no better. They were set to end this day at Gastonbury, the fortress home of her cousin's husband.

Gastonbury. She shivered. She had heard tell of Lucien de Montregnier, a dark and fearsome lord who had conquered the lands in a sweeping campaign of vengeance and taken her cousin, Alayna of Avenford, to wife. The thought of such a man, mingled with her other fears, set her to nibbling on her fingernail.

In truth, it was not so much Gastonbury, or even its fierce lord, that sparked her dread as what lay *after* the visit to her kinswoman. Berendsfore Manor. Sir Robert, and her one, greatest fear.

Which brought to mind her dream. Or was it a memory? She never really knew for certain, and the wondering preoccupied her to madness.

It had begun, as it so often did, with the deceptively mild realization that she was in her bed at Hallscroft, her home since she was a child. In the dream, she was but a girl of ten and two. She could detect the soft smell of rain and wood fires that wafted in through the window. A band of moonlight fell across the pale carpet of rushes. It was so real, she often wondered upon waking how it was that each sensation had felt so vibrant, each perception clear and acute.

When the woman entered, she was only a shadow, but her scent was familiar and beloved. Soft contentment drifted over her at the woman's presence. The faint touch of fingertips at her brow, then along her cheek, felt like cool silk.

"Beautiful Rosamund," the woman whispered, and Rosamund reveled in her mother's love.

Then she spoke again and the words that came

across the years, borne upon the wings of memory and given breath in the netherworld of sleep, were just beyond Rosamund's comprehension. She saw her mother's lips move, heard sounds come forth, but could not understand.

Her mother stood and turned, her profile jarring. The protrusion of her belly was evident now, with the moonlight behind her. Her slender, delicate mother thus encumbered had been strange and somehow disturbing to Rosamund, as though she had known at the advent of her mother's pregnancy that the visible advances in the woman's condition would bring them both closer to loss.

Going to the window, her mother had spread her arms. She set herself adrift on the air. She was flying. The world fell away, and Rosamund knew this was no beautiful soaring of the falcon. Her mother's hair, so like Rosamund's own, floated and she smiled, turning her face away from the tormented visage of her little daughter and into the death before her.

Rosamund screamed, but no sound came forth. No tears came though she wanted to weep. She reached for her mother but her limbs refused to obey her will.

She always awakened with a bilious sob caught in her throat.

The wretched dream came often these days to haunt her with its truths and lies, fed by the terror of her own fearful destiny.

She was hot. Sweat glistened on her brow and made her hands clammy. The draperies of the litter were drawn against the dust of the road, blocking out the cool breezes that heralded the waning of summer. The air was so thick in the dim interior of the horse-drawn conveyance, she could scarcely breathe. She smoothed the pale blue material of her surcoat absently.

"Up ahead," someone outside called, and the litter slowed.

"What? Who? Have we arrived?" Hilde inquired, opening her eyes. "Is this Gastonbury?" The maid stretched out her toes, extending her chubby legs in front of her. "I am starving. No doubt your cousin shall have a great repast for your reception." She all but clapped her hands together and rubbed.

"How can you think of eating?" Rosamund's irritability went unnoticed. Of course, no one would heed if she were screaming like a madwoman and tearing at her hair.

"Oh!" Hilde cried as they lurched forward. Branches ruffled the curtains on either side of them, poking through the slits as if sticking their heads in for a brief greeting.

"It must be a narrow part of the road, or a pass," Rosamund explained. She hid her growing tension.

The litter drew to a stop.

"What is it?" Hilde wondered, pulling back a corner of the draperies.

Rosamund peered over her shoulder. "Nothing out there. Only trees, Hilde, as we have seen every day."

Then a dark realization came over her. The sounds. The men talking, the movement of the horses—they had ceased altogether.

"Mayhap we have come upon some barrier," Rosamund suggested brightly to fight the threat that seemed to pulse in the very air. "An unforged stream, possibly. Or a bridge toll to be paid."

All at once, shouts came—sharp, harsh. Urgent. The driver seated above them called a command to the horses as he whipped the team forward. The two women were tossed back onto the velvet cushions as the conveyance quickly accelerated.

Behind them, the clash of steel against steel signaled they were under attack.

"God's breath, Hilde, what—?" The question was cut off as they flew over a rut at breakneck speed. They were tossed into the air for a moment, then down together with a painful clash of limbs.

"Oh, Lord. Oh, Lord. Oh, Lord." Hilde began the prayer as she wound her thick arms about her mistress. Rosamund was not averse to the comfort of the embrace, although she had to push mightily against Hilde's clinging fingers to allow herself to breathe properly. The maid flung a leg over her, as if she were prepared to climb up onto Rosamund's lap.

The litter picked up speed.

"Hold on to the sides, for God's sake," Rosamund called to Hilde over the clatter of the wheels.

"Oh, Lord. Oh, Lord," Hilde continued.

"Hilde!" Rosamund choked as the maid's grip tightened.

One shake of the head—meaning Hilde was not about to release her hold on Rosamund—was all the answer she received. They rounded a bend and, if not for the white-knuckle grip Rosamund had on the frame of the conveyance, the pair of them would have tumbled out the side.

The thunder of horse's hooves next to them set Rosamund's teeth on edge and caused Hilde to bury her face in her lady's neck.

"Hilde, please. I cannot move. I want to see what is happening."

"Would it comfort you to see the faces of our murderers?"

"Aye!" Rosamund shouted, and gave her companion a great shove. Once clear of the weight, she flicked back the draperies. In an instant, she drew them closed once again.

"What, mistress?" Hilde asked hysterically. "What did you see?"

Rosamund's eyes cast about the small space as if an armory of weapons would suddenly be discovered in her hour of need. "There are not enough of them. Hilde, I am afraid…"

She did not need to finish. Her stated fears would be obvious to the servant and very similar, as well.

There was a loud crash over their heads, as if something large and heavy had hit the roof. Hilde screamed, "We are boarded!"

"Shush," she commanded, cocking her head to listen.

"They are fighting!"

"Shh!"

The carriage took a dip in the road with a bone-jarring crunch, settling Hilde back to curling against her mistress's side. Rosamund began to pray. Her lips moved rapidly over the Paternoster, then the Ave Maria.

They rode hard, faster and farther. The heavy clatter of the wheels jostling them along the beaten dirt path filled their ears—that and the muted thump and crash of the struggle up in the driver's box. Suddenly that, too, stopped.

The litter was brought to a standstill.

Hilde peeked up from Rosamund's tear-soaked bosom. "Is…is it done? Are we safe, mistress?"

"I know not." Rosamund barely breathed the words.

There was the sound of someone landing on the ground from above them, then the soft crunch of footfalls.

Hilde made a soft squeak of terror. "My lady…"

The curtain lifted, exposing the two of them to the man who stood beside the carriage. Rosamund got a glimpse of a leather tunic, a hard, dark-complected face and cap of tight curls upon which sat a jaunty red hat with a hawk's feather stuck into it.

Beside her, Hilde let loose a brain-scrambling scream and fainted, falling limp across Rosamund's lap.

Chapter Two

In the nearby castle of Gastonbury two men circled each other on the lists of the lower ward, crouched, tensed, weapons drawn and at the ready. The dark one held a sword in one hand, a shorter weapon in the other. Across from him, the blond man brandished a Viking broadsword in both fists. His body moved lightly despite the massive breadth of his shoulders and his great height. His controlled movements were a match for the pantherlike stalking of his slightly shorter opponent. Sweat trickled down from his forehead and into his eyes. He dashed it away with a quick swipe of his arm.

Off in the corner, a trio of beauties giggled.

"Perhaps you would like a hair ribbon to tie back your lovely locks," the dark one taunted. "I am certain any of those lusty wenches would be happy to offer one of theirs."

The huge blond man only snarled, showing his teeth to be even and very white. Another man might have flinched, but his adversary only chuckled.

The dark man moved quickly. Their blades came

together with a ring of steel. A single spark flared for an instant.

The blond man tossed his head. "You used that move before. Are you getting tired, or bored?"

"Shut up, you cursed Viking," the dark man growled. "Have you something better to offer?"

"Do not force me to shame you before your villeins, Lucien."

Again the beauties tittered. Lucien scowled. The Viking grinned.

"I should think you would wish to take more care not to goad my temper."

"I do not fear it," the Viking assured him.

Lucien moved, launching his body directly at his opponent's midsection while bringing his sword up from the other side. With no room to maneuver, the Viking could only strike a short blow aimed at Lucien's gut. Lucien saw it and brought his left hand down to the thick wrists, numbing the other's grip.

The great broadsword fell. Before the clang of it hitting the hard-packed earth died out, the Viking took a step back and retrieved from his belt a weighted net. He laughed as he swung it back and forth. "I am just as deadly without my sword."

"We shall see," Lucien said. No sooner had he uttered the words than he found himself down in the dirt. Jabbing with the shorter weapon, he wrapped it around the net and yanked it out of the other man's hand. He pulled the Viking off balance and felled him.

"A draw?" the Viking asked, flat on his back.

Lucien's top lip curled in a sneer. "Never." He scrambled to his knees, both hands wrapped around the hilt of his short sword, his eyes locked with the

Nordic blue of the Viking's as he raised it high. The larger man stayed on his back until the last moment. Then he reared up. The sword came a hair breadth from slicing into his side.

Lucien was suddenly furious. "Sweet Jesu, Agravar, why did you move? Did you see how close that was? It could have struck you."

The Viking shook his head. "If the blow had been aimed to kill, the twist would have caused it to glance off my side. Since you meant no harm, it had the opposite result."

With that blithe explanation, he planted a booted foot on Lucien's chest and tossed him on his back. In a flash, he was over him, the same short sword Lucien had wielded against Agravar only a moment ago now pressed into the flesh of his neck. "Yield," he demanded with a smile.

"Bastard!" Lucien swore.

"True enough," Agravar said, withdrawing the weapon and standing. The trio of giggling nymphs waved. He turned his back on them with a grimace.

Beside him, Lucien stood and brushed himself off. "'Twas only luck you had this day."

"Luck is the fruit of skill and preparation."

Not a gracious loser, his friend and liege lord glared at him. "I set you on your arse last time."

"And I laid you low the time before that. As I recall, you were spitting out dirt until supper." He was distracted by a familiar form coming from the direction of the keep. "Pelly!" he hailed.

"Captain," the young knight answered, bowing first to him. To Lucien, he executed a similar motion. "My lord. My lady has bid me ask if you had forgotten your promise to ride into the village and escort her cousin's party to the castle.''

"Damn, I *had* forgotten." Lucien swept a hand through his hair and gave Agravar an enigmatic glance. "Was she...did she seem...upset?"

Poor Pelly looked stricken. He glanced at Agravar for reassurance. "Never mind, boy," Agravar said, giving him a slap on the shoulder that knocked the slight-framed youth forward a few steps. "We know the mistress's temper is short these last days of her confinement.''

Lucien let loose a string of expletives and stalked off. Rolling his eyes, Agravar dismissed Pelly and retrieved his weapon from the dust. As he followed Lucien off the training field, the three women smiled and nudged each other, casting flirtatious glances his way.

In the stables, Lucien was working up a fine temper. "Why do you not simply bed those wenches and give us some peace?"

"All at once or one at a time?" Agravar asked innocently.

"It makes no difference to me as long as they cease their annoying simpering."

"You shall have to get used to it because they do not interest me."

Lucien grumbled something intelligible.

"Is my lady in good health?" Agravar asked with studied nonchalance. "I have noticed your normally disagreeable nature even more trying of late."

Lucien gave one shake of his head. "Agravar, by the blood of Christ and all that is holy, the woman is more precious to me than my own life, but I fear I will go mad before this babe is brought into the world. She is not herself. Never content, fickle to the extreme, and apt to spring into tears at the slightest frustration of her whims. She is fast becoming a tyrant.''

"She will be restored when the babe is born," Agravar said blandly. He was a great admirer of the Lady Alayna and knew her to be a gentle lady with a heart as fierce as her husband's, but never petty. And though Agravar could understand his friend's impatience at Alayna's uncharacteristic moodiness, he had no tolerance for any complaint Lucien might make.

For, as Agravar knew, the kindness of the Fates was fickle. Lucien had been gifted with the miracle of a peerless love. It was something the Viking had never known in any form. And he had, at the advanced age of thirty and four, resigned himself to the disappointment that he never would.

These thoughts kept him in sour company as he threw the saddle over his destrier and tightened the cinch. When Lucien spoke, his voice was barely a whisper. "I cannot think straight until she is delivered safely of the babe. Her restlessness...it has given me a bad premonition. I am...I..." He bowed his head.

Chagrined, Agravar said nothing to his friend's mangled confession. He had been thinking Lucien consumed with self-pity when it had been worry that tore at him.

Recovering quickly, Lucien asked, "Tell me where you learned that maneuver you used back there? It might be useful, if one is unlucky—or unskilled—enough to find oneself on one's back in battle.''

"I learned it from the gypsies." To Lucien's incredulous look, Agravar shrugged as they mounted their horses and kicked them into action. "I gather techniques wherever I can."

Lucien grunted, pointing up ahead. "Pass yonder, Agravar. As we speak of techniques to be tried, it has reminded me that I had the smithy forge finer, lighter weapons from the steel I had imported from Spain. I am told it is far superior to our domestic blends."

"Impossible," Agravar scoffed, but he was happy to oblige the change of direction when he noticed the three women lying in wait who would be avoided by a diversion to the forge.

"Garron!" Lucien called, and the smithy shuffled out to see to his lord's bidding. "Show my captain the new swords you have fashioned."

"Oh, lovely beauties, they are, sir," Garron exclaimed, fetching one of the blades.

Despite himself, Agravar was impressed. The weapon was sleek and quick, cutting through the air like a whisper. "I doubt it would cleave a man in two as deftly as this," he said, tapping the heavy broadsword resting at his hip. "But it feels extraordinarily clever in one's hand, almost as if it has a life of its own." He passed it to Lucien, who made a few swipes with it and gave it back.

Untouched in Lucien's scabbard was his father's sword. There was no question of him relinquishing that blade, even for an exceptional weapon. It was a symbol of what he had come back from hell to recover, along with his lands, his life, his soul.

That quest had given Agravar something to believe in for the first time in his lost, uncharted life. He had become Lucien's right arm. Good God, he had even committed one of the most heinous acts known to mankind in order to save the friend he counted as brother.

But now, in this time of peace, he would gladly trade his bloodletting broadsword for this delicate instrument, a weapon as elegant as the soft, peaceful life it bespoke. Aye, he'd once told Lucien he'd be content to mount his weapons upon the walls as monuments to his bloody past, and it was true enough.

True enough.

"I shall test the weapon," Agravar said. Tossing his broadsword to the smithy, he ordered, "Give it a good sharpening while I test this and I'll tell you what I think of this new steel."

The soldiers took the short but roughly cut route through the woods as they were dreadfully late. Lucien, anxious not to further upset his disgruntled wife, had assured Alayna that he and his men would beat a quick path to see her cousin escorted from the edges of his lands to inside the castle gates.

They were just about to clear a scruffy copse into a meadow when, to their astonishment, two riders appeared, a man and a woman, cutting across to disappear into the woods.

"Strange," Lucien said in a low voice.

Agravar exchanged glances with him. Then a sound from behind caught their attention. Twisting in his saddle, Agravar listened. Was that weeping?

Casting a glance back at the two riders, he saw they were at the other end of the meadow, just entering the forest that extended all the way to the north road.

"Out for a ride, do you think?"

"Probably." Lucien squinted. "But I do not recognize them. Of course, it is some distance."

"We should make certain. I shall go after them," Agravar said with a nod in the direction where the riders had disappeared. "You best take the others and investigate that caterwauling."

Lucien scowled at having drawn this duty, but he pulled his destrier around as Agravar kicked his into action and raced across the meadow.

Chapter Three

Agravar came upon them at the stream by Fenman's forge. He spotted a flash of color through the trees. They had stopped, perhaps watering the horses. Reining his destrier, he slid onto the ground and crept up on foot, staying close to the thicket. Quietly, he unsheathed the new sword from his scabbard and held it low lest some of the sunlight filtering in through the canopy catch the steel.

They were just ahead, the man and woman. She was bent over by the stream. Her hair, the color of dark honey strewn with sunlight, was loose and thick, left unbound in the maidenly fashion. Her face, in profile, was striking in its clean lines—straight nose, strong chin, generous mouth and deep-set eyes under a delicate pale brow.

A noblewoman. Could this be Rosamund Clavier? Agravar wondered, for she was no one he had seen before in these lands. If so, what had happened to her traveling party? And who was this man with her?

The man in question watched the woods as the woman bent over the shallow waters to ladle water with her cupped hands. He wore a jaunty red hat with a ridiculous plume stuck in it. It appeared he was nervous, but he allowed her to linger long enough for Agravar to move closer.

"Come," the man said, touching the woman on the arm. "We must make haste." When she didn't respond, he said more insistently, "Lady Rosamund."

Her head snapped up. She stood. And Agravar stood.

First he caught her eyes, bright, rounded orbs of pale honey brown. Agravar cleared three long steps before anyone moved. Raising his weapon, he crept up behind the man in the red hat. That one finally realized someone was coming up behind him and whirled about.

"Step away. I am Agravar the Viking and have come to fetch the lady to safety."

The look of horror on Rosamund's face, her single, reflexive step backward as if in recoil, stung him. He was used to people reacting to his Nordic looks, his size, his heavily muscled frame, but the stark fear in those grave eyes slipped under his defenses like a stiletto wheedling inside the links of mail.

His gaze snapped back to her companion, who had drawn his sword. Agravar raised his own blade to meet the challenge and issue a silent threat. The damnable thing felt like a feather. Agravar wished for the comfort of his old familiar broadsword.

He spoke. "Be reasonable, wretch. You cannot hope to best me. Your ransom is lost, if that was your aim."

The man with the ridiculous headgear advanced nonetheless, holding his weapon in front of him as if it were a cross wielded to ward off evil spirits. "You'll not take her whilst I stand."

"Fool—the game is lost."

The man's dark eyes glittered. "I will not leave behind my gain, sir!"

But the gain left without him. The lady in question whirled in a gentle swirl of hair and skirts and fled without a sound.

Agravar decided he had tarried long enough with this nonsense. He struck. The jab of his weapon was lightning quick but lacking in substance. Unused to the lighter weight, he felt off balance, cursing under his breath. Mentally correcting for the difference, his next try made more of a threat as it sliced a neat little gash across the man's tunic.

The man brought the hilt of his dagger down in an unskilled move, hoping only to deflect the blow. A strange sound split the air as the fine, gleaming steel—imported from Spain for its superior quality—snapped off!

It fell into the dirt with an inauspicious ping. Amazed, Agravar held up the hilt and its paltry stub of steel.

"You broke my sword," he bellowed in an accusing voice.

The man seemed horrified to see what he had done. "Sir, I am sorry. I—"

He said no more, for Agravar took advantage of his consternation to close the gap between them in two quick strides and lay a crushing blow to the man's jaw. His red hat flew off in one direction, the feather in the other, and the brave fool crumpled into a heap.

Agravar shoved his embarrassingly damaged weapon into his belt and set off after the woman.

If she reached the horses, she might have a chance, Rosamund thought, hiking her skirts up and running as hard as she could. Not since she was a child, romping in the forests of Hallscroft with the peasant children from the nearby farms, had she pushed her body this hard.

She would never outrun that terrifying Viking. The thought pushed her harder, her legs pumped faster. The horses—if she made it to them, freedom was hers.

The need to know if he was behind her was hard to resist, but she was not about to lose one precious second in glancing back. Wait! She skidded, caught her balance and turned. This was not the way to the horses. This path didn't look familiar at all. She circled again, panic rising.

A loud, splintering crash sounded from up on her right, where a slight ridge ran parallel to the path she had just come down. Whirling, she saw him as he leaped into the air, his face grim, teeth bared in a bone-chilling snarl that drained the blood out of her body in a single heartbeat. His hair streamed out behind him, pale and shiny, catching dappled sunlight and throwing it back into the forest.

She was so shocked she didn't think to get out of his way. He landed in front of her, squarely on two feet, but his momentum carried him into her. His hands clutched her waist as they fell, twisting them both so that when they struck the loamy turf, it was he who landed on his back. She fell on top of him, cushioned nicely on his great chest.

He let out a sound that was half grunt, half sigh as the hard ground and her slight weight compressed his mighty form from either side. His arms held her, but loosely. She waited only a moment to catch her breath before pushing herself up and away.

The thick arms tightened immediately, making her struggles impossible. But her hands were free. They struck something solid and cold, giving her an idea. Stilling her body's movements, she stretched out her fingers, grazing their tips against her boon. Nimbly she worked her hand forward and closed her grip.

He rolled, bringing her under him. She found herself trapped by his arms on either side of her and the broad-shouldered mass of him overhead. As neatly caged as a prisoner, she peered up at the face that hovered only inches from hers.

"Are you the Lady Rosamund Clavier?"

His voice was deep, and at this proximity, the rich tone reverberated throughout her whole body. He smelled vaguely of sweat and a faint hint of soap, perhaps from his shave, for his chin and cheeks were bare.

She nodded, not wanting to try her voice.

"I am sent by your cousin, the Lady Alayna. Be easy, my lady, for I mean you no harm. If I allow you up, will you listen to what I have to say?"

Again she bobbed her head.

He hauled himself up, moving quickly and with surprising agility for one so large. She slipped her hand behind the long panel of her surcoat as she climbed slowly to her knees and then to her feet, her back to him.

"Lady Rosamund, I—"

In one giddy, unpracticed motion, she whirled and

brought up what she thought was his dagger in both her hands. "Let me be!" she cried, and jabbed the weapon out at him in a threatening gesture meant to ward him off.

The broken-off hilt of a blade was displayed before her.

Her eyes fastened on it, then shifted to his face. He was watching her with dancing eyes. They were very blue, like a cold north sea. Perhaps that was just her fanciful association from the knowledge that he was a Viking.

"And exactly what do you intend to do to me with that?"

She blinked rapidly, trying to think. "It is more weapon than any you can claim," she said bravely.

"And what makes you think I am in need of a weapon, my gentle woman?" A blur caught the corner of her eye. And then her hand hurt. She looked at it to see what could be causing the pain and was amazed to find it empty.

"Now we are evenly matched," he said, stepping forward.

"How can you think so? You are twice my size." She fell back a few paces. He advanced again, closing the gap and then some.

"I would guess three times or more, but what difference does it make when you possess such cunning?"

"What will you do with me?"

"Nothing worse than rescue you, my lady."

"Ha! You think I will come easily under that pretty lie?"

A great shoulder lifted and fell. "It matters not,

for I'll have the result either way, although it would be less of a bother if you would cooperate."

His steady advance, and her retreat, had backed her against a log. It caught under her knees and she stumbled. In a trice, he was beside her, his hands at her waist to steady her and pull her upright.

"Safety, my lady," he said, and his tone was completely changed from the sharp admonishment of only a moment ago.

His touch was unbearably hot, encompassing part of her back and the side of her hip in one broad palm. His breath fanned down against her cheek, whispering across her flesh and making her shiver...from terror, she thought.

"Please do not touch me." It was a soft, ineffectual plea.

But he complied. He dropped his hands and stepped away. "Will you come willingly with me, or shall I fling you over my shoulder and bear you like a sack of grain to Gastonbury?"

"You are taking me to Gastonbury?" she asked.

"First I must gather your companion and your horses, then find your guard and my other men, but we should clear the castle walls before darkness."

At her quiet consideration of this news, he asked, "Does that not reassure you, my lady, that what I have pledged is true? 'Tis not harm I intend you, but deliverance to the safety of your cousin's care."

She thought good and long before replying, considering her options, and the possibilities. "Aye, sir. You have my trust."

By his dubious expression, she could see he was not completely reassured.

And well he should not be, she reflected as she followed his lead.

Chapter Four

With the highwayman slung over one horse, Rosamund seated on another and Agravar in the lead, they came to the clearing just east of the stream.

Other men were assembled, Rosamund saw; both her soldiers and presumably Gastonbury's. A great welcome went up at their arrival. A man approached the Viking and he dismounted. She heard the name Agravar. The Viking's name, she supposed. Yes, he had said it before. Agravar.

The man who approached looked like a demon, with a wild mane of dark hair and eyes that were almost black. He turned to Rosamund and she tensed, causing her horse to shy.

The Viking—Agravar—was beside her in a flash, grabbing the reins and steadying the beast. "Come, this is your cousin's husband."

This was the legendary Lucien de Montregnier! He stood beside the Viking and nodded. "I know you have had a trying adventure. We shall rest and refresh ourselves before setting out for home. My wife will be anxious to see you." He ran his hand through his hair and tried to smile. He was almost handsome when he did so. "And I would be grateful if your nerves were made calmer before we resume your journey, else I be taken to task as it was my tardiness that was at fault."

"Aye, of course," she said. Agravar helped her dismount. His nearness was as disconcerting as it had been before. She wriggled away from him once her feet touched the ground. His hands fell to his sides.

A screech split the air and Hilde came charging toward Rosamund from the other side of the glen, arms outflung, skirts flying. Rosamund braced herself.

"You are safe, ah, praise the saints and the sweet Lord in heaven!" Slamming into her mistress, Hilde squeezed until tiny pinpoints of light began to dance on the periphery of Rosamund's vision.

"Hilde," she choked, pushing the woman away. Hilde pulled back, took another look at her and swept her to her bosom for a second strangling clinch.

"Come," Agravar said, wrapping strong fingers about Rosamund's arm. He managed to get her away from the effusive maid without a struggle, mostly because the woman gaped at him with a mixture of awe and terror that made her grip go lax. As polite as any courtier, Agravar led Rosamund to a good-sized rock. "Take your rest while the men water the horses. It will be but a moment to prepare them for the short ride back to the castle."

Rosamund kept her eyes averted, fighting a flush of shame at his surprisingly gentle attentions. She stared at his boots and gave a perfunctory nod. The boots turned and she lifted her gaze, watching him walk back to the horses and untether his prisoner.

The man with the red hat—that affectation now

stuffed unceremoniously into the top of one battered boot—was awake now. As he was led to the opposite side of the glade, just along the edge of the brush that formed a semicircle behind them, she saw his eyes were on her and they blazed bright and vigilant.

She lowered her lashes again, thinking fast. After a while, she said to Hilde, who was engaged in a manic monologue about the dreadful events that day, "I am thirsting. Please fetch me a tankard of water."

"Yes, my lady. Oh, certainly, my good lady. How happy I shall be to do it, my sweet, safe lady."

Agravar gave his report to Lucien as Lady Rosamund's guards were rounded up, their wounds seen to as best as could be arranged before they got to the castle. Agravar overheard one of them saying, "The man had me down. He could have slain me, but he rode on."

Stopping, he inquired, "Do you claim these bandits showed mercy?"

"Not to me," another, older man grumbled, showing three stubs where the fingers had been severed. "Dicky here was lucky enough to get a young one. You get 'em young, an' they don' have the taste of blood yet."

Thinking of the single member of the bandits they had managed to capture, Agravar asked, "What is the significance of that ridiculous hat? Did others wear one?"

"Nah. He's the only one I saw, bloody cur," the grizzled soldier said, turning his head to spit, as if to illustrate his opinion of the whole lot of them. "The rest of them scattered, like they knew these woods."

Agravar frowned. "Local thieves."

A woman's voice—an annoyingly familiar woman's voice—startled Agravar. "Oh, Lord, she's taken again. Ah! He's got her!"

Muttering a curse under his breath, Agravar turned to Hilde. "What is the matter now, woman?" he demanded.

"My lady! She's gone again, and him as well— the bandit. Fine ones you are at protection when an innocent lamb gets stolen out from under your very noses. He took her, I say. They're gone!"

"God's breath!" Agravar swore. "That woman has proved to be a great deal of trouble this day. Lucien! She is missing again."

Hilde leaped up and hung on to his arm, holding him as steadfast as an anchor. "Oh, no, sirrah! She is the most darling, sweet child, she is."

The woman clutched so desperately as she regaled him with the many virtues of the Lady Rosamund, Agravar feared he might be forced to strike her to disengage himself. He did finally manage to get away without resorting to such measures. The woman's plaintive wails followed him as he trotted up to his men.

"Pelly, go see to that servant," he ordered, ignoring the other knight's sudden pallor. "Put the guard on alert. The rest of you, with me!"

Swinging up into his saddle, he paused and nodded to Lucien, who himself was already mounted. "A-Viking," he said. It was their old war cry.

Lucien nodded, yanking his horse around to follow. "A-Viking," he agreed.

Agravar and the others raced into the woods.

* * *

The man in the red hat veered down into a gully, ducking under a tight weave of low-lying shrubs. Behind him, Rosamund plunged, hissing in pain as tiny branches tore at her hair and the delicate wrists exposed by the trailing sleeves of her dress.

"Here, my lady," he said, reining in his steed to point the way. "The meeting place is up beyond the ridge. I arranged it just after we separated for escape. The others shall be waiting there." He paused. "At least, they should be. I paid them well enough."

Rosamund drew her horse up beside him, taking note of the path to which he pointed. When she saw him pitch forward slightly and put his hand to his brow, she reached out a solicitous hand to his shoulder, "Davey, are you well?"

He shook his head as if attempting to rid himself of a cobweb in his brain. "That cursed Viking knocked me but good. My head's a thick one, I was always told, but it'd have to be made of iron to withstand that mighty fist." He shot a sheepish grin at her. "Come to think of it, 'twas my lord, your brother, what told me that most times."

"Then it must have been true, for Harold never lied."

Davey tried to laugh, but it turned into a wince instead and he pressed his fingers hard against his temple. "Come. It will not be long until they find we are gone. You have earned us one slim chance at escape, though I do not know if it was brave or foolish. Let us not waste it in conversation."

"I couldn't let them hold you, not when you have done so much for me."

He looked at her with adoring eyes. "All that and more, I do gladly."

Noises behind them spurred them into action. They came out of the gorge and began climbing a ravine.

Rosamund's heart began to pound heavily with excitement. Almost there! The top of the ravine was just ahead. Once they cleared it, they would be out of sight. She was thinking they were actually going to succeed when Davey fell off the horse and rolled back down into the fertile gully.

She reared her mount when she turned it too sharply, but was luckily not unseated. She raced down to Davey's side and slid off the horse.

He was dazed. Whether from this recent tumble or still scrambled from Agravar's blow, it was difficult to tell. He pushed away her frantic hands. "Go without me. Go! This is your only chance."

"No, Davey. Come, please. That Viking beast will kill you if he catches up with us." But as she helped him to his feet, she saw he was in no condition to outrun a band of trained soldiers—two, for her own guard would be on them as well as the men from Gastonbury. With a sinking feeling, she knew they were outmatched.

It was over. There would be no freedom for her.

The daring escape, cleverly disguised to seem an abduction, had seemed a brilliant inspiration. Now it seemed merely desperate and not inspired at all. A folly to cost a dear friend's life, for Davey, who had been her only companion through her years of solitude after her brother had died, would almost certainly be killed.

That made her decision easy. "What—?" Davey murmured, for he was slipping into confusion again as she helped him into the saddle and lashed his hands around the horse's neck with the reins. Giving the beast's hindquarters a strong whack, she watched as man and horse disappeared into the brush, still verdant in these late days of summer.

He would find his way out of the woods later. For now, he need only be hidden. As for herself, her independence would have to wait another day.

She began to run, this time back the way they had just come, in the direction of the soldiers.

It might be of helpful effect if she were to scream, she thought, trying to imagine how Hilde would do it and set about in a fair imitation of the chubby maid's hysterics.

In a trice, they found her. De Montregnier arrived and was about to dismount when he was eclipsed by the massive Viking. Agravar swung his leg over his horse's head, dropping to the ground by her side before the huge beast had come to a full stop.

His gaze raked her from head to toe. It was all she could do not to flinch from his searching eyes. His closeness made her feel trapped. Could he suspect she was false, she wondered, or was that merely conscience pricking her?

She drew in a shaky breath. "The man…he was taking me away when he fell into the water, on the cliff path that runs along the river." She was hopeful her very real anxiety would help her appear convincing. "The current took him. It was horrible. I saw him only for a moment, and then he and his horse went under, never to reappear." She shut her eyes and feigned a shiver. "I was afraid I would fall as well, so I dismounted and ran back here."

She had seen such a place on their way, and thus knew it was a feasible tale she told. There was a

pregnant moment while she waited to find out if they
would find it so.

Lucien said, "We will watch for the body to wash
up when the tide comes in. Let us go home. It is a
long enough day without dredging a river." .

Rosamund bit her lips to keep from crying out in
relief. Davey was safe, she thought. But she was as
cursed as when she had started this dreadful journey.

She made no protest as a strong pair of hands en-
folded her, lifting her up as if she were but a babe
being borne in a father's arms. A soft voice instructed her to put her leg here, the other there, and
she found herself astride a horse. A very tall horse.
Looking down, the ground seemed dizzyingly far-off.
Then the saddle jerked as the one who had carried
her to this lofty perch swung up beside her. She knew
who it was. She remembered his scent and recognized the muscled arms with a fine feathering of fair
hair upon them. They came around either side of her
to take up the reins. She knew the voice as it called
out the command to proceed homeward.

She was in the arms of the Viking, and she began
to tremble.

It was a curious thing to have a woman in the
saddle with him, Agravar thought. A curious and new
thing. He had never shared a saddle like this before.

Not unpleasant, no, and yet by the time Gastonbury's walls came into sight, his nerves hung in
shreds.

There was her perfume. It was a blend he was not
used to. It made him slightly light-headed. And the
way her rounded bottom rested . neatly against his
thighs, which drove him to distraction. Her long legs

dangled on one side, tucked neatly under his. Her hair tickled his nose when the wind caught it. It was soft and curly, like spun gold.

He scoffed at such poetic thoughts, then bent his head slightly and inhaled. Mayhap he was growing used to the scent of her, for the pleasant aroma did not make his head swim too much this time.

"How far is the castle?" she asked.

"Just up ahead. 'Twas lucky you were so close when the bandits struck, else we never would have reached you in time."

There was a long pause. "Lord Lucien seemed concerned as to the welfare of my cousin. Is she ill?"

"Not ill, no. Just beside herself with worry at your delay, and will be quite upset, I'll wager, when she learns of what occurred."

"Are these dangerous lands?"

"They are some of the safest you will find in England, but what place is completely impervious to evil?"

"Evil abounds everywhere, sometimes even in those we trust."

It was such a strange utterance, and so soberly spoken. "It can be true," he agreed.

"Oh, it is true," she said, then fell silent.

Lucien rode up to them after a while. "You do not seem the worse for your trials, Lady Rosamund. We shall offer you comfort and rest soon enough inside the walls of our keep, and therein my lady wife shall be glad to welcome you."

Agravar felt her tense, saw her glance down and away, her only response an incomprehensible mutter he could not hear. He exchanged a look with his friend, and as Lucien was not well-known for his facility or tact with the fairer sex, he quickly kicked his destrier to move on past them.

"Has my lord and liege displeased you?" Agravar asked gently.

Her blond head shot up, almost striking him in his chin. "Nay. I...I am sorry. Did I seem unpleasant to him, do you think?"

"Rest easy, my lady. Lucien doesn't know what insult is—his hide is too thick to feel anything less than full assault."

"Then I have not angered him, do you think? Oh, bother. I shall try to make it up to him when next we speak."

Agravar was disconcerted by her anxiety. Lucien's reputation was of a formidable warrior, it was true, but there was no reason for a maid to fear him as much as she seemed to.

The mystery deepened when Gastonbury came into view—pale yellow sandstone walls spread in a swath across the meadows under a cerulean sky. Yet, at its first sight, Rosamund stiffened and Agravar would swear he heard a soft, mewling sound from her, like a soft cry of fear.

"Gastonbury," he said softly into her ear.

"Yes," she whispered in a rusty voice.

Was this the same woman who had brandished his own weapon—albeit a maimed one—against him? How was it she was so suddenly cowed and almost unrecognizable from the defiant little virago he had met in the wood?

Stranger still was how her intriguing blend of courage and fear affected him. He found himself fighting not to tighten his grip, to draw her up against him, shield her in a way he didn't fully understand.

It was a pleasant feeling, somehow, but it was a wanting as well.

It was then he remembered why Lady Rosamund had come.

She was here for a short visit, no more, on her way to Berendsfore Manor, home of the distinguished knight, Sir Robert of Berendsfore, where she was to become the good man's bride.

And so he said nothing, did nothing to indicate he had even noticed her strange, pained tensions as they drew nearer to his home.

Chapter Five

Once they were through the castle gates, the group bypassed the stables and headed directly to the upper ward. The comforts of the hall beckoned. The men were tired and hungry and there were servants who would see to the horses.

Rosamund was bone weary, bedraggled, caked with mud and covered in dust from riding in the open. She was heartsick. And deep down, she was terrified.

Taken out of her thoughts by the sound of her name being called, she saw a beautiful woman rushing toward her. Agravar dismounted and his large, capable hands lifted her down.

"Rosamund, welcome," the woman said. "I am your cousin, Alayna." Rosamund turned to her, unexpectedly finding herself in an embrace.

The momentary closeness brought a shock. Alayna was heavy with child, her rounded belly unmistakable as it pressed against the slim lines of Rosamund's own body. Rosamund froze, a cold strike of shock slicing straight down her spine.

Her mother in silhouette, her ripe form swelling

*before her. Her hands laid over it, folded, as if to
protect the wee life within. Turning now to Rosamund, her lips parting as she said...*

Alayna held her out at arm's length with a smile
ready, then frowned. "What has happened? Was
there some mishap?"

Thank goodness, Alayna was in no way similar to
Rosamund's mother's ethereal golden beauty. This
woman was strong featured, with dark hair and blue
eyes. The lack of resemblance brought Rosamund
back to herself quickly.

"Some highwaymen, I am afraid," Rosamund
supplied in a voice still a tad shaky in reaction. "We
had a chase. Or two."

Alayna's eyes widened. "Lucien, how did this
happen?" she demanded, whirling to face her husband, who had come up behind them.

A tiny tick showed at his temple as he ground his
teeth together. "We shall discuss this later. *Privately.*"

Rosamund's heart skipped a beat at the low sound
of the warning in his voice. "All is well, cousin,"
she said, placing a restraining hand on Alayna's
shoulder.

Alayna ignored the plea in Rosamund's tone. "Did
I not ask you to ride this day to the edge of your
lands to see my cousin safe? Did you not promise
you would?"

"'Tis my fault," Agravar said, coming to his
lord's side.

"Oh, hush, you overgrown Viking. My husband
hardly needs you to defend him."

Rosamund covered her mouth to keep from crying

out in alarm. But Agravar only tucked his chin to his chest. She noticed his shoulders were shaking.

"Well?" Alayna demanded, once again facing Lucien.

"I did forget my promise, Alayna." The words were nearly choked, as if they cost him much to say. Rosamund's heart raced as she waited for the explosion to come. Yet, he continued, apparently remorseful. "Forgive me." He paused and then nearly growled. *"Please."*

"I want to hear what happened before I grant my pardon. Honestly, Lucien. Do you think I make idle requests...ah!" Placing her hand over her belly, she stopped.

Lucien turned pale and was upon her in a flash. "What is it? Is it the pains? Oh, Jesu! Pelly, call the apothecary! Call the midwife!"

Alayna slapped him away. "Nay, nay, you madman, stop hovering over me. 'Tis only a twinge. You shall not escape the questioning I have planned for you. Come." She whirled and moved with ponderous steps toward the studded oaken portal to the hall.

Lucien raked his hand through his hair a few times and glared after her with a murderous scowl. Softly, and to no one in particular, he muttered, "More likely 'tis the gibbet you'll have me dangling from if the whim suits you."

Rosamund cringed at his angry words. She nearly fainted with alarm when Alayna whirled and narrowed her eyes at her disgruntled husband. "Did you say something, Lucien?"

"Nothing of import," Lucien called back. Casting a dark look about that dared anyone to snicker, he fell into stride behind the stately lady.

"Come, Lady Rosamund," a soft voice said at her side. She recognized it as Agravar's.

"Will he beat her?" Rosamund cried, whirling to face him. She forgot herself enough to place a hand against his massive chest.

He appeared taken aback. "Beat her?"

"Oh, please stop him—" She snapped her mouth shut when she saw the look on his face. "She meant no harm," she finished lamely.

"Rosamund, Lord Lucien would never lift a hand against his lady wife. She is beloved to him. Why, he would cut off his right arm for her. He would never do anything to cause her the slightest pain."

Wrapping her arms about herself, she turned her face away from him. She was suddenly chilled.

He didn't know. He didn't understand. No one had known about Cyrus, either.

She could never make him see. "I would like to freshen up," she murmured.

"Go with Margaret. She will show you where Alayna has arranged for you to sleep. I shall see you at supper, Rosamund."

"Aye." She almost said thank you, then thought better of it. He had robbed her of freedom and delivered her to this, the next step closer to a dreaded destiny. She had little to thank him for.

She followed the servant he had indicated. As she passed a small gathering of women, she caught one—a buxom lass with hollows under her cheekbones and a bright head of pale hair spilling about her shoulders—staring at her. With a hand on one jutting hip, she regarded Rosamund over her shoulder with a sneer curled on her bee-stung lips.

One of the two others with whom she was standing

said something and there was a chorus of laughter. The woman smiled coldly and turned around with an arrogant sniff.

"My lady, this way," Margaret said politely.

"Oh, aye." Dutifully, Rosamund fell into step.

Lady Veronica of Avenford, an older, slightly shorter, and perhaps less spectacular version of her daughter Alayna, smoothed the last of Rosamund's garments and handed it to Hilde to place in the trunk. "There," she pronounced with a flash of a smile. "Everything seems to be in order. After all of that jostling, they just needed to be refolded and laid again."

"It is kind of you to help," Rosamund replied.

Hilde said, "I'll take out your green gown for you to wear to supper."

It was Veronica who replied, "Nay, Hilde. She is to rest this night. Was a difficult day for your mistress, and you, I imagine. Let her have her supper on a tray in here, and then you both can find your rest early."

Rosamund drifted to the window. "You need not trouble yourself, Hilde. I am not very hungry."

"Go fetch it," Veronica said in a tone that was gentle but commanding. Hilde—who had a tendency to be bossy herself and was never docile—shocked Rosamund when she muttered, "Yes, my lady," and scurried out the door.

Veronica had a manner about her, Rosamund considered. One simply didn't disobey her. "Rosamund, come here. You are restless."

"My thoughts disturb me," Rosamund admitted. She sat in the seat indicated.

"I know it has been a trying day," Veronica said. "Your maid is busy with setting your clothing to rights and fetching your supper. Let me brush your hair for you and you will be ready all the earlier for bed."

On the small table, Hilde had set out her silver brush and a matched set of pearl-encrusted combs. Veronica picked up the brush and admired it. "Lovely," she commented, then came behind Rosamund and began to stroke her hair.

"'Twas a gift from my stepfather," Rosamund said stiffly.

"Ah. It must be a beloved memento."

Rosamund did not reply.

After a while, Veronica chuckled softly. "I hope my daughter has not given you a poor view of our home here at Gastonbury."

"Alayna? Why ever would that be so?"

"She is not herself. Lucien is worried sick over it. Oh, he would never admit it, but he fears for her. I can see it in his eyes, the anxious way he watches her. And she makes it not one whit easier with her disposition so sour and her reasoning utterly gone. Bless him, he tolerates much. Even Alayna knows it, yet she says she cannot stop herself from some of the most obnoxious fits of temper I have ever witnessed. And I am her mother!"

They laughed together, then Rosamund asked, "Are you worried about her?"

"Aye. Nay. Oh, I suppose. A mother always worries, but I know 'tis merely the heat and the heavy weight of the babe that makes her cross. 'Twas not like this with the others. This is the third, you know. I have a grandson who you will espy running around the keep. And then there is the pretty little angel who just coos the sweetest song. Bah! What a foolish woman I am to go on so.''

''Nay, my lady. 'Tis pleasant to hear the pride and delight in your voice.''

''You indulge an old woman.''

''''Tis not true. 'Tis I who benefit from your great kindnesses, and I am grateful for your attentions.''

''If my daughter were feeling better, she would be seeing to you and trying to comfort you after your terrible day. I know she feels dreadfully responsible.''

''Nay, my lady, she must not. I cast no blame.''

''Lucien has sent word to Lord Robert. He wishes you to stay with us until we receive a reply.''

''Oh.'' The mention of Robert of Berendsfore set Rosamund's pulse thumping a bit harder.

Veronica twisted the dark blond tresses into a thick braid and fastened the end with a leather thong. ''There, now I shall leave you to your supper and your rest.''

''Thank you, good lady.''

Veronica smiled down at her, touching her slim hand to Rosamund's cheek. A look of uncertainty passed over her features, then was gone. ''Rest,'' she said with a renewed pleasantness.

''I shall.''

''And *eat!*'' she called over her shoulder.

Rosamund laughed despite her distractions. ''I shall try.''

The darkness was absolute when she awoke, panting and sweating from the dream. Her mother falling…

She shook her head, refusing the wispy ghost of memory. Sitting up, she pushed her hair out of her eyes. Tendrils had sneaked out of the braid and stuck to the thin sheen of sweat along her brow and cheeks.

At the washstand was fresh water and a towel for the morning. She wet the linen and rubbed it over her face and neck, down her arms, until gooseflesh pricked her skin.

The night was warm but there was a sweet breeze, and now that she had cooled herself down, it was quite pleasant. She wrapped a sheet about her and went to the window, pulling up a small stool so that she could lean out and listen to the night sounds. The pleasant chorus soothed her. She folded her arms on the windowsill and rested her chin on her crossed wrists.

The dream was gone now, but she was wakeful and troubled. She thought of Alayna, who had been so upset on Rosamund's behalf. Alayna's mother, the Lady Veronica, had also touched Rosamund's heart with her kindness and solicitude. In some ways she reminded Rosamund of her own mother. There was nothing overtly similar save those things common to all mothers. The phrases they are apt to say, a look, a smile—all full of nurturing warmth.

Rosamund thought of Lucien and his terrible scowls, and Agravar and the surprising gentleness of his hands when they had touched her.

She wondered where Davey was, and when he would find her. And she wondered what she would do if he did not.

Chapter Six

There was a break in the heat, and the denizens of Gastonbury came forth from the shuttered dark coolness of the castle where they had dwelled in exhausted and sweltering stillness for the past fortnight. A large tent was spread out in the meadow just outside the curtain wall. Alayna brought her small children to play there, under the fond regard of her mother and the silent companionship of her cousin.

The outing was treated with all the celebration of a high feast day. Veronica, Alayna and Rosamund reclined on cushions under the canopy, the men lounged nearby. Couples wandered off together, or gathered under shade trees for more intimate conversation. Spirits were high and musicians played gentle, lilting music, which drifted on the refreshing breeze to mingle with laughter.

"Margaret, sing us a song!" a man cried out.

"My lady?" Margaret asked her mistress, eager to comply with her admirer's request.

Alayna nodded. Despite the lessening in the heat, she still seemed rather wan. "Yes, go ahead."

Margaret scrambled up off the cushions to stand

primly beside a grinning lyre player. She muttered something and he began to strum.

Her song was lovely. Rosamund smiled and closed her eyes, leaning back against the soft pallet upon which she reclined and let the peace of the day seep into her.

"She sings like a lark," Veronica whispered in her ear. "But the chit is insufferably vain about it."

Another voice, harsher, brimming with violence, spoke from somewhere deep in Rosamund's memory. *Vain harlot!*

Her eyes flew open and locked with the steady, placid orbs of her companion. Veronica smiled and the flash dissipated, leaving only the steady thud of her heart pounding in her ears. Then that steadied as well.

She made some reply and they fell silent again.

Rosamund rubbed her temple. Sometimes she feared madness. But the pain was fleeting, like a streak of lightning that is brilliant and stark in the darkened sky, filling the watcher with awe and terror, but when its brief moment of glory is spent, so is its threat. All it leaves behind is the strange scent that curls one's nostrils and the dread that it could happen again and that harm might not be avoided.

Her past was like that.

"Rosamund?"

"Aye? Oh, aye, my lady."

"Are you unwell?"

"Nay. Not at all."

Forcing a smile, she lifted her gaze and attended the song. But her feelings of disquiet returned. She caught Agravar's eyes on her. That Viking seemed always to be watching her with more than passing interest in his eyes.

The knowledge terrified her and thrilled her at the same time, the latter of which she understood not at all. She looked away, feeling an overwhelming self-consciousness all of a sudden, as if that white-hot gaze could see inside her. And know all her secrets…

A wicked whack on her shin brought her out of her thoughts in a snap. She yelped, "Ah!"

Young Aric de Montregnier, who was four years old, stood before her with wide eyes and gaping mouth. His was the panic-stricken face of a child who knows he has gone too far.

"Uh-oh," he said simply.

"Aric!" Alayna exclaimed.

"I am sorry! I am sorry!" Alayna's son exclaimed. "I did not mean it, Mother. I was fighting the infidels. Bryan was Saladin and I King Richard and I missed and—"

"Lucien," Alayna said calmly, slipping the wooden sword out of her son's hand, "have you been telling Aric tales of the Crusades?"

Lucien managed to look wary and stern at the same time as he sputtered some sounds that were neither denials nor confirmation.

Looking at Aric, Rosamund had never seen so small a face beset with such misery and she was overcome with sympathy. The poor lad had simply gotten carried away with his game, and although she understood his mother's annoyance, the boy's gorgeous countenance undid her.

She found herself moving before she even thought. She came to her feet and put her arms around the boy. "Pardon the child, Alayna. Aric knows how I

love to play soldier.'' Aric looked up at her as if she
had sprouted horns from her brow. She continued,
''We both have a fascination for the great Crusades
and the grand adventures of the knights who under-
take the holy quest.''

The child knew lying when he heard it, but he had
also been taught to respect his elders. The resultant
turmoil—should he agree to her fibs or denounce her
for honesty's sake?—was apparent in his trembling
grimace. Rosamund had to smile, and stroked his
small cheek, touched by his distress. ''Oh, we have
never spoken of it, I admit, but kindred spirits know
these things about each other. And so Aric probably
knew I wouldn't mind playing his game with him.''

''You mustn't go about whacking ladies,'' Lucien
chided gently.

''Aye,'' Alayna added more emphatically.

''I shan't, Mother. I promise,'' came the solemn
vow. Aric cast a grateful glance up at his protectress.

''Very well. Come for your sword after a space,
and we will see if you can find better uses for it than
harassing our guests.''

Rosamund looked down as he nodded bravely, biting his lips to conceal his disappointment at losing
his toy for even this little while. She could not resist
a brush of her fingertips along his silky hair. Dark,
like his mother and father, and softly curled and feeling like silk.

She had not been around children often. She had
not thought to like them this much, nor to think of
the child she might bear someday. Not with this gentle longing, anyway. It had always been a bitter dread
that took hold of her when she anticipated an existence as a wife and mother.

Now she found this sprite's antics could make her smile, and there had been a curious impulse to hold his baby sister. Watching the infant Leanna totter about had put a near-physical ache into her arms.

Aric scampered off and as she watched him go, she saw Agravar coming for her. He gave a small bow. "A devotee of the Crusader knights, are you?" he asked.

"In truth, I know nothing about any Crusade or knight." She paused, considering. "Not true. I *have* heard of King Richard. But who was the other... Sanhedrin?"

His mouth twitched. "Saladin was Richard's great nemesis. A clever adversary and brilliant tactician, he kept our good king in check and safe from victory."

"You sound as if you are an admirer."

"That would be heresy, would it not? Therefore, I shall amend my opinion to say Saladin was a soulless infidel who had the devil on his side and therefore frustrates the righteous aims of our blessed monarch."

Despite her wariness, she was amused. "Rest assured, sirrah, I shall not denounce you."

He laid a hand over his chest. "A great relief." He indicated a spot next to where she had been sitting. "May I?"

"Of course," she replied, surprised that the prospect of conversing with him was not nearly as untenable as it should have seemed. They sat together.

She looked over at him, hiding her curiosity under her lashes. His angular features seemed sculpted out of granite. He seemed content to just sit, his leg drawn up, his elbow cocked on one knee, and watch the gathering in comfortable silence. A warrior angel, both golden and mighty, at rest.

She was curious about him. "You say 'our monarch,' yet you are a Dane, are you not?"

His head dipped a moment, then came back up. "I am English," he replied. It was the tightness in his voice that warned her off.

"Oh."

He seemed to regret his harshness after a moment. "My mother was an English lady."

"Oh."

"How do you find Gastonbury?" he inquired, taking a fresh tact.

"Pleasant."

He nodded, then fell quiet again.

She took in a long breath and expelled it slowly. Her fingers drummed idly on the blanketed ground. The silence stretched on.

"Why are you so nervous all the time?" he asked suddenly.

She started. "Nervous? Me? Why, I am not nervous."

He laughed, though not unkindly. "Aye, nervous. *You.* You are more skittish than an unbroken colt."

Her hand fluttered to her hair, smoothing and tucking in absent movements. "Mayhap you merely think I am because 'tis your nature to be suspicious."

"My lady, I have a most congenial nature. Not suspicious in the least. However, I *find* it most suspicious that you should think me so."

Her lips quirked. "Therefore you confirm my opinion, and admit you are suspicious."

He opened his mouth, frowned in puzzlement, and then shut it again. "'Tis a silly conversation."

"Then let us end it."

"Aye."

It wasn't long before she demanded, "Why do you always stare at me?"

He grinned without even glancing at her. "Your great beauty, of course."

"But I am not a great beauty, sirrah."

He looked at her then, rather critically and with intense eyes as his gaze slid over her features. "Are you not? Perhaps you underestimate yourself."

"No troubadours shall sing verse to my face, I think. Homage like that is deserving of beauty such as Alayna's."

"And yet I have observed that kind of attractiveness can be as much a curse as a blessing. There are other kinds of allure a woman can posses. Mystery, for example."

Her heart lurched. *Mystery!* "How absurd. What mysteries can a woman have?"

"I would say a great deal."

"We are not allowed mysteries, sirrah." She could not help a touch of bitterness from entering her voice.

"Allowed? What do you mean?"

"Why, we have no rights, no choices. We are at the mercy of our men."

"All the more reason for your hearts to be held in secret," he observed blandly.

"Secrets, aye," she conceded. "We women have many secrets. But you used the term *mystery*, and that denotes a secret that would be of interest or consequence. I fear that our secrets are of little meaning to men. They are simply our own, and matter only to us."

"How tragic to hear you say so. And I think your

new friend, the Lady Veronica, would chastise you
sorely for such sentiments. She would give you a
different view of woman's attributes, and a much
fairer one, I'd wager.''

"You disagree with me? How odd, when we seem
to be of a like mind in so many other things."

"My lady," he said with a slow grin, "I would
be the last man on this good earth who would profess
even the most meager wisdom of women."

"You must have some knowledge." Her tone was
sly.

"None."

"Then why do those three women yonder keep
staring at you?"

He started. She saw she had him off guard, and a
playful urge asserted itself. "Is it that one of them is
your woman? If she is, will you please go to her so
that I will be spared the daggers shooting from her
eyes."

He seemed deeply displeased at this. At first,
Rosamund thought it was she who had angered him
so well, but he turned his scowl to the trio of blondes
whispering behind their hands. They immediately adjusted themselves, thrusting out their chests and donning alluring smiles.

Agravar made some sort of sound. Kind of a
growl. "Those idiots plague me."

With feigned innocence, she asked, "Then they
are not beloved to you?"

He appeared appalled. "Damnation, they are not,
I tell you."

She wanted to giggle in delight. This huge hulk of
a man was *embarrassed*. "You need not be awkward
if you are of a mind for a romance, sirrah. Why, I

would think any one of them would be willing to entertain your attentions, seeing as they are always smiling this way."

He rubbed his chin roughly. "Aye, Rosamund, I know what it is they are willing to oblige me, and I have no interest in it. Now may we please quit the subject?"

"Very well. 'Tis of no matter to me, of course. 'Tis only they seemed so disturbed by your—"

"May we speak of something else, madam?"

She shrugged. "But, sirrah, we seem to have nothing else to say to one another."

He narrowed his eyes with ill intent. "Mayhap a return to our earlier topic of how you are more than you seem."

"I thought 'twas decided 'twas your suspicious nature that made it only appear so."

He grinned. "My lady, I might be persuaded to think you do tease me by the quick parries of your skilled tongue."

Skilled tongue—her? He had been more to the truth when he had called her skittish. At least, that was how she was used to seeing herself. However, she *was* matching wits with him, and doing a not altogether horrible job of it.

It was a satisfying realization. She began to relax and enjoy herself a bit more.

"I? I think not, sirrah. Your vanity is addling your brain."

The way the smile toyed with the edges of his mouth stirred a tiny flutter of excitement inside her. His was a broad mouth, and expressive, the only feature of softness in that hard, handsome face.

"Is it?" he said smoothly, leaning toward her a

little. "'Tis the first time I have been accused of such a vice as vanity. Pride, aye, that I have heard. Stubbornness—that seems to be one of my chief faults. But vanity…never before."

"You are an unusual man, indeed, to admit failings at all, let alone recount them with such ease. Men usually think themselves infallible."

"Nay, 'tis human I am, and all too ready to admit it. Yet, in fairness, may I also make mention of my assets. Chief among them is modesty. Naturally."

She couldn't suppress a laugh. "Naturally."

"And bravery. And then there is my great charm."

"Unquestionably."

The flash of his smile, the smooth sound of his laughter sent a jolt of pleasure through her. "I am possessed of other attributes, of course, but since I am so modest—as was mentioned before—I am forsworn to avoid bragging."

"Ah, what a shame."

"And how is it a shame, my lady?"

She tossed her head and smiled and realized with a start that she was actually *flirting*. "I was learning so much about you."

And then he stopped. He simply stopped. The smile faded in degrees and the crinkles in the corners of his eyes smoothed. His jaw tightened and began working. He glanced away.

What was wrong? What had happened?

"What inane conversation. We must have an abundance of idle time." He rose, dusting off his leggings and looking around, as if suddenly unsure. "I tarry too long." Then he left her.

Rosamund felt stripped. Confused, hurt, more than a bit angry, yet the most strongly felt emotion was an acute sense of loss. And questioning shame—had she said something amiss? Spoken wrongly? What *had* she done?

Only that she was learning much about him. But 'twas part of their game, a trivial folly that had been…it had been…something she had never felt before. It had been *fun*.

Of course it was silly and of course it was a bit inane. But it *was* fun, wasn't it?

Perhaps not for him. Perhaps, as always, she had gotten it wrong. Which was just as well, she supposed, because the whole matter was far more confusing than she had the energy for.

Gastonbury was proving to be a most disconcerting place. And yet, she could not long for the end of her stay, for the only deliverance she would have from this place would be to hell. Marriage.

Which was the same thing.

Chapter Seven

He was always watching her. Like fingers of pressure on her spine, the touch of his gaze was with her whenever she ventured out of her chamber. They talked on occasion—nothing consequential, nothing light and sparring like the day they had lounged together under the tent. But he watched her.

So when she spotted Davey sitting at one of the trestle tables one evening at supper, she knew she had to proceed very, very carefully.

Something was wrong with Rosamund Clavier. Agravar knew this for a certainty. Exactly what it was, he was not certain. But he was determined to find out.

Lord Robert had sent a message to say he would be journeying to Gastonbury himself to collect his bride. In the aftermath of his betrothed's ordeal, he wished to personally see to her well-being himself and offer his own guard as greater protection for her journey to her new home at Berendsfore.

Therefore, Agravar had little time to find out what it was that haunted the graceful lady with the sad eyes. He never bothered to examine why it was so devilishly important.

He just watched.

Then one night at supper, when she gave a furtive look about and exited the hallway into the turret stairs, he followed.

Stealth was not his forte. Brute strength was. He was light enough on his feet, however, to get into the turret without too much noise.

It was dark on the stairwell. And silent; he heard no footfalls. He began to climb, his palm sliding over the outer wall to guide him.

He heard her farther up the stairs. Following, he moved faster lest she evade him. The five turret stairs of the castle connected the different chambers and corridors of the three-story structure. This particular turret had doors that opened onto chambers used for the laundry, bedchambers, the sewing room, the ladies' solar and the topmost chamber sometimes used to house guests.

There was no reason he could think of why she would wish to go to any of these places at this time of day.

He could see her now, a form of dark gray among the shadows. She had heard his footsteps and was racing up the steps. His hands shot out and snatched her. Crying out, she wrenched against his grip.

Her scent assailed him. That perfume, he thought. What the devil was it, some enchanted scent?

His voice came out like gravel. ''Rosamund, 'tis me, Agravar.''

She twisted away. His hand slipped, sliding across her waist. Hissing in a startled breath, he felt how slender she was. Strong, yet fragile in his large hands.

Damn her perfume! His head was completely befuddled. His hands moved without him even thinking he wanted them to. Oh, he did want them to, but he shouldn't. He knew he mustn't. This was a lady. A betrothed lady, guest to his friend and lord, cousin to his lord's wife…ah, hell. He dipped his head giving in to impulse.

Her breath fanned against his cheek, rapid, ragged gasps. His own grew unsteady. He pulled her closer. A bold, conscious need stiffening him and defying his self-control, he pulled her closer still.

A remote part of him, some observer untouched by the searing presence of her willowy form so near to his, warned him. Honor. Aye. *Honor*. It was what defined him, the penultimate antithesis of what his hated father had been.

Honor.

She made a sound, a kind of whimper as if he might be hurting her. It was a small thing, but it gave an edge to reason and he let his grip go lax.

Stumbling, she scrambled up a few steps to a window slit. Grasping the sill, she gulped in the fresh air.

"You frightened me!" she said accusingly.

Her hair was nearly undone. Its combs hung loosely, still caught up in the tousled tendrils. Her cheeks were flushed.

He found he had to physically restrain himself from going to her side and putting his arms about those delicate shoulders. Asserting dominion over the impulse, he crossed his arms.

"Who did you think it was?"

"Why did you follow me?"

"You speak first."

"I thought…it could have been anyone."

The challenging spitfire from the other day was gone. Here again was the cringing waif. He said, "Surely you know you are safe. Who would harm you here in your cousin's home?"

She tucked her chin into her shoulder. "Do you think there are only certain places where evil can reign? It can enter anywhere. It resides in homes like this one, I can tell you."

"Are you an expert on evil, Rosamund?"

When she turned back to him, her eyes were a bit wild—large and round, lost in that pretty face. They startled him. So did her answer. "Aye. Of a sorts, I am."

He blinked, trying to absorb it, trying to think what it meant. In the end, he only held out his hand. "Come. Let us back to the hall."

She was so artless, so utterly transparent. Casting a look up the stairs, into the rising treads that disappeared into darkness where the weakening strains of daylight could not penetrate, she hesitated. "I… I thought I might roam a bit. Get to know the castle."

"What a poor liar you are."

Her head whipped around. She was all fire again. "What an insulting man you are! What reason have you to question me?"

What reason had he? Only that every inch of his flesh screamed with instinctive uncertainty whenever she was in sight, only that something deep down in his gut seemed somehow connected to this woman—a woman he had known but a sennight. Only that his soul spoke to him of her, and it told him disturbing things.

It was true he didn't seem to know what he was about when with her. But it was hardly seemly to tell her this, so he only smiled and shook his head. "I can take you on a tour. Shall we go to the top of the turret and see what we find?"

Suddenly she was all nerves again. "Nay. We have been overlong on these stairs. The air is stale. Let us to fresher areas. Perhaps outdoors."

"But I insist, my lady. You should not change your plans for me." He grabbed her hand and pulled her along up to the top of the tower. "We will go together to conquer the challenge of the turret."

She resisted a bit, but it did not impede their swift progress up the stairs. The small chamber at the top was empty.

"See," she said, but her voice trembled. "The air is close in here. 'Tis unhealthy. Let us to the garden, or better yet, the grove. 'Twill refresh us."

Agravar let his eyes travel about the small chamber, quickly assessing there was no place for anyone to hide.

What was he thinking? It was ridiculous to suspect Rosamund had been sneaking off to some kind of secret assignation. To what purpose? And who would she know here at Gastonbury whom she could not speak to out in the open?

And yet...

There were so many doors leading into the turret. The top chamber may not have been her destination at all. Or, perhaps, if there had been someone waiting, they could have easily slipped away without anyone the wiser.

She took his proffered arm stiffly and they descended the steps. Bypassing the hall entrance, they went down one flight farther and then out the doorway that led into a small enclosed yard.

The sun was low, stretching long, cool shadows that made the little area pleasant. Rows of vines clamored over one another, bare now of their spring fruit. Trees clustered in uneven groves laden with apples and pears. They stood hunched against the sun, weighted by their burdens, like sentinels to guard and protect.

'Twas only an illusion, he knew. At Gastonbury, *he* was the captain of the guard. *He* protected. If need be, even from unlikely threats in the form of shapely maidens with cascades of golden hair and eyes of soft, pale brown.

She moved idly, lost in her own thoughts. He trailed behind, keeping a seemly distance. His body still felt singed where he had brushed up against her on the stairs.

"The grove is cool," she stated.

"Aye." There was a pause. "'Tis pleasant."

She bowed her head, silent for a space. "Our grove at home was not so sheltered as this, and not nearly so comforting. I like it here."

"Do you mean the grove, or Gastonbury?"

"I like Gastonbury. I have found kindness here—in Alayna and her mother. The Lady Veronica is patient with me." Her hands fluttered, betraying her nervousness. "I shall hate to leave it."

The statement jarred him. He had nearly forgotten. Lord Robert would soon bring her to live with him at Berendsfore. A strange sensation of loss twinged the edges of his awareness.

She said, "Have you kin here at Gastonbury? You are not from Denmark, you told me."

"My brother lives in this castle."

"Brother? I have seen no other Vikings here."

"Yet you have met him. I do not think you are fond of him, however. 'Tis Lucien who I call brother, and he is the only family I acknowledge."

"No others?"

"None."

She paced off a few steps and lifted her head to the lurid sky. The colors of sunset cast her fair aspect in bronze. "I, too, am alone."

It was the last thing they said that night. They stayed together for a bit more before she wandered back inside. He remained until dusk had settled in full, and her words stayed with him.

Chapter Eight

Gastonbury must be a place of enchantment, Rosamund thought. It had done the impossible.

She had forgotten.

Life seemed to have been given to her anew and her past…her past was somehow irrelevant. Comfortable and safe this last fortnight, she hardly recognized herself any longer.

For the first time, she knew deep contentment and she was happy.

In the ladies' solar with Alayna one afternoon, she sat on the floor with Leanna, who was just shy of her second year and as placid and pleasant as her brother, Aric, was brash. Lucien and Alayna's second child was doted on by her parents, and was her grandmother's delight. Veronica sat on a cushioned chair, smiling indulgently as her granddaughter built tiny towers with the colored blocks Rosamund handed her.

"She is an angel," Veronica mused. "Though I am sure I do not know from where she gets it. Her mother was a handful, always tearing in my embroidery basket and unraveling my loom. She never sat still, not for an instant, that one. As for her father, I have little doubt he was a full-fledged terror.''

Rosamund stayed wisely silent. Her own opinion of Lucien was hardly flattering. The fearsome lord of Gastonbury's visage set her to quaking even now, a full month after being welcomed to his home.

Veronica continued, ''I shall have to ask his mother when next she visits. She comes every Easter, a week as uneasy as you are like to find in this castle. The rest of the year she spends in a convent.''

''How odd.'' Rosamund looked up at Veronica. ''Why is it she only comes for such a short time? Is she unpleasant?''

''Not at all. She is very polite, but a bit cold. When one understands her past, one can see why. She made many mistakes in her life. What a wretched fate it is to have to live with the fruits of one's labors when they are fraught with mistakes and folly. Ah, Rosamund, when you are old like she and I, and realize much of your life is behind you...sometimes it weighs heavy on you.''

Rosamund's brows rose. ''Surely you have no regrets, my lady.''

''Regrets? Nay, not exactly. Yet we all have things we would do differently. Say what was in our heart more often. Perhaps not have bothered with a quarrel.''

''You think of your husband. Do you still miss him?''

Veronica smiled slightly. ''Oh, aye. And I always shall. He was a great, great man. I loved him.'' She shook her head and let the matter drop.

''I lost a brother when I was ten. He took ill and passed away. And, of course, I shall always miss my mother," Rosamund said quietly. "'Tis a very sad thing to lose someone you love so much."

Veronica placed a comforting hand on her shoulder. "Of course 'tis so, child."

It was an invitation, such a gentle segue for Rosamund to confide in her. And strangely, Rosamund found she wanted to.

"I was only twelve when she died. The night it happened, she came into my room and sat by my bed. I was sleepy, not yet dreaming but not awake, either. I felt her hand on my brow, brushing away my hair as she often did. Her touch was always cool and soothing. She wished me pleasant dreams, just as she did every night. She said good-night." *And something else. Something she couldn't quite remember; didn't want to remember. It was always there in her dreams, the unknown...the threat of what she might recall if she thought long enough....*

"Rosamund, dear, do not speak of it if it troubles you."

"Nay, 'tis not difficult."

"Of course it is. But sometimes memories are like poisons in an old injury. They fester if we don't lance the wound. As painful as that is, it is the only way we can heal it."

Yes. It was like that. Poison inside, eating at her.

"She died from a fall from the ramparts. She must have gone up to gaze at the night sky. She sometimes did that, when her mind was restless. Somehow, she leaned too far out and fell." *Or was pushed.* Rosamund studied her hands, clasped together. The knuckles were white. "I do not suppose I will ever know what happened."

Liar.

"Poor child." Veronica leaned forward and clasped Rosamund's locked hands in hers, stroking them until the tension eased.

Rosamund bowed her head, fighting the tide of emotion. Her eyes were squeezed tight. Wetness spiked her lashes, making them hot against her cheeks. She could cry right now, if she would let herself. She could weep for ages.

She pulled her hands away with a deep, halting breath. "Thank you, my lady. You are kind to indulge me."

Veronica smiled, reaching out to touch her fingers to Rosamund's forehead, smoothing aside a twisted tendril. "You may find there are more words after these have settled. When they come, seek me out, child. Sit at my knee and I shall listen."

Rosamund only nodded. Leanna toppled another tower and the two of them turned their attention back to the pretty babe.

Lucien sat by the corner hearth in the hall, clutching a pewter cup in both his hands. Agravar sat on a stool, hunching toward the cold grate, his elbows on his knees, his hands dangling limp.

"You look like hell," Lucien said, and drank. "Did the trio of trollops finally get their hands on you?"

"Who? Oh, those three. God, is there no way you can banish them or something?"

"Can't do it. They've committed no crime. We've had common law in England for two kings now." He took another drink.

"Is Alayna in bad spirits?"

"She's...she's weeping. I have no idea why. I do

not think she has any idea why. I think..." He stopped, clenching his teeth until the tick showed in his temple. His next words were whispered. "Something is wrong, Agravar. She was never like this before. Something ails her and it goes beyond the babe inside her."

"The barber and the midwife have both pronounced her well, you told me so yourself."

"'Tis not right. I feel it."

"You are sounding like a mystic, Lucien. Next I will see you burning tallow and transmuting into ecstasy."

"You may yet, old friend. If I thought it would save her, I would paint myself red and dance naked upon the drawbridge."

"No need for that yet, I trust. The harvest is nigh, and with your villeins made ill after such a visual treat as that, the food will spoil in the fields."

It was a weak effort, but it got a ghost of a smile, anyway. "So I have an excuse for my wretched state. What of you? Have there been breaches over the curtain wall by Vandals that I am not aware of?"

"No Vandals." Agravar paused. But breaches had been made.

"How is that little ninny, my wife's cousin? Lord, the chit wears on my nerves. She is always looking at me as if I am a wolf about to devour her." He held up a staying hand. "And none of your comments about my looks—I have taken a care to be very kind to her." Glowering into his cup, he added, "I fear she is simple. And I am beginning to think it runs in the family."

"Alayna's maladies shall pass when the babe is safely birthed."

"Agravar, the first time someone tried to slay me, I was sixteen years old. They have been trying ever since—men twice my size and expertly skilled in battle. And still I sit here today. However, I do not know that I will survive *this*." He gave his friend a baleful glance. "Be grateful you have no woman to twist you up in knots, my friend. Aye, you are wise. Away with your conscience—tumble the three wenches who pant after you and be done with them. Then drink with your comrades at arms and be glad you own your own heart. 'Tis safest, I think, than to live in this wretched fear."

Agravar said nothing. He had lived a lifetime of brutal neglect and abuse, yet never had he heard words more cruel. Rising, he left Lucien to his drink and his self-pity and went to fetch himself a serving of the former to wash away the sour taste of the latter.

Chapter Nine

The man in the dung-brown monk's robes said, "My lady, the longer we delay, the worse are our chances of success."

"I disagree, Davey," Rosamund replied, pacing a tight path before him. "The longer I can pretend all is well, the less on guard they will be."

"But who can suspect you? There was no reason to doubt you were being abducted."

"All the more reason for us to take care. We have the element of secrecy with us. Thus, you are never to risk this foolishness again. Do not come to me unless I summon you. Many of Lord Lucien's soldiers saw you when you were captured, you know."

"They do not expect me to be sitting beside them in the hall." He smirked, waving his hand at his tonsure. "And I have sacrificed my locks to appear the harmless friar."

Rosamund shook her head. "That Viking will know. He sees everything, and he has the instincts of a cat."

Davey's eyes sharpened. "Has he been troubling you?"

"He watches me." A shiver rippled through her, an exquisite blend of heat and cold. "I try to avoid him as best I can, but he dogs my steps and asks far too many questions."

"You do not have to suffer him, he is not lord here. Simply command him to leave you alone. He is merely the captain. You must not allow him to bully you, my lady. You are a noble. He is not."

She gave a little laugh at his simplistic opinion. "Agravar the Viking is not so easily dismissed."

"You are too soft. 'Twas always your weakness."

"Please, let us not quarrel."

"Then please listen to me, my lady. We must get you away soon. There is a new moon a few days hence. The night will be black, giving us excellent cover. We can slip away to the river. I can have made arrangements for a boat—"

"Nay. No boat, no escaping in the night. Don't you see, Davey, they will have us back by supper the next day. My cousin's husband is legend. With that Viking with him, they are near invincible." She placed a hand on his arm to calm him. "We must not act rashly. We must be clever."

His look was fierce. "Then be clever, my lady. Find some way. What do you think Lord Cyrus will do when he finds there has been a delay in the marriage he so covets?"

That knocked the breath out of her. "I hadn't thought of that. What do you think he would do?"

"Lord Cyrus is not predictable, I am sorry to say. More the reason for us to make haste to see you away from his reach."

"Aye." The press of panic was like a weight against her chest.

"Lady Rosamund, I am yours to command. You need only tell me what I must do."

"Alas, I have no plan." She paused, swallowing hard against the knot in her throat. "I should be the craftiest of creatures. I spent years watching Cyrus. Surely observing the most vile being in all of Christendom should stand me in good stead. I shall put my mind to deception and give you an answer before too long." She locked her eyes with his and spoke with force. "I *will* not be married. And I will not go to Berendsfore, Davey."

Davey watched her, silent. When he spoke, his voice was edged with excitement. "I shall try as well to think of something. We must away as soon as possible."

"Aye." She looked about her, nervous. "We dare much."

"I shall leave you. Soon, my lady. I promise you. Soon."

He left the grove. She lingered a moment longer, recalling another night when a different man had tarried with her here.

Nay, she chided, forbidding herself such indulgences. She must leave Gastonbury, and all she had come to love. Alayna and her children, the Lady Veronica, who had seemed to instinctively sense Rosamund's need for a confidant.

And she would leave the Viking who had shown her, in their few brief encounters, that she might be different than what she was. That she might want something she had never thought to want.

Forever would she wonder if she could have, indeed, found a different self from the shy, cringing girl she had always been. Now, it seemed, she would never know.

Rosamund came to supper dressed in a dark gold surcoat over a cream kirtle sewn with bronze-colored thread. She looked breathtaking, Agravar thought, watching her every movement as she crossed the hall and came to the dais. She moved to the left to sit with the women, next to Veronica as she always did. But there was the glance, just a brief check in his direction before her gaze skittered away.

He made her nervous. This he understood, although it did not please him. He made many people nervous. It was his size, and his coloring that branded him Norse. He was used to this sort of reaction. At least, he told himself he was. Reason dictated he should be by now. Since childhood it had been so. It was not pleasant, but 'twas better than abhorrence, which he had seen in the eyes of a lady before, a particular lady whose affection he had craved above all others.

Mere aversion he could tolerate. He told himself this, but it didn't ease his tension.

"Agravar," Lucien called. He stood with another man whose skullcap and clerical cape showed him to be a priest. Agravar did not recognize him as one of the friars who made regular visits from the nearby abbey. This man's pinched features and small, close-set eyes glittered with cunning as Agravar approached. Huge front teeth protruded as he smiled. At least Agravar assumed it was a smile. It could just as easily been an expression of pain.

Lucien said, "This is Father Leon, from Hallscroft. His lord is Cyrus, Rosamund's stepfather. He has been sent to see about the delay in Rosamund's marriage.''

Father Leon bowed. "Aye, you see, when my Lord Cyrus—a good man, a pious man, a most excellent and conscientious guardian of the fair Lady Rosamund—well, when he heard of her unfortunate mishap, you see, he was beside himself, simply beside himself and he has therefore sent me to address the matter with you and acquaint myself, as it were, with the situation and advise him in all due haste— for he is most anxious, most anxious indeed—on the arrangements to deliver the lady to her betrothed and seal the marriage bargain posthaste, that is, without delay—''

Lucien cut him off. "Agravar has had the honor of rescuing the chit…ah, the lady and so he is the one you should speak to on the matter. For myself, I have notified your lord and Lord Robert of Berendsfore, and he has replied that she is to await him to fetch her here. Therefore, I have turned myself to other matters. If you will excuse me.'' He all but fled.

"Quite right,'' Father Leon said, smiling after him, his unbelievably huge teeth bared unselfconsciously. "Excellent man, wonderful reputation. Just, wise. A goodly man, indeed.''

Agravar frowned. "You are from Rosamund's home?''

"Ah, aye, I am. A priest for her father, or stepfather as you would have it.''

"How long have you known her?''

"Oh, quite a while, you see, quite a while indeed. I knew her mother, aye, I did. Beautiful lady, lovely lady. Quiet, chaste, an example to the less holy matrons who do not know their place. Lord Cyrus doted on her, aye, he did indeed, quite so, and so it was that her passing was ever so tragic, you see, and never spoken about since, not even her name, and Rosamund—such a meek child, quite an example of virtue, I daresay—kept on by the good graces of my lord, who saw fit to continue to provide for her, although she was a mere woman and no relation to him—"

"Come," Agravar said, indicating the dais. He would repay Lucien for this. "I shall let you see the lady for yourself to assure yourself she is well."

"That would be quite lovely, you see, for I am sent to remind her of her duty, as it were, for Lord Cyrus is quite set for this marriage. Important family, you see, and much at stake and the girl was not completely willing at first—ah, there she is. Greetings, Lady Rosamund, I am sent by your honorable stepfather to convey his wishes for you to return to the objective of your journey as soon as possible. Now, I am to understand that your intended is traveling to Gastonbury so that the nuptials can take place as planned, which is an excellent plan, it really is, and so... Goodness! Where is she going?"

Agravar had observed her every reaction. From the moment Rosamund spotted the priest, a parade of shock, fear, revulsion, anger and determination flew across her features. The garrulous man had prattled through it all, oblivious to her florid reaction to his presence. When she finally acted, it was to leap to her feet and run away the cleric, out of the hall and up the great stairs to her chamber.

Father Leon stared after her. "Oh, dear."

Agravar bit the insides of his cheeks. "She seems rather distressed today."

Father Leon wagged his head sagely. "'Tis the curse of the inconstant female, I fear. Be ever wary, my son, for she is wicked and embodies all of the temptation that would take men from their simple tasks that serve our Lord and enslave him to her minions. Oh, the poor witless creatures are sly in their pretenses, warping the sensibilities of good men, stout and strong-hearted men—"

"Did you just say 'witless' and 'sly' to describe women, father? I fail to see how a creature can be both."

"'Tis the paradox of the feminine mystery, you see, which is encrypted in the Holy Scriptures in the judicious warnings for men of God to fear and mistrust their life mates, lest they be judged unworthy to follow the paths for God."

Agravar resisted the urge to throttle the fool. But more, he was overcome by a dawning sense of horror that this idiot had had his clutches on Rosamund, if his claim of having been her instructor was true.

"I am interested to hear more. Come and refresh yourself and sit. There. Barnard! Wine here. Take your ease, Father, and tell me about Lady Rosamund's home. Is Lord Cyrus of the same mind as you?"

"Oh, aye, most assuredly so. That poor man was bedeviled most gravely by the enchantress he had married. Of course, I may not speak outside of the sanctity of confession."

"Naturally, but one would assume your wisdom on these matters comes from many sources."

"True enough, good sir, indeed it does and in that event, I have observed *in general* that many a man must labor under the yoke of...of..." Father Leon glanced surreptitiously about. "Of *carnal desire!* It can enslave a man, even in the bonds of marriage, for God does not excuse our duty to him, you see, because of matrimonial vows and so procreation is the goal for all devout men and…well, the other thing can enslave a man and rob him of his pious goals. Such is the lure of women, and their evil must be contained. Low voices, heads bowed and such, these are the marks of a goodly wife and daughter, as Lord Cyrus has been conscientious to show his stepdaughter, you see—"

"You say Lady Rosamund was…er, successfully taught these attributes by her stepfather."

Father Leon sighed. "Indeed, I see you are doubtful after that willful display we saw just now—quite so, understandable I do say—but I beg you not to worry, young man, she will pay for her sin in her own conscience, for her training has been sound. Aye, her rebellion is to be anticipated, for it was precisely the fear of this very eventuality that Lord Cyrus sent me here, because he knows well that the female soul is wayward and a constant vigil must be kept to insure it will not revert back to its inherent wickedness."

Agravar was beginning to feel slightly ill. He said unenthusiastically, "Ah. Of course."

Father Leon took it as encouragement, and expounded further on his opinions of the fairer sex. Agravar's thoughts drifted under the drone of the idiot's speech. Since the priest seemed to need no responses to encourage him to elaborate, Agravar was saved having to listen.

So *this* was how she was raised. Shy, fearful— skittish he had called her. Ah, but Lord Cyrus and this ignoramus were right in one thing. She *had* begun to blossom away from the oppressive dictates of their women-hating theology.

"It really is crucial that women mind their station," Father Leon was saying. He had apparently paused long enough to take a sip of the wine the servant had brought him, and his bottom lip glistened with bloodred droplets. Agravar passed him a linen napkin. Leon took it, thanked him absently and set it unused on the table as he continued.

"What are women for but to bring honor and wealth to their lords and masters? Women are essential in the political aspirations of their betters, but they are filled with silly notions—courtly love and other devilish ideas—which in turn are their weapons—"

Agravar raised his hand and called down to the other end of the table. "Lady Veronica!"

"Huh?" the priest muttered, snapping out of his diatribe.

Veronica rose and came in response to the summons. Agravar grinned slyly. "Father Leon, this is Lord Lucien's mother-in-law. I believe she will be…interested to be acquainted with your philosophies. If you will excuse me."

He rose, and as he passed the rather puzzled lady, he bent quickly and murmured in her ear, "Resist murdering him, my lady, for we may have need of him in the future. Otherwise, feel free to exercise no restraint short of that one thing."

He did feel a bit guilty for leaving her with Father Leon, but the first shriek of indignation that reached his ears was just too satisfying. Aye, he had chosen wisely. If anyone could give Father Leon what he deserved, it was Lady Veronica.

Leon was about to receive a dazzling instruction on the female character.

Chapter Ten

Rosamund almost jumped to the ceiling when the rap sounded at her door.

Her heart beat so hard, she thought it would tear out of her chest. *He was here*—that vile beast who posed as a man of God. Her stepfather's puppet, filled with the same sick poison as Cyrus. And now he was going to take her back with him!

Circling the room, she tried desperately to clear her mind of the cloying panic. Why hadn't she flown when she had the chance? Davey might have gotten her away if he managed to procure a boat, or a diversion could have been—

The knock came again, this time frightening a small squeak out of her. She slapped her hands over her mouth and eyed the window—which hovered over the packed earth three stories below—with consideration.

"Rosamund, 'tis Agravar. I must speak with you. Open the door."

She did not think at all, merely acted. Racing to the portal, she threw back the bolt and swung the door wide. He stepped inside, shutting the door behind him and placing a finger to his lips.

"Where is the priest?" she demanded.

Agravar grinned. "I let loose Lady Veronica on him. It should keep him busy for a while."

"Then he is still here?"

"Be calm, my lady. I have come to assure you that you are safe."

"He is talking to Veronica?" Shaking her head in disgust, she whirled and paced to the window. "How could you expose her to him? She doesn't deserve to hear those horrible things."

"Neither did you."

She sucked in a breath, as if he had hit her in the stomach. After a short silence, she said, "What do you know of it?"

"Nothing, Rosamund. But I can imagine. I can imagine it was most...unpleasant for you."

She stepped quickly to put more distance between them, seeking the farthest corner of the room. "Please, do not try to understand me."

He spread his hands out helplessly. "I fear I am ever destined to fail in that."

"Shall I hear you lament the inherent wickedness of women, too? Is your opinion the same as that...that...man?"

"The only mystery I seek to solve is why you resist me when I offer you aid." He started coming for her. She backed away, stopping when her heel hit the wall behind her. He said, "Rosamund, if I had known of this, I would have helped you."

"Helped me?" She was incredulous. She slid along the wall, inching away from his advance. "And how would you have done that, Viking? Smote

Cyrus with your sword? Or perhaps it is Lord Robert you shall challenge?''

''Lord Robert is a good and just man from all reports.''

''He is a man!'' she flung.

He paused for a heartbeat, stopping in his tracks. ''So am I.''

She had noticed. A man like other. A man, but not terrifying, for all of his fierce looks. A man—the only man she had ever met—who just might have a heart.

Oh, aye, she had noticed.

She bowed her head. ''Do you not understand…to have you hear these awful things…to pity me—I cannot bear that.''

''''Tis not your shame to bear. It is they who should be embarrassed.''

''But if they spew it at me, am I not despoiled?''

''Stop it!'' he commanded, and for the first time, she heard his voice sharpen. He took three strides and grabbed her by her shoulders, giving her a little shake. ''Do not do that. Your dignity is yours. Do not surrender it, not for anything. They can hurt you with words, but only if you let them. Do not allow it, Rosamund. Never listen to that filth.''

His words were far too profound. She tried to shrink away. ''What do you know of it?''

His head fell forward, his forehead brushing against hers. ''Would that I did not know anything.''

''What kind of answer is that?'' she accused.

She could see his jaw clench in spasms as his nostrils curled against his inner thoughts. ''No kind of answer.'' He released her and stepped away. ''God, I do not know why I even came here. He said those things and you fled and I…I acted without thinking. I do not do that often.''

''Should I be grateful?'' Her voice was rising. In a detached manner of observance, she considered that she might be becoming hysterical. She had never felt closer to the brink of losing control.

''I will tell Lucien to send him away if you wish,'' he said, ignoring her question.

''It matters not, Agravar. He is down there in the hall.'' Tapping a slender finger against her temple, she added, ''And he is in here.''

He bowed his head. It was a sign of defeat. ''I shall leave you. Accept my apologies for disturbing you.'' He left.

She felt worse for him being gone. Why had she fought with him when he was only trying to help her?

Why *would* he want to help her? She was too confused to contemplate it. All she could fathom was that Leon was here, and that meant Cyrus was here, in spirit if not in the flesh. Thus, everything was changed now. Gastonbury was no longer her refuge.

It was that thought that brought on the tears. She fell onto the bed and cried. She wanted to die, like a rabbit when it cannot bear its fear any longer. It just dies of fright.

If only she could, she thought. What a great relief it would be.

''If you are angry with me, I am certain I deserve it,'' Lucien said as he and Agravar walked along the edge of the training field. From the iron frame that housed a few dozen long-handled spears, he picked one out and examined it. "How long did Father Leon abuse your ears with his prattle?"

"You did me a favor, actually." Agravar squinted into the sun. "'Twas enlightening."

"Enlightening? You mean to say you found his opinions worthy?"

"Not at all, but his ridiculous philosophies go a long way to explain the strange behaviors of your wife's cousin."

"Oh. I suppose." Lucien cast his friend a curious glance. "What care you about the chit? Unless…"

"Nay, do not think it," Agravar warned, stalking off toward the lists. "She is but a bother, and soon to be gone."

"Oh, admit it, you fool. She has interested you from the start." Lucien was on him in an instant. "Aye, of course she has. If I wasn't so bound up with my own worries, I would have seen it sooner."

"Lucien, you are perpetually bound up in yourself. You rarely see beyond that huge beak of a nose of yours."

"I will allow I am not the most delicate of men when it comes to other people's sensibilities. 'Twas what I always relied on you for."

"You say it as if you are proud of it."

Lucien shrugged. "It is what life has made me. And you have no prettier tales to tell than I." He regarded his friend with something dangerously akin to compassion in his hard face. "Ah, perhaps worse. At least my early years were spent with a father whom I loved, and my mother, although a wretch, never loathed me as did—"

"Enough. Are we going to spar with blades or will you torture me with these clumsy words?"

"Let us have at it then," Lucien conceded.

Agravar stalked a few paces away and whirled, sword drawn and at the ready.

Lucien met the first blow. "You surprise me, Agravar. You have never been unwilling to talk of your past."

Agravar lunged, striking hard. "I am not unwilling. What is the point? Aye, you had love once, and have it now again. And I do not." He struck again. "There is no disagreement."

"Then why are you angry?" Lucien asked, ducking as the great broadsword came at him, slicing the air just beyond his ear.

"Because, you stupid cur, you are an ass!" To his surprise, Agravar saw how Lucien braced himself for the Viking's next blow. Maybe he even cringed. Was he striking at him that hard?

The realization sobered him out of his rage. With a grunt, he tossed his broadsword into the air where it arced in the sunlight, throwing off glints of fire, then landed with a thunk in the dust.

But he was not done with Lucien. He stalked a tight circle around his puzzled friend. "Does love trouble you with fits of temper, Lucien? How unfortunate. My heart aches for you and your surpassing trials. My God, are you a complete dolt? You tell me to guard my heart and how fortunate I am not to have a wife to trouble me. Do you have not the slightest inkling of how unthinking you are?"

Lucien stayed very still, following the stalking Viking with his eyes. Agravar tossed his head and scoffed, "What trials you bear, friend, when your happiness is so great your only care is that you will lose it. What pity I hold for you when I see that incredibly lovely woman whom you hold as wife watch you with devotion in her eyes, and when those children whom you have sired run to you with smiles and shouts of happiness.'' His voice had risen to a shout. ''You think I am better off with my lonely heart, Lucien. I ask you what do you know of it? *What do you know of it?*''

Lucien shifted uncomfortably at the interest they had drawn from those nearby. ''Peace, friend. Do not forget I am no stranger to suffering. I was once as lost as a man could be—''

''*You* have forgotten. Aye, long ago you were as troubled a man as set foot on this earth, but the love of your wife and your children is too sweet to see clear into that distant past. You are soft, Lucien. You have lost your edge, and I envy you that, but don't, for God's sake, pretend for a moment that it wasn't the luckiest damned thing that could have happened to you. And do not ever begrudge one moment of pique, one instant of worry or vexation or anything else your lady gives you, because you are the most fortunate, undeserving bastard on God's earth.''

Lucien hung his head and breathed in deeply, letting it out in degrees. ''You are wrong, Agravar.'' He looked up and tried a smile. '''Tis you who are the bastard. 'Twas your parents who were unmarried. Mine own were safely sealed in the blessed union of wedlock.''

All at once, Agravar's anger drained out of him. He shook his head and grinned. '''Tis the poorest excuse for a jest I have ever heard.''

Lucien grew serious. ''You are unwanted no longer. Your home is here. You have chosen it so. When I would have given you the lands of my own birth to compensate you for your service, you chose to stay here at Gastonbury, by my side. And so you have, because you are not merely my captain, but my brother, as well. Never say you have nothing. You do have family.''

Agravar went for his sword, taking a long time to wipe the dust off the blade. He held it up and examined its edge, concentrating on the honed steel. "'Tis your family," he said without taking his eyes off the weapon. "I am happy to have it. But mayhap, Lucien, for the first time, I want something of my own.''

Lucien came up beside him and spoke softly. "I am sorry for the desire you may hold in your heart for the girl, but it does not change the situation. You cannot have Rosamund.''

Agravar swallowed and sheathed his weapon. "I know it.''

Chapter Eleven

"I must speak with you," Veronica said, taking Rosamund's elbow as soon as the younger woman entered the ladies' solar.

"I—I..."

"Come here, by the window. Sit."

Rosamund did as Veronica instructed, and settled herself at a discreet distance from the others who were busy carding wool. Folding her hands on her lap, she kept her eyes downcast.

"Look at me, child."

It took a moment, but Rosamund complied. There was never any refusing the quiet command of the older woman.

"Now, you listen to me. If I ever look at you and see by your eyes or your posture that you are even *remembering* the things those vile men taught you, let alone *believing* in them, I vow before you right now to take you over my knee and wallop your backside."

Rosamund's mouth fell open. Veronica raised a chastising finger. "Do not make the mistake of thinking I am bluffing. If it takes treating you like a child,

I will do so to retrain you away from those hateful beliefs. I have lived a good many years, and though I am not old and frail just yet, the value of my experience allows me a certain perspective on these matters. In all modesty, I assure you I am a most excellent judge of character.''

Taking Rosamund's trembling hands in hers, she continued in a softer tone. "Now, Rosamund, heed me. The men who speak so against women are weak. They do not understand our mystery, our very differentness from them. They perceive it as a threat, and thus must try to control that threat because of their very fear of it. They are not strong, masterful men, but inadequate, frightened boys who use their superior position to dominate what they cannot fathom, or appreciate. These men are loathsome, and the farthest thing from godly that can exist on this earth. But their most insidious danger is what they can make us believe about ourselves.''

That last statement made Rosamund wonder. "Were you ever under the power of such a man?''

"Nay, not I, child, but a very dear friend of mine made a disastrous marriage. 'Twas almost her undoing, but she gained courage in the end to defy her husband and prevent him from strangling all that was precious and unique out of her. This story had a happy ending, for she survived the wretched man and is happy today.'' She paused, pressing her lips together. "But she nearly went a different course. At times, I feared for her life.''

Rosamund snatched her hands out of Veronica's grasp and stood. Flustered, she said, "I will remember your kind words, my lady.''

Veronica came around to her side and placed a

reassuring arm about her shoulder. "Use them as a shield in your weak moments, Rosamund, when your thoughts slip back to those horrid lies."

"Thank you, my lady," Rosamund said with feeling, and gave her a quick hug.

And she did feel better. Veronica's insights had the ring of truth in them. The more she thought of all the lady had said, the more she recognized that Cyrus and this knave in priest's garb were exactly the weak, feeble-willed men Veronica had described.

In the ensuing days, if she did not exactly walk about the castle freely, leaving herself open to meet with Father Leon, she did not cower in her room, either. Only in the evenings did she see him, at supper, but luck gave Father Leon no chance to get close to her. He did not approach the high table, being much too intent on making himself as drunk as possible. She felt protected, thinking that perhaps it was because Lady Veronica was always nearby that he dared not speak to her.

She spent mornings with the other ladies in the solar, afternoons on her own, sometimes in her chamber, sometimes venturing out to the children's rooms to play with sweet Leanna or laugh at Aric's antics. That one was showing the beginnings of developing into a tyrant, despite his mother's sharp reprimands. He adored his father, and only Lucien's stern scoldings checked his exuberant, if overbearing, personality.

"He orders the older boys about, and they let him," Alayna lamented one day. "And the younger ones think the sun rises and sets on him, but he will have naught to do with them. He says they are a nuisance and dismisses them in the most abominably rude way.''

''He struts about like the lord of the manor already,'' Lady Veronica added, but there was a twitch in the corners of her mouth.

Rosamund thought for a moment. ''I promised him I would tell him stories of the Crusades. I have been working very hard to learn some.''

''Ah, that will serve his bloodlust,'' Alayna said with a disapproving click of her tongue.

''Mayhap not. I was thinking I might relay instead a story to teach a lesson, and put in a moral or two.''

''An excellent idea.'' Veronica beamed at her. ''An indirect approach is sometimes best.''

Alayna nodded, apparently liking the idea. ''Aye, and 'tis better coming from you. Sometimes little boys have enough of mothers telling them what to do.''

''And grandmothers,'' Veronica added. ''Our thanks to you, Rosamund. It is good of you to help us with our little problems.''

It wasn't all good, at least for Rosamund. She was getting too involved with the people here. It would only make them all the harder to leave, when the time came.

She liked the little orchard where she and Agravar had once shared quiet company and flirted with confidence. She would often sit and read in the cool shade late in the afternoon, when the heat was at its worst.

She liked to read. It was something her mother had taught her, a secret thing—an evil thing, if Cyrus was to be believed. It was the one rebellion her mother had indulged, and well worth it, for Rosamund loved to pore over the illustrated manuscripts and dream of the classical heroes depicted in picture and word. She had a wonderful imagination and a gift for leaving her cares behind and losing herself in fantasy.

It was that gift that had gotten her through many of Father Leon's sermons and lengthy discourses on the evils of the flesh. She didn't really know what that meant, even after hundreds of woeful warnings, since she never paid much attention to them. But best of all, she could spend hours in her lonely chamber flying upon the wings of a gigantic swan, or climbing Olympus only to be so admired by Zeus he awarded her special status as a demigod, or sailing on a ship bound for the Holy Lands disguised as a boy, intent on glorious war in the name of the Christ.

These were her fantasies—of adventure, like the ones she read secretly. And of freedom. Always freedom.

On this day, she went to her garden with a particular manuscript and a sullen little boy who would rather be running about with his friends than holed up with a *female*. However, there was the lure of the promised stories—war stories, no less—of knights and dreaded Saracens and heathenish infidels and that was enough to appease his inquisitive nature.

"I like to hear about Antioch. Tell me how it fell and how all the knights put their enemies' heads on pikes along the walls."

Rosamund cringed. "Who told you such a thing?"

"Dervel, the groomsman."

"No such thing happened. I am not going to tell you stories of the Crusades today. I have something else I want to talk to you about."

"Does it have fighting?"

"Aye, 'tis a war story, but this war was very long ago," Rosamund told him. "Come and sit by me here."

The little boy perched his bottom on the edge of the stone bench, for he would never be openly disobedient. Neither did he trust that the promised tale would prove entertaining. He gazed at Rosamund skeptically. "Did the men wear armor and carry swords?"

"Aye. They certainly carried swords, but their armor was much different than what you are used to seeing." Rosamund opened the book and found a particular illumination. "They relied much more on their shields, because they had no way to make it possible to move in the armor plating. Therefore, they used it sparingly. See, here is a picture."

He peered at the parchment. "That looks foolish."

"It is merely different. They were Greeks, and they lived in a part of the world that was much warmer than we are used to here, so they dressed differently."

"I think they look like girls. That one is wearing a kirtle."

Rosamund sighed. "'Tis a gown of sorts, true, but all men wore it back then. 'Tis called a toga."

He lifted one shoulder, a gesture identical to his father's. "I suppose." He peered at the manuscript and pointed to a heroically drawn figure with impossibly blond hair. "What is his name?"

"This is Odysseus. See, Aric, how big and strong he is?"

"He looks like Agravar. Agravar is big and strong."

"Aye, I know."

"Where is his sword? What kind of soldier is he? He has no sword."

She rolled her eyes in despair, then got an inspiration. "He keeps it on his ship."

"That is very stupid. A soldier must always have his sword. Agravar would never be caught without his, nor my father."

Rosamund remembered once when the mighty Viking had indeed been caught without a weapon. She chuckled softly remembering her own chagrin when she had discovered her great prize was a blade stump. Distinct in her memory was the sparkle of amusement in Agravar's eye.

"Was Odysseus a great fool?"

"Oh, nay, not at all, Aric. Odysseus was a hero. He fought in a long war, called the Trojan War, and won a fabulous victory for the Greeks. But you know what he did then?"

"Chopped off all their heads and put them on pikes to warn others?"

Rosamund blinked in shock. "Nay. He angered the gods, and refused to admit that it had been with their help he had won the war. His arrogance nearly cost him his life, several times over. As it was, he was doomed to wander for many, many years in search of his home, lost and yearning for his wife and son. This is the story of his adventures and how he finally had to learn humility. I want to read it to you."

"That's sad that he had to stay away for so long," he said, then brightened. "Did he kill any dragons?"

"They have different monsters where he lived. But he did slay a Cyclops and outsmarted a few nymphs who wished to hold him prisoner."

"What are…nimps?''

She sighed and shifted uncomfortably. It was not possible to explain how Odysseus had fallen under the enticements of Circe, or how he and his men had languished in the land of the lotus-eaters. She had never understood it herself. In fact, it had made her rather disappointed in the tarnished hero. How could he be ruled by his base self, allowing it to divert him for one moment from his noble mission?

But she might be able to imagine the thrall of such temptations. A wanting that great…it might be that 'twas possible. There had been moments, in Agravar's company, that she had felt a strange, aching sort of need.

This wasn't working as she planned. "Never mind.''

"Do you have a picture of these monsters in there. The Cyclops and nimps?''

"Perhaps. They come later, as part of the long, adventuresome journey Odysseus makes to return home after angering the gods with his arrogance. Come, let us read the story together and you will see—''

But Aric had already lost interest. "Let us see if we can spy the practice field from here!'' he cried, leaping up from the stone bench and running to the garden wall.

"Aric, come away from there. I thought you wanted to hear this story. Aric!''

Paying her no mind, he clambered up onto a pile of rocks until he could just about get his chin over the edge of the limestone. "Aye, I can! See, there is Agravar! I told you he would have his sword—he always has it. See?''

Rosamund stood and placed the manuscript carefully on the bench. "Aric, really," she said primly, but it was only a halfhearted chastisement. She went to stand by his side and followed his pointing finger.

The grove was an enclosed yard on a hillock that overlooked the rolling paths that led to the lower wards, where the lists and other training fields were spread out on large, dusty flats. The forge was down there, where the armorer and the smith labored, as well as the stables, which were accessed by a narrow passage from another enclosed ward. The entire area was thick with soldiers in mock battle, squires scrabbling for this weapon or that, craftsman being consulted about the repair or construction of armor or swords, and a host of other activities that were the everyday fare of a soldier's world.

Yet among all this chaos, the Viking was unmistakable.

Stripped naked to the waist, with a thick sheen of sweat glistening on his exposed torso, he strode among the others with confidence. His hair was wet, dark and clinging to his skin. Someone said something to make him laugh, and the flash of his teeth made him appear softer for a brief moment.

His body was magnificent—wide, powerful. His legs were long and thick with muscle, his waist lean, narrow, with a tight, flat abdomen with small ridges on it. From there on up, his body flared out to meet the impossible width of his shoulders, his sculpted chest smooth and hairless. His arms were as large as a young tree, bound with sinewed strength that shifted and bunched in the most fascinating manner when he swung his blade, flat side landing with a *thwack* on another man's posterior.

The other man jumped and rubbed his rump, then charged.

Rosamund gasped, stuffing her knuckles between her teeth.

Aric looked at her with disgust. "He's just teasing Will. They are always fighting like that. He's here for his service to my father. He's nice. He gave me a ride on his horse. Do you want to see his horse?"

"No, thank you," Rosamund murmured absently, too absorbed in the little battle going on below her. Will, whoever that was, was agile and lean. Agravar was larger, less swift, but the might of his swing was impressive. Each blow bent the other man's knees as he met the weighty parries.

"Agravar will best him. He is bigger. When I get big, I am going to beat everyone, just like Father does. Only even he can't beat Agravar. Sometimes he does, but then Agravar gets him the next time. It is kind of a rule they have. Mother fears one day they will kill each other."

Intent on the men sparring, she absently murmured, "Aye, that is nice." She cringed when Will swirled his weapon in an arc. It caught the sun, flashing fire for a moment before it came down. Rosamund let out a small cry.

"He's all right, see? None can harm Agravar! Come," Aric cried excitedly. He leaped down from his perch and raced to the gate. Undoing the latch, he demanded more imperiously, "Come!"

"What? Oh, nay, Aric. Return here at once!"

But Aric was off in a twinkling.

The fighting men had paused to catch their breath before going at it again. Rosamund cast one last look, then followed the gleeful boy, forgetting all her good intentions of morality stories and lessons on humility.

In the end, she allowed the boy to persuade her to take him to see the fighting. They arrived down at the lists as the combatants were ready to go at it again. Aric jumped up and down at Rosamund's side, shouting, "Agravar! Smite him!"

Agravar looked over with a smile on his face. He stopped when he saw Rosamund. She tried to smile, but the gesture froze on her face and she was suddenly overcome with an acute self-consciousness.

Will pretended offense at Aric. "Take sides against me, will you, you little bloodthirsty demon? That is the last time you ride on my horse."

Agravar hadn't moved.

"But you cannot beat Agravar! He is my father's captain!"

"And I your father's villein!"

Rosamund could not tear her eyes away from a thick rivulet of sweat as it traveled with excruciating slowness from Agravar's neck to the sharp furrow dividing his chest. It glistened as it slid lower, making its way to the waistband of his breeches.

Will sauntered toward them, wiping his brow with the hem of his loose-fitting shirt. "Who is this, your new nursemaid?"

Aric said, "Nay, 'tis Mother's cousin. The Lady Rosamund."

"Well—a relative of Alayna's. Delightful to meet you," Will said.

Rosamund wanted to reply, but the strange numbness hadn't released her yet.

"She's scared of everyone," Aric explained. "I heard Father say so. He doesn't like it. Mother told him that he should visit the devil for saying something not nice about her kinswoman and then Father swore, but not at Mother. I heard it all.''

There was an awkward pause. ''I fear that conversation was meant to be private,'' Will said softly.

At last Agravar moved, and Rosamund could once again breathe.

''Greetings, Aric,'' he said to the little boy, then lifted his gaze to Rosamund. ''Good day, my lady.''

''G-good day.'' She felt—and this was completely irrational—*guilty* somehow, as if she were somewhere she had no right to be. Or seeing something she had no right to see. He was still half-naked, after all.

She rushed to explain herself. ''I was with Aric in the grove, reading Odysseus, and he saw you and said that Will gave him rides on his horse and he wanted to come down and I thought we could…are we interrupting?''

Lord, it was all she could do to keep from staring at that expanse of flesh in front of her, beautifully sculpted, purely masculine. His chest rose and fell slightly as if he were still winded. She felt her knees go a bit weak and concentrated on keeping her eyes fixed straight ahead.

Aric was dancing around, showing off his own imaginary skill at the thrust and parry. Will laughed and made admiring noises and the boy beamed.

''We were just about to end,'' Agravar said.

Will looked over, obviously surprised. ''We just—''

''Wait here,'' Agravar said, cutting him off. He trotted back to the water barrel and doused himself with a dipperful, then rubbed a towel quickly over his skin.

At the sight of this, Rosamund's mouth went dry and her head felt suddenly light and floating, like the time when she had the fever and could keep nothing in her stomach for nearly a sennight. She watched, not aware that Will was there or what he might think. As for Aric, she had ceased to be conscious of the little boy altogether. A distant part of her brain was horrified by her capriciousness at abandoning the noble task she had set for herself that day, but she dismissed its nagging without much trouble as she watched Agravar pull on his shirt and head back her way.

"I say, Lady Rosamund, how long are you staying?" Will spoke loudly, as if this were not the first time he had asked the question.

"Uh? Oh...a short while, I think."

"She got bandits on her! Agravar went and got them off."

"Aric!" Agravar admonished.

The boy looked puzzled. "Well, you did. You were the one who got her back. Now she is going to marry Lord Robert."

Will looked more confused than ever.

"I shall explain the whole high adventure later," Agravar said, slapping Will on the back and flashing a grin. "Rosamund, shall we leave these two clodheads—"

"Hey!" Aric protested, looking as though he wished he had his wooden sword with him just then.

"—and head back up to the keep?"

"Of course," Rosamund said smoothly, grateful

that her voice didn't tremble. "Lovely to make your acquaintance, Will."

"I…" He looked thoroughly confused for a moment, then shrugged. "I shall look forward to seeing you at supper."

As they left, Will frowned after them. Then he swatted the little boy and began to chase him around the lists.

Agravar felt an incredible excitement vibrate through his body as they walked. What was she doing here? Had she come just to see him?

"Young Aric has a great deal of energy," he commented.

Beside him, she strode with her back stiff, facing straight ahead. Mutely she nodded.

Agravar's mind puzzled. Sometimes, when a knight was wooing a particular lady, she would come down to the field and observe her beloved's prowess. Agravar had always considered this a damned nuisance. The whole practice session would be disrupted. The knight would usually begin to swagger about, bloated on conceit as any strutting peacock would be at catching the eye of a peahen, and all the while maintaining an affected casualness as if it mattered not in the least that admiring eyes were directed his way.

For the first time he could understand why. He had scoffed, scolded, even cuffed a few of his men when they had become stupid in the presence of their female audience. Yet now Agravar himself felt an indescribable rush of pleasure, a lightness inside of him, a deliriously idiotic fixation on the mere fact that she had come. It was the first time she had sought him out and he was silly over it.

His first thought, his only thought, upon finding her watching him, had been to get her away from the curious stares of his men. Nay. His first thought was to put his shirt on. Odd how her presence had made his near nakedness seem carnal all of the sudden.

Then he wanted to take her away from the prying and curious stares of the others. He wanted her all to himself.

This elation was quickly waning. Whatever magical obsession had seized them both back there on the lists—surely the feeling of sensual energy that had come upon the two of them was not only his imagination—it was gone now. From Rosamund's posture, one might assume they were marching in some vigorous, not very well appreciated, exercise. From her demeanor, one might guess she cared even less for the company than she did the activity.

"Where would you like to go?" he asked, not knowing what else to say.

"Nowhere in particular."

"I thought we might walk a bit, if you wish."

"Aye, 'twould be pleasant."

He all but rolled his eyes as they trudged on in silence. He was more dumbfounded than ever. First she seeks him out, then she spurns him. He lapsed into silence.

She burst, "I did not come to see you today. Aric ran off and I but followed. I do not wish you to think I came down to spy on you."

"I would not think any such thing." Dismally, this was true.

They rounded the inner wall and headed out over

the narrow bridge, which crossed a stream that cut through to the outer wards. Walking at a brisk clip, arms swinging, head held high, she appeared more to be marching into battle than strolling with... A friend? Surely not. But what, then?

A flood of foolishness rushed through him like a scalding heat. Look at him—a man over ten and twenty years—skipping attendance to a maiden who had demonstrated time and again her indifference to him, a woman who could not, in any event, be his even if his feelings were returned.

His feelings? The thought stopped him in his tracks. Rosamund took a few more steps before realizing she had lost him.

Looking back, she asked, "Is something amiss? Are you tired?"

The question caught him off guard and he laughed. "Tired? My lady, not to seem a braggart, but I am used to riding three days in the saddle only to battle for another four. Nay, 'tis not weariness. Never mind it. Let us go on."

She hesitated a moment. "You know, there is someplace I'd like to go, if you will take me. I used to study the healing arts with the apothecary at Hallscroft. If you will escort me outside the gates, I would like to see if there are any herbs or roots that I could make use of."

Agravar replied temperately. "Certainly. Let us go."

Never mind that Alayna's old nurse, Eurice, was a most accomplished healer and could have handed Rosamund more dried herbs, roots and any other materials of consequence than she could carry. They set off into the woods.

Chapter Twelve

Agravar's laughter was rich and deep. It flooded the glade in the wood where he was sprawled on a carpet of moss, ankles crossed, leaning on one elbow as he toyed with some long blades of grass.

Across from him, Rosamund laughed, too, quieter, almost to herself. It was a secret laugh, quite apart from the jest they had just shared.

Seated on the same springy moss, she had her feet tucked up under her as she sorted the plants strewn on her lap. Her dress would be hopelessly grass stained, she knew, and this would earn her a thorough scolding from Hilde. But Rosamund didn't care.

She had a taste of freedom, and it was exhilarating.

This is what it feels like not to be afraid anymore. This is what it is to wake each morning with anticipation instead of dread.

How odd she would find so much ease in the company of so fierce-looking a man. Agravar, for all his Nordic looks and knight's bearing, was not terrifying at all.

"So he was unmasked," he said, finishing his lively tale.

"And what did the lady do?" she asked with a chuckle.

"She had the cad cast into the moat and closed the castle gates!"

"Good. I would have done the same."

His smile flashed again. "Of that I have no doubt. Rosamund, you are positively formidable at times."

"I? You who are the Viking say this to me. With all your warrior ancestors weeping from the shame of it, you tell a mere girl that she is formidable?"

"I am only part Viking," he corrected. "Thus my fighting nature is tempered with wisdom. Had I not mentioned that when listing my virtues?"

"Oh. Aye, I had quite forgotten."

"That was from my English side."

"Your mother's side?" she asked, forgetting for the moment how he had displayed such reticence about his mother before. Too late, she wished she could bite back the words.

He seemed to consider something for a moment. When he spoke, his voice was hesitant. "My mother was English, aye."

She kept her voice soft. "I recall you saying so."

"My father...my father was a Viking raider. He came ashore and swept over my grandfather's lands, storming the manor house where the family slept one night. It was over before 'twas begun, they say." He drew in a deep breath, as if it were a labor just to imagine it. "Those who fought were killed. The rest were rounded up."

He looked down at his hands as they busily twined the grass into a weave, then unwound it, then tied it up again. "My mother was…" He took a deep breath. "She was taken and…used by my father. I suppose the other women were given to the men, but he kept her for himself. She hated him, I know, and his regard for her went only so far as the diversion she gave him in bed."

Should she say something? She wanted to ease the furrows in his brow, but no words seemed to come to her.

"'Twas not the last time he abused a maid thusly, nor the first. God only knows how many brothers and sisters I have scattered about England and Denmark. I am a bastard. Half English, half Danish Viking, and the living mark of my mother's shame. She never recovered after he sailed for home, and there were those who would forget how unwilling she was. She was never the same. The Vikings have a reputation for using their slaves badly. Lucien will tell you this is true. When they left, laden with all their booty and the strongest to serve them in their homelands, the only thing those bitter remnants of the village could remember of my mother was that she had been spared much as the favored of Hendron."

"Agravar…I am so sorry."

"'Tis not your fault, of course. But I understand why you say it. It serves, does it not, when one has nothing else to offer. How many times did those words fly to my lips when I would see her, my mother, and know what I was to her. Even as a child, I knew 'twas not my fault, not really, but still I wanted to say it. I felt it. I *was* sorry. I wished so desperately that it could have all been different."

With a quick indrawn breath, he brought his head up and tossed aside the tangled blades of grass. "You know, there may be some who would be looking for you. We told no one where we were headed. Perhaps it would be wise to get back now. Supper will be soon.''

His retreat from the weighty subject of his birth suited her, for she had no means to express the awkward emotions pressing against her chest. What a coward she was, she reflected. "Hungry are you?'' she said lightly, donning a smile.

He stood and brushed at the green stains on his leggings. "I can hardly be content on those few handfuls of berries you fed me. Here, let me help you up.''

She gathered her boon and reached up for his hand. Warm, strong, soft and hard, it felt like touching her fingers to a smoldering coal.

Grasping at some semblance of composure, she observed, "'Tis not my duty to see you fed, Agravar. Why did you not find a rabbit or squirrel, or—''

He did not release her hand right away. Instead he pulled it, drawing her closer. Her hip brushed the top of his thigh.

"Because I wished to remain with you,'' he murmured. Her eyes lifted, wide with surprise. And pleasure. Those words let loose a cascade of tremors that left her feeling as if her insides had turned to liquid.

Father Leon and Cyrus had not succeeded in stifling her female perfidy, after all, she thought distractedly as her body swayed forward into Agravar's. There seemed to be some force as immutable as that which anchored things to the earth winnowing away at the space between them.

Catching himself, he let go of her hand and added,

"As you do have a penchant for misadventures in woods."

Despite his flippant words, she saw something naked in his eyes that came at her like a blow to her chest. It was intense, unbearable. She turned away.

Her gaze was caught by something moving out of the trees behind him. Stealthy, fast, with a short ax in one hand, the kind for chopping wood. His face was in a snarl, but it was still Davey's face, easily recognizable. And there was no mistaking his intent.

"Nay!" she shrieked. It came out before she had even thought.

"What is it?" Agravar demanded, instantly alert. He grabbed for her. "What? Rosamund, tell me?"

She could not allow Davey to murder Agravar, yet neither could she give her man away.

"Run!" she shrieked, snatching his hand and whirling to race in the opposite direction of the approaching menace.

"Rosamund!" Agravar cried, trying to haul her back.

"Run!" she yelled, letting loose of his hand and hitching up her skirts. Looking over her shoulder, she saw that once she was in flight, he was right behind her.

She dove for the tree line, her skirts getting tangled in the bracken of the low copse. It slowed her down. In a few strides, he grabbed her, yanking her to a halt.

"What the devil are you doing?"

She swallowed and turned.

Davey was gone.

Her relief made her go limp. Quickly her mind

searched to invent an explanation. "A…a…bear! I thought I saw a bear."

His head whipped around. The glade was empty, of course.

"Ridiculous. Where did you see it?"

Pointing, she indicated the general area from which they had come. "There. I thought 'twas there. I must have been mistaken. Mayhap 'twas just shadow. Aye. Probably only shadow."

He stared at her so long and with such doubt in his face, she feared she was found out. Drawing his short sword from the cuff of his boot, he waved her on. "Come. I am certain you were mistaken, but we best not take chances."

"Aye. Let us away."

They came out of the woods to cross the short meadow strewn with long, purple shadows from the setting sun. They were almost at Gastonbury's gates when Rosamund said, "Agravar?"

"Aye?"

"Thank you." She stopped and faced him. "It was good of you to take me."

He looked annoyed for a moment, then wordlessly they crossed the drawbridge.

Whatever pleasure the outing with Agravar gave her, it was gone the moment Rosamund saw Father Leon the following day.

As he walked rapidly to her, she stood stuck on the spot, never even thinking of retreat. It was as if invisible irons held her fast to await the inevitable end to her brief flight into contentment.

Leon wore an expression of determination on his pinched features. His small, close-set eyes slid over

her, taking in her appearance. "You are impertinent
to avoid me. Look at you and your brazen eyes, staring openly and not at all as you have been taught. I
see you have already succumbed to vanity." His eyes
glittered malignantly. "Lord Cyrus was right to send
me—such a brilliant man, a wise and prudent man—
for how well he and I both know your wretched nature. Just as my lord always claimed, you are like
your mother and it can be nothing short of Satan's
work to have you bedevil my master and thwart his
plans."

Grasping desperately at the rapidly shredding remnants of the confidence, Rosamund choked, "'Tis
not I but his own conscience which plagues him."

"How dreadful that you malign him."

"He is a murderer. And…and you are no better.
He killed my mother and you know 'tis the truth."

His smile was ugly and cruel. "What is this? Has
the serpent been whispering in your ear again, girl?
'Twas not Lord Cyrus who caused her death but—"

And then a strange thing happened. For a moment,
Rosamund feared she might have gone mad, for the
priest seemed to float in the air. The one thing that
saved her from being convinced her sanity had
snapped was the amazed expression on the man's
face and the gradual widening of her peripheral vision, which had narrowed to the pinpoint of Leon's
ratlike features, to reveal a huge, blond-maned Viking behind the friar.

Then the priest was fading away, getting smaller.
It occurred to her, through the haze of fear and panic
that had crowded her brain, that Agravar had the
priest by the scruff of his neck and was hauling him
out of the keep.

She merely watched the incredible sight—a giant of a man with his burden dangling ignominiously in his fist. He gave Father Leon a shake every now and then, but spoke not a word as he bore the man out the door and into the upper bailey.

Rosamund blinked, pulling herself out of her shock, and stumbled after them. She followed silently all the way to the stables where Agravar dragged the old man's donkey away from its feast of sweet, fresh straw and dumped the priest onto its back. Flustered, indignant, the priest was beginning to work up a response when Agravar jerked him close and whispered something in his ear.

Rosamund could not hear it, but the widening of Leon's eyes, the look of horror on his face testified that it was no declaration of fondness the Viking uttered.

Agravar drew back and slapped the beast on the rump. The sound of the blow rang out crisply. The animal took off at a clipped pace, the friar bouncing jauntily on his backside as he kicked his heels for the inauspicious steed to go faster.

Those who had observed the event began to laugh until the sound of it filled the yards and people were clutching their middles and wiping away tears. Agravar turned, his face bearing testament to his snarling fury.

Rosamund took a step back. He had been gentle with her; he had teased, he had laughed. He had been awkward when he confided his ancestry. He had been intense when he had tried to protect her, but he had never been like this. It frightened her a little. It filled her with a kind of awe and a vaguely stirring sensation when she realized it was on her behalf that he raged.

That frightened her even more. But a different fear, an almost giddy, delicious kind.

Stumbling backward, she fled. She collided with someone, muttered an apology, and was about to take up her flight when that someone gripped her wrist.

"My lady!" a voice rasped.

"Davey!"

Glancing furtively back to Agravar, Rosamund saw that he had turned away.

"What is it?" Davey demanded. "What is happening with the Viking? What has he done?"

Rosamund grasped at his thin shoulders. "We must make haste. Come to me tonight by the orchard gate and we will discuss our plan. I must away, Davey. Cyrus sent Father Leon...I was wrong to ignore him. Cyrus will never let me be. In any case, Lord Robert will be here any day, and my time will have run out."

Davey drew a tongue over his lips. "Finally. I am ready, my lady. Come see me tonight, just after sunset," he agreed.

If Agravar was a man prone to wager, he would have staked his half of his father's treasure that things regarding the Lady Rosamund could not get much worse.

It was a wager he would have lost.

He was intercepted in the outer bailey by one of his men. "Sir," the man said smartly, "there is a traveling party spotted, flying the colors of Berendsfore. 'Tis believed Lord Robert has come for my lady's cousin."

Berendsfore. The world tilted crazily for a moment. *Come at last for Rosamund—his betrothed.*

"Sir?"

Agravar looked up and blinked. "I am coming to the watchtower to see for myself."

Within the quarter hour, the men were clearly visible. It was not much longer when the entire retinue passed through the fortified gatehouse.

Agravar's attention focused on the man riding a destrier, smartly dressed in expensive traveling clothes. Perhaps two score and five, Agravar guessed his age to be. Robert was distinguished looking, with salt-and-pepper hair and shoulders still square in defiance of the advancing of his years.

He had heard talk of the man. Only good had been said. He had been an excellent fighting man in his day, and peace had reigned in his lands since he had taken them over. He was well-thought-of by the other barons and often served as emissary from them to the dyspeptic Prince John, for his skills in diplomacy were noteworthy.

A fine husband he would make, Agravar thought, but it was a bitter sentiment.

Agravar said, "Send word to the keep that Lady Rosamund's betrothed has arrived."

Chapter Thirteen

Lucien welcomed Robert of Berendsfore and brought him directly into the great hall. "This is my captain, Agravar Hendronson," Lucien said when Agravar approached.

It was Agravar's true name, but he disliked it, mostly because in Danish tradition the son's last name was derived from the given name of his father. There were not words to describe the revulsion he felt at being identified as his father's son.

He went by Agravar the Viking, or Agravar of Gastonbury, but he rarely needed the distinction beyond his first name. There were not many half-Viking bastards named Agravar loose on English shores.

Robert inclined his head, a respectful gesture that impressed Agravar. This man was a powerful baron, and not required to take notice of a commoner like himself.

"Your legend precedes you," Robert said. Turning back to Lucien, he added, "As well as yours. I am honored to be welcomed into your home and thank you most sincerely for keeping my betrothed safe from harm." His brow furrowed as he looked about. "I must say I am anxious to see for myself that she is well. I have been concerned since news of her near-abduction reached me."

Lucien answered, "She is indeed well. My wife and mother-in-law shall bring her shortly."

Robert nodded and switched to other topics, displaying a keen interest in Gastonbury and finding out whether the myriad of tales circulating about how exactly Lucien had won it from the hands of its previous lord held any truth.

Agravar was amazed when Lucien, who was normally reticent to the point of rudeness when curiosity was aimed his way, told the story.

"When I was but a youth, my father was murdered by Edgar du Berg, Lord of Gastonbury, and I would have found the same fate if not for the greedy wastrels whom he sent to do the deed. Instead of killing me, they sold me into slavery for the extra coin it gave them, and told Edgar I was dead. I came to the longhouse of Agravar's father in Denmark to live as a slave. 'Twas there he and I became friends, for Agravar had come to the lands of the Norse for his own purposes. I...escaped, with Agravar's help, and we stole the Viking's fortune."

Agravar thought how cleverly Lucien spoke, leaving out the most salient of details, like cold-blooded murder. Like Agravar's own crime of patricide.

"I had sworn to take everything away from Edgar," Lucien continued. "And declared war on him as soon as I could mount an army and return to England. The defeat was easy and I won all that had been his."

"Even his bride, so I have heard."

Lucien seemed a bit awkward. "'Twas advantageous for me for political reasons to take Edgar's widow to wife."

Robert smiled. It warmed his noble features and made him look younger. "I daresay, it was more than strategic advantages that visited you upon the union. You are to be congratulated. A good wife is a gift beyond any measure."

Lucien looked rather guiltily at Agravar. "Agreed."

"Which brings us back to my present quest. I myself have not made the acquaintance of my bride-to-be. I am anxious to meet the girl."

"You have not even seen Rosamund?" Agravar inquired. Although this sort of thing was not unusual, it intrigued him. He wondered if some clue to Rosamund's strange behavior could be found here.

"'Twas an arrangement made with Lord Cyrus of Hallscroft."

Was this why Rosamund was so ill at ease, so prone to nervousness? Did she dread Lord Robert because he was friend to her stepfather. He knew she despised Cyrus. "Do you know Lord Cyrus well?"

Robert seemed to think this an odd question. Agravar supposed it was. And the way he had asked it made it sound like an accusation, he knew.

Robert answered nonetheless, his tone never breaking from the courteous. "Passingly acquainted I would say. I met him at court. He was looking to make a good match for his stepdaughter, and I was seeking a wife. It was an advantageous arrangement for both of our houses."

Lucien was looking at Agravar as if he had just sprouted horns. The Viking feared he might have given himself away with his questioning, or perhaps it was just that Lucien knew him so well. Of course, marriages were made for advantage. One didn't have to be the odious Father Leon to believe that. It was business, nothing more.

Lucien, in a rare display of sensitivity, intervened. "My wife and her mother are quite fond of the Lady Rosamund, and I believe Agravar knows how distressed they shall be to lose her friendship when she leaves us. Therefore, he is a trifle protective of our guest. For their sakes."

That Robert let the matter drop was pure tact, nothing less.

The ladies entered, first Alayna who made a surprisingly graceful curtsy, considering her ungainly form. Lucien came quickly to her side and put an arm about her. Apparently, the lady's mood was docile today. She took her husband's aid and gazed warmly up at him. Lucien closed his free hand over hers and Agravar had to look away. Sometimes it hurt to see their love. Lately, it did, anyway.

"My wife's mother, Lady Veronica of Avenford," Lucien said. Veronica dipped low with infinite grace.

Robert's voice was warm with pleasure. "My lady."

"My lord," Veronica replied as she rose. Her eyes took in everything about their guest, making no secret of her assessment. She had always been a lioness when it came to her own daughter, and now their shy, retiring cousin was apparently included in her fierce protectiveness.

It appeared that she was pleased with what she saw. "May I present my cousin, Rosamund Clavier."

Rosamund was as pale as a ghost, her honey-brown eyes round and staring. With jerking movements, she came forward. When she executed her curtsy, she wavered as if her balance failed her.

Agravar took a step forward, then stopped.

It was not his place.

Robert put his hands out. Rosamund stared at them a moment, then must have understood that he had extended them to her as courtesy. She slid her trembling palms over his and rose, her eyes downcast.

"How good it is that we finally meet, Lady Rosamund," Robert said gently. "You are as lovely as I was told."

Agravar fought the urge to snarl and yank them apart.

Alayna suggested they adjourn to the head table for refreshments.

"I believe we have some acquaintances in common," Veronica said after everyone was settled. "Lord Garon and his wife were dear friends of mine and my late husband."

Robert seemed delighted. "Garon of Lockenland? How is it you know such an old curmudgeon?"

"He and my husband served the same overlord. He mentioned you from time to time."

"Oh, I pray you do not judge me by that," Robert said, and laughed good-naturedly.

Veronica's eyes sparkled. "Nay, my lord. He spoke well of you, rest assured. I did, however, get the distinct impression that the two of you had some interesting adventures while on crusade together."

"Misadventures, rather. How is Garon? Have you seen him?"

"I do make an effort to return to London whenever possible. Not as often as I would like since coming to live here, but as much as I can manage. I was there just last year and saw him at court.''

"Wait a moment!'' Robert said, stunned. "You are Veronica of Avenford!''

"Aye, I know it,'' she responded with amusement.

"When I saw Garon years ago, I believe he spoke of you. He called you...''

Veronica looked uncomfortable. *''Le petite marshall.''*

Robert slapped the table. "Aye, that was it!''

Veronica tossed her dark head in a gesture that was imperious and feminine at the same time. "Garon was always incorrigible.'' Meeting her daughter's amazed stare, she added, "Well, he was. Your father seemed to think well of him, but I always thought his character was questionable.''

"Aye, Mother,'' Alayna said softly, biting her cheeks. "Is that why you speak so fondly of him? And visit him whenever you are in London?''

Veronica waved away the questions. She appeared years younger, nearly of age with her daughter, as she talked animatedly with Robert. They swiftly found they had many other friends in common.

Off to the lady's other side, Rosamund was silent. Never had a soul looked more lost, Agravar thought.

He was gripped with a strange feeling looking at her sitting there like that. It was frustration that drove him away—the knowledge that there was nothing he could do for her. The realization struck him that there was no place for him here at these proceedings. 'Twas family, he reflected sourly.

Rising, he bowed and muttered an excuse. No one noticed he was taking his leave, except Rosamund.

She caught his gaze for a moment before she veiled her eyes once again.

He headed back to the guardhouse.

"Rosamund, child, why were you so quiet today?" Veronica asked, crossing the threshold into Rosamund's chamber.

Hilde was twisting Rosamund's hair into a coronet wrapped with a thin string of pearls. Never shy, the maid offered her opinion. "You should be putting your best face on, my pretty. Lord Robert—ho, Lord, he's a handsome one. He came all the way here to bring you to your new home, and that shows he's got a kind heart. Protective, too. Doesn't want anything to happen to his woman. And that is what you are, mistress. You are his now. Oh, to belong to a man like that." Looking up at Veronica, she flashed the woman a grin of rapture at the thought of such a thing.

Softly Veronica said, "She understands this, Hilde."

Hilde held her hands out to Rosamund's stiff back. "This one here is like a frightened little doe, she is. Shyness is fine, in fact it is often pleasing to a man. But too much and the man will think she is simple. Honestly! She just sat there like a log, not doing anything to present herself in an attractive light to her future husband."

Shooing the garrulous servant aside, Veronica took the brush out of her hand. "Allow me, please." Her deft fingers loosened the weave of hair and smoothed away the artless bumps that marred the lines of the coif. "Is it true, child? Is it that you are shy?"

"Aye. I suppose." Rosamund looked at Veronica through the glass. "He seemed rather...imposing."

From behind Veronica, Hilde let out a small cry of denial. "Well, of course he is! He's a fine figure of a man, I say." She clapped her hands together with glee. "Oh, my lady, he is superb! Did you see his tunic, how rich it looked? And his hair, with just that touch of age in it to lend distinction. Ah!"

"Hilde," Veronica said gently. "Please go to the kitchens and fetch your mistress sweet wine and something to eat. She was too overcome to eat earlier, and she will need her strength for tonight's revelries."

The thin ruse did not fool Hilde, but she could not argue with Veronica. No one in their right mind would dare. She muttered, "Aye, mistress," and left with a resentful look cast over her shoulder.

"There, now we can speak without being interrupted."

A wavering smile appeared on Rosamund's face. "Hilde is a trial at times, but she is devoted."

"No one can fault her for her lack of it, I agree. Rosamund, I sense a great unease in you. It has been there since I met you, but today it seemed...stronger. Is it Lord Robert? Does he frighten you?"

"Nay," Rosamund said quickly.

"Child," Veronica soothed. "Do not be too quick to deny it. I know 'tis intimidating to contemplate marriage to a man you have never met, but thank the good Lord in heaven that Robert is indeed a man of unsurpassed character. A finer husband you could not select. He is wealthy and, as Hilde is so apt at noticing, very pleasing to the eye. True, he is older than you, but still handsome and strong. He will give you many children...." Her voice trailed off and she considered the pale face staring at her through the mirror. "Ah, 'tis a foolish old woman, I am. Is it that which troubles you? The marriage bed?"

Rosamund was so startled, she actually jumped. "Oh, nay, my lady. My stepfather had his priest instruct me in the duties of a wife in that regard."

"Oh, child." Her voice was heavy with pity. "I daresay you were horribly misinformed. No doubt that little beast made it seem atrocious."

The convulsive reflex in Rosamund's throat confirmed Veronica's suspicions. She laid her hands gently on Rosamund's shoulders and spoke. "Robert will be kind to you. It is true you must submit, and the act will seem strange to you at first."

Rosamund's face flamed vivid scarlet.

"I know 'tis embarrassing," Veronica continued, "but you must know that you will come, with the good grace of God, to view this part of marriage as more than just duty. It will bring you both pleasure, and not just from the act. The closeness you share, the tenderness and feeling, 'tis a mighty thing, and lovely. I hope you will find this pleasure, Rosamund."

Rosamund merely nodded, biting her lips. How could what Veronica was saying be true? From what Father Leon had told her, the marriage act was the most vile depravity she could ever imagine. The fact that so many women allowed it was mind numbing. The way she saw it, this particular humiliation was just one more burden that women bore at the hands of their husbands. How could it bring pleasure?

Then she thought of Agravar.

What if she were to lie with him? That way. To

have his hands on her, his rod between her thighs as she was told it was to be.

A shudder went through her, but it was not one of revulsion. The thought of him touching her body—of touching his, feeling the firm masculine contours she had once glimpsed—slammed her with a startling, sudden heat that made her weak, stealing her breath for an instant.

The ragged flutters that winnowed down her spine were stunningly delicious. She felt confused. When Father Leon had taught her of the "sins of the flesh," she had never, *ever* imagined that she might feel this way.

But then, she was so very different from the girl who had left Hallscroft months ago. Almost unrecognizable.

The face staring back at her from the glass looked the same. Dark eyes, strong nose, a mouth formed of two shapely lips that tended to look pouty in repose. In truth, the outside of herself hadn't changed, but inside, but she would never be the same, never be as she had been before coming here.

Before *him.*

Veronica stroked her hair in a gesture of affection. "You are such a lost lamb."

"I…I am merely overwhelmed," Rosamund muttered. She glanced down, not wanting her friend to see the questions in her eyes.

Veronica sighed. "There, your hair is finished. Now, I want you to eat what Hilde brings you, and no arguments, please."

Rosamund offered her benefactress a weak smile. Veronica continued to look stern, but her eyes were soft. "And I want to see a cheerful girl at the supper table. And definitely no cringing!"

Rosamund's lips twitched. "Yes, my lady."

"All right, then. I shall see you down in the hall."

And when Hilde came with the tray, Rosamund forced every morsel down her dry throat.

Chapter Fourteen

Rosamund did her best to appear brighter and more pleasant during the meal that evening, she truly did, but every time Lord Robert bestowed his dignified attentions her way, she could do nothing but stammer out some incoherent reply. She had no idea if any of the garbled statements she made were even sensible. He was kind in not calling attention to her inane presentation, although his puzzlement was apparent. Finally the man stopped trying, though from pity or disgust, she was unsure.

She knew she was disappointing Lady Veronica, who for some reason was most anxious Rosamund make a good impression on her future husband. When it was apparent this hope was fruitless, the good lady kept the conversation flowing by diverting Lord Robert with her own lively discussion. This left Rosamund free to contemplate her misery and examine in morbid detail the utter idiot she was making of herself.

And Agravar's blue eyes stayed on her every moment. He saw too much. Sometimes, it felt as though he saw everything.

Her earlier conversation with Veronica kept running through her mind, unleashing a myriad of questions to taunt her.

What would it be like to belong to Agravar?

She tried not to dwell on the enticing prospect. It did no good to crave what one could never have. Cyrus had taught her that. Her stepfather had been excellent at crushing tender hopes that might have spurred rebellious thoughts, or worse.

She dared not look again at Agravar, but she knew he was there, and that his gaze never strayed. She fixed her gaze over the heads of the crowd down at the trestles. It was then a face caught her notice. It was Davey.

He was off in a corner of the hall, seated at a table with a rowdy bunch of soldiers. Still dressed as a friar, the shiny top of his tonsure was slick with sweat and gleaming in the light cast off from the torches. He stood as soon as her gaze fell to him. He had obviously been trying to get her attention and was in motion the moment he succeeded. Inclining his head to the corridor leading to the kitchen, he headed out that way.

Rosamund remembered to breathe. She put her head down, feeling heat creep up from her neck to set the tips of her ears on fire.

Had anyone seen? Had *he*?

Glancing slyly to the side, she saw Agravar seemed at that particular moment to be otherwise occupied in conversation with a knight. Was she safe, then? He hadn't seen her reaction when Davey signaled her?

Rising, she waited silently at her place. Lucien looked over first, a bit taken aback by her just standing there. Robert said, "Rosamund, is something the matter?"

"Your pardon, my lord. May I be excused?"

There was a silence. She saw people were staring at her. Then Lord Robert cleared his throat and replied, "Of course, Rosamund. You need not ask my permission."

"I am sorry, my lord. I shan't trouble you again."

On her way off the dais, she saw Agravar was scowling.

She sensed she had done something to shock them all. What? Had she offended, as well? Had she embarrassed Lord Robert?

And what would he do to her if she had?

She rounded the corner and entered the corridor. A hand gripping her upper arm brought her swiftly into the shadows.

"Where have you been?" Davey whispered harshly. "I have been trying to get you to come for the past hour, but you refused to look at me."

They stole together along the darkened corridor. Rosamund glanced behind to make certain they were not seen. Once she was certain they were safely out of sight, she whirled on Davey. "First, I did not spy you until just now," she said, snapping her arm out of his grasp. "I came as soon as I did. And second, though I am in your debt for the efforts you have made on my behalf, I am still your mistress. I do not take orders from you, Davey."

"Who do you take them from them? Your Viking?"

"What? What has he to do with anything? And he is certainly not *my* Viking, as if it is any concern of yours."

"You will not take orders from me, you say? You dawdle in the woods and laugh sweet enough to make the birds jealous while I scrape and plot to make you free? You cannot toy with me this way, Rosamund!"

She was incredulous. "Davey, what has happened to you? You have no right to address me in such a manner."

He seemed to catch himself. Checking his burst of anger, he hung his head, the tip of his shoe scuffing restlessly in the scented rushes. "That is because I have never felt like this. I have never been through what I have in these last weeks." His head shot up, his eyes feverish. "I wait. I watch every day, my lady, and I see you grow more and more content and forget that your own disaster lies just ahead. Why, 'tis here—Lord Robert is here and your time of peace is nearly done." He sneered. "You think that Viking will save you. You think *he* will protect you."

"I do not!"

Davey was vehement. "He can do nothing for you. A giant he may be, and mighty, I'll grant. But he cannot help you, Rosamund. He serves Lucien and neither one of them will go against the law. Only I can win you your freedom. Can you not see? *He* is your enemy. Only I am your friend."

"Do not scold me," Rosamund said firmly, but inside she was trembling. "I know well that Agravar cannot save me, for all his kindness and sympathy. I would not ask it of him. He might pity me, but he serves Lucien." She paused, considering what she knew of Alayna's husband. "And Lucien would never stray from the ranks of what men of his position deem *right* and *honorable*. He of all of them terrifies me the most, with his dark looks and terrible scowls. I know he is gentle with Alayna, but he has never liked me. I do not believe he would ever be made to feel sympathy for my plight.''

She swallowed against the lump rising in her throat. Her voice grew harsh. "I am depending on *you*, Davey."

Davey fished in the folds of his monk's robes and brought out a pouch of a size that might carry three or four pears. And then he told her what to do. "I shall await you at the postern gate," he said finally.

Rosamund nodded. His plan was good. Daring, with no small degree of risk, but it just might succeed.

And yet she wasn't certain she could do it.

A deep sadness settled inside her breast. How difficult it would be to say goodbye to her pleasant days at Gastonbury and the good companionship of the kind folk who dwelled here, who had welcomed her and made her feel loved.

Silly thought! The happy existence she had found here was lost to her, whether she went on to Berendsfore or made good her escape with Davey.

And yet she *had* found a home here, a home like no other she had ever known. Friends were here. And Agravar. In some ways—in so many ways—it was he who was the hardest to leave. He had shown her parts of herself she hadn't known existed. And he had looked at her with something tender and fiery in his eyes. She did not fully understand it, but her body responded every time it happened. And she liked it. She wanted it.

She wanted him.

She did not want to leave, she realized suddenly.

Not him, not any of them. But she could not stay, either.

Someone was coming! Rosamund stuffed the pouch behind the front panel of her surcoat as Davey ducked away into the shadows.

"Rosamund? What are you doing?" It was Agravar, of course. He was ever on her heels, ever watching.

He looked troubled, a slight frown of concern on his hard-featured face. Her hand itched to reach out to those furrows between his brows and smooth them away with soft words and a light caress. But of course, even if she dared, what comfort would she offer when those lines were caused by his suspecting only what was true?

She stared mutely, all too aware of the pouch she had secreted in her dress.

"Why are you hiding?"

What would he say if she told him, *Help me, Agravar, I need to run away*?

The insanity of her thoughts troubled her. She refused to look at him. "I..." Her own words came back to her. *He would have no patience for my intrigues...I could never depend on him.* "I got lost. The castle is still unfamiliar to me and I got all turned around on my way back from the guarderobes."

His eyes narrowed, then darted a quick survey of the darkness around them. Head cocked, he listened, but no sound betrayed her lie. Davey was swift and already gone.

She looked at him in profile, taking in the strong chin, the high, narrow cheekbones, the hawklike nose. His blond hair, loose and looking like a skein of silk—if one could imagine such a delicate thing a part of such a rugged man—fell past his shoulders.

His head whipped back to hers, his golden-lashed eyes still suspicious. "I thought I heard voices."

"'Twas me. I was singing."

A doubtful scowl was her reply.

She said, "I must return to the—"

"I will speak to you a moment, lady. I would like some answers."

"To what questions?"

"So many they confuse my brain." He crossed his arms over his massive chest. "Let us start with why you have been behaving as if Robert is your executioner instead of your intended husband?"

"That is not true. Lord Robert is a good man." She said it like a catechism.

"Indeed, I have seen it to be true. So why are you reacting as if he were a demon sent from hell to claim your soul?"

Her voice trembled. "You are ridiculous."

"Am I? I find your behavior too peculiar, my lady, to be explained by your feeble excuses."

"I need not explain myself to you."

"'Tis true enough. I am of no account. Perhaps, then, I should go to Lord Robert with my concerns. You certainly have to explain yourself to him."

"Nay!" She grabbed at him with her free hand. "I beg you do not."

Agravar shook his head in amazement. "I should think you would be grateful to be wedded to a husband like him. I cannot imagine your life at Hallscroft was anything you shall miss."

She recoiled. "You know nothing about my past."

"Recollect, dear lady, that I met the priest who

was sent by your stepfather. 'Twas I who sat while he regaled me of his particular beliefs that I must admit was singularly disgusting to me—and I have, in my years, seen and heard a goodly amount to sour any man's stomach. I ask you to recall, fickle lady, that 'twas me who sent the repellent cad bouncing home like so much baggage.''

The mental picture evoked by his words was accurate. She paused, savoring the image. Despite herself, the corners of her mouth began to curl. '''Twas only what he deserved. He was rude to you and Lady Veronica.''

'''Twas for what he said to you that I did it.'' His voice was soft.

''I did not ask you to do it.''

''You ask nothing of no one, and yet we clamor for the privilege to give. Have you noticed? Lady Veronica, Alayna, myself, even poor Lucien does his pathetic best to be cheerful for your sake. Why do you resist it, Rosamund, when all around you is naught but kindness? 'Twas not a man, woman or child in this castle who didn't despise that priest once they realized what he was about.'' Agravar grinned. ''Did you see how his heels dangled down so far they scraped two furrows in the dirt?''

'''Twas a very undignified exit,'' she agreed with a quick giggle. Her heart felt full and light. How easy it was to forget herself in his presence.

He was doing it again—making the impossible happen. Making her feel like another woman altogether, with other choices.

He stepped closer, his blue eyes clouding to a darker shade. When he spoke, his voice was husky. ''I nearly killed him. I wanted to. 'Twas the first time

I had felt the urge like that, outside of battle. He had hurt you.''

Fighting the draw of his words, she tried to breathe normally.

He touched his fingers to her chin and tiny darts of pleasure crawled over her skin. Did he know what he did to her with his touch? ''I hate that,'' he murmured. ''I hate to think of those things being said to you, taught to you all your life. It is horrid to have lies fed you. When you are raised with them, you get so confused. Right and wrong get turned upside down and you do not know what is real anymore.''

Her head swirled. The touch of both his fingers and his words was like a drug.

''Rosamund…''

He was stroking her flesh. A strange feeling came over her, something akin to a trance.

She waited, not daring to breathe.

She was afraid he would kiss her. She wanted him to, she was desperate for him to take that one final step and she would be his completely. She would melt in his arms and tell him everything and weep on his strong shoulder. But that would only make the leaving all the worse.

Much, much worse.

Casting about for something—anything—to give her back her head, she murmured, ''Lord Robert may be looking for me to return.''

It must have been the right thing to have said. He stopped those titillating sliding motions with his fingers. His features hardened. ''He will not mind,'' Agravar said, but his voice was sharper, stronger.

She was regaining control of her senses. ''Still, I should not like to anger him.''

He seemed to struggle with some reply he wished to make, but he chewed the inside of his cheek and kept silent. Her body felt weak, but she drew on her reserves of strength. Slipping past him, she went only a few steps before she paused.

With a bit of distance between them, she turned to look at him. She thought about what had almost happened. She thought about kissing him. What did it matter? The pouch was in her hand, safe and secret. Tomorrow she would be gone and it would not matter at all.

What if she placed herself in his capable hands and lay with him, giving in to the desire that scalded her heart? What if she offered him her innocence in this last night together?

Tomorrow, she thought wryly, she would be dead. Would it matter that she was not a virgin?

"Go on, go to your bed," he commanded. "I know you do not wish to return, and frankly we will all be relieved of your nerve-racking presence. I will make your excuses to Robert."

Aye, she could not go back in there. The wonderful thing about death was that while it cheated passion, it also freed one from fear. Robert's anger was no longer to be dreaded.

She slipped away, almost racing up the stairs to the exile of her lonely chamber to do what she must. Death and resurrection awaited her, and the mighty Viking Agravar could be no part of it.

Chapter Fifteen

It was a clear morning, with just a touch of mist. It would burn off later, but it was early yet and the tendrils clung low to the ground like wisps of ghosts reluctant to be banished from their midnight reveries by the clear, pure light of the sun.

In the armory by the east wall, Lucien, Will and Agravar stood inspecting the fine array of steel.

They were together again, the three of them, sharing the treasured camaraderie. With swords in their hands and their laughter mingling, it was as if the years that had changed them from the three soldiers fighting for a uniting cause had never passed.

Agravar was amazed how familiar it all seemed. Familiar and pleasant. Lucien was as relaxed as was possible for him, a state denoted by the small smile playing on his lips, with himself and Will forming a brotherly circle around him—the kind of fond affection expressed by tormenting and ruthless jests. Will's quick wit and lighthearted antics were part of it, as was Agravar's occasional, slightly snide comments, or brutal observations that Will wouldn't dare.

A figure appeared in the doorway, cutting off the

deep echoes of masculine laughter. The three turned
to the woman. Agravar recognized her immediately,
although they had met only once before, at Will's
castle, and she had looked…well, quite different.

Olivia was pretty and slim, a quiet woman who
had first appeared wrapped in rags and mystery, both
of which Will had made short shrift of last Christ-
mastide. They had been wed the New Year's Day
just passed. Her gentle influence had healed the
breach between Will and his overlord and brought
Will back to the friendship from which he had become estranged.

She now looked to Will and smiled, but remained
where she was when he held out his hand for her to
come to his side. To Lucien, she dipped a curtsy.
"My lord. I beg your leave."

"Good God, Will, tell your wife to leave off such
formality. Has she been taking lessons from Rosamund?"

Will grinned, gesturing to his shocked bride.
"Come, love. Lucien detests such displays. Say what
you need."

"I regret to disturb you, but there is some problem
with the Lady Rosamund. Veronica has sent me to
fetch Lord Lucien."

Lucien grunted in disgust. "Call Lord Robert, for
she is his responsibility now." At Olivia's taken-
aback expression, he amended reluctantly, "Oh, very
well. What is the problem with the Lady Rosamund?"

Olivia, unlike Rosamund, was not at all afraid of
Lucien's bluster. She explained, "She has bolted her
door against us. Her maid has been trying to gain
entry, but the lady will not answer."

Agravar felt the first flutter of alarm. He stepped forward. "Are you certain she is inside?"

"Sir, the door is locked." She blinked prettily, showing her consternation. "If not she, then who could have thrown the bolt?"

"What does she say?"

"She says nothing. She has not answered our call."

"God's boots, what is the chit up to?" Lucien's tone was curt. "She has been nothing but a trial since the moment she arrived on my lands. For all that is holy, she tests my nerves."

"Surely you cannot fault her for falling victim to miscreants," Agravar snapped. He was surprised at the irritation he felt at Lucien's unsympathetic opinions.

Something was wrong. Very wrong.

Undaunted by their bickering, Olivia interceded. "Lady Veronica sent me to fetch you. She fears you may have to force the door. Will you come?"

Agravar took off at a run, caring nothing for those who chanced into his path. Without apology, he shoved them aside, landing several unfortunate folks on their rumps. Up the stairs to her bedchamber he flew, his mind focusing on a single pinpoint of fear.

What had the little fool gotten herself into?

Arriving at her chamber, he tried the door first, futilely jiggling the latch.

"We have tried that," Lady Veronica said dryly. He hadn't seen her, waiting off to one side of the corridor with Rosamund's maid.

He looked over the portal and raised both his fists. Bringing them down on the oak planks until it shook on its hinges, he called, "Rosamund!"

Veronica looked impatient. "We tried that as well, Agravar!"

Hilde flew up to him and grasped his arm. "I have been calling her, sir, but she comes not! Oh, I know 'tis disaster. I daresay, that child has come to an evil end. Oh, my good, sweet Rosamund, so gentle, so fair—"

Hilde's wails were cut off abruptly as he disengaged himself and turned his attention again to the door in front of him. His eyes quickly scanned the perimeter of the portal, assessing, weighing options.

Behind him, Hilde clucked and retreated behind Veronica.

"Break it down," Lucien ordered.

They arranged themselves three across, each with their shoulder turned in toward the door, hunched, legs bent. Agravar counted, "One, two—"

On three, they surged, crashing painfully into the wood. The sound of it splintering was crisp, but it did not give way.

"Again. One, two—"

It took two more tries before a plank succumbed. Agravar stepped back and drew back his mighty fist, thrusting it through the broken wood. His hand groped, found the bolt and threw it from its brace.

He drew in his hand, gritting his teeth against the splinters sliding under his flesh. The maid shrieked at the blood dripping from his hand. "My Lord, your arm is in ribbons."

He didn't even glance at the wounds. Opening the door, he and his companions rushed into the room.

There was no one there. The bed was not slept in, not a thing was disturbed. He stood in the middle of the floor, taking it all in with a sweep of his eyes and not moving another muscle.

Hilde brushed past them. ''Mistress Rosamund? Mistress? Oh, my dear, where can she be?''

Veronica was calling Rosamund's name in a gentle, shaking voice. Olivia crept in, wary, looking about with wide eyes.

She shrieked and Agravar followed her line of sight. He saw the blood. His heart froze in his chest.

Several things happened in the space of a single instant. His vision converged on the thick, brownish puddle by the window. He saw that there were touches of it on other things—the chest, the dressing table, a long, grisly smear against the wall. Another by the hearth mantel.

Then he heard a scream. Hilde, probably, just now spotting the blood. A gasp followed, and some muttered words behind him. Veronica.

Will stepped forward and began to inspect the stains.

Lucien spoke softly from behind Agravar. He was ordering the ladies out of the room.

Will went to the window and peered down. Glancing back over his shoulder, he shook his head at Lucien then continued to search the room. Agravar instantly understood what he was doing. He was looking for her body.

Nay. She isn't dead.

Agravar's brain was crowded with snatches of memory. Phrases, visions. The turret stairs, the garden. The woods. Just last night, in the alcove off the hall.

Lucien placed a hand on his shoulder. ''Agravar,

you know her best. Do you have any knowledge that would help us?''

Will came up just then and said one word. ''Nothing.''

No body, then.

''Agravar,'' Lucien prodded.

He closed his eyes, turning away from the press of emotion in his breast. Think, he commanded. What the devil was going on here? *Think!*

The priest. She had been terrified of him. Had he returned and done this out of revenge? Or had whatever secret she had harbored driven her to take her own life?

But if that were so, where was she? Even if she were murdered, why would her assailant take away her lifeless body?

Agravar snapped his lids open. ''The blood means nothing. We must assume she is alive.''

''Agreed.''

His thoughts churned. She had said once that she was an expert of sorts on evil. What did that mean? What evil was done here last night?

''Agravar, did you hear me?''

''We must ride out.'' He drew in a bracing breath before he spoke. ''If her body is not here, the blood means nothing. Even if she is...is dead, then her murderer cannot be far-off.''

Lucien was unsure. ''Perhaps we should search the castle first.''

''Nay,'' Agravar shot impatiently. ''I say we waste no time in getting under way.''

Will was uncomfortable. ''The stains have already turned stale. It has been hours.''

Agravar looked at Will with such intensity the

other man actually blanched. Through grinding teeth, Agravar growled, "Then we best hurry, hadn't we?"

There was nothing else said. They went to make ready.

In the open, in the meadow, the world seemed unreal. The color of the sky seemed lurid, a distastefully gaudy blue clashing hopelessly with the sour greens of the fields.

Agravar was numb. He kept trying to shake himself out of it, for he needed his senses sharp, but his brain was stuck on the unspeakable question of what he would do if he lost her.

It was his fault. He was captain—it was his duty to see to the safety of the castle and all within. He had known there was something wrong with her, some trouble, some…secret thing she held away from him. He should have known to watch her more closely, to question her with greater force.

Lord Robert had joined them, riding between Lucien and Will. His face was ashen, his wide-shouldered body taut. His men rode with Lucien's guard as they swept into the woods.

Agravar had an odd thought. The last time they were in these woods, he had ridden down her abductors and gotten her back. Twice, in fact. *Please, Father,* he prayed, *let me be lucky one more time.*

Twice. He had saved her twice.

His brain kicked into action.

They rode on, not talking. Listening, searching the ground for hoofprints, the horizon for a flash of color, a sign.

Twice she had been abducted. This time being the *third.*

Three times? What were the chances of a maid coming to harm *three times* in so short a space as a few fortnights?

And then he remembered that the very first time he had spotted her, it had been from across this very meadow, riding with the kidnapper toward the woods that led to the river.

Riding alongside the man in the red hat. With no tethers on her. Why had it never occurred to him before?

Unfair, he thought. That would not, in itself, have meant anything. A terrified maid would follow orders under duress, or threat, without need of binding.

Perhaps only now, after knowing her restive nervousness, her fears, her haunted face and all of the secrets she clasped so desperately to her heart, could he suspect such a thing.

Could he suspect such a thing?

Lightning fast, images flashed through his mind again, this time with a purpose.

Are you an expert on evil, Rosamund?

Aye, I am. Of sorts.

Sneaking off to the turret, alone in the darkened corridor near the kitchens.

The man in the red hat.

Why had the kidnapper wanted only her—not even her jewels had been stolen. Ransom? Some grudge, perhaps?

Reining in his horse, he stopped.

"Lucien," he called, "I...my brain is nagging me."

Interested, Lucien stopped and twisted in his saddle. "What is it?"

He suddenly felt ridiculous. "I do not know. Something. I cannot explain."

"Speak, Agravar. Your instincts are always keen."

When he had fetched her back before, she and her companion had been headed to the river that ran through the woods up here. Following it north, it wound around the foundations of Thalsbury, Will's demesne. South, it led into the Dove, which fed into the Trent.

Such a clever abduction, so close to the waterways and easy access to escape. As if the kidnapper had known she would be along just at that moment in the opportune place where they could away to the sea.

"Let me go to the river. I go alone. We cannot spare the men for the search of the woods. If 'tis but my imagination, I'll not risk her life on mere suspicions, but I have to see for myself if what I suspect is possible. You go on and comb the forest."

"Go ahead, then, but take some men."

"Nay. It may mean the difference in the ground you can cover, and yours is the more plausible route for them to have gone. If naught comes of my hunch, I shall join you presently."

Lucien paused, considering it. Nodding, he murmured, "A-Viking."

Agravar jerked his destrier about. "A-Viking."

Rosamund paced the banks of the river.

Davey was hunched over the small fire he had built, chuckling and rubbing his hands together against the encroaching chill. "The blood will scramble their heads," he crowed. "They will search the castle, high and low, and they will sit and puzzle and puzzle. 'Where has she gone? What has become of her?' they will wonder, all to no avail.''

"But why did we bolt the door?" She rubbed her arms briskly. "Does it not make it seem more suspicious?"

"Of course, Rosamund." He was calling her Rosamund now. No more "my lady." It made her uncomfortable, as did his swaggering confidence. "The intrigue of it all shall have them tied into knots for hours. That was my plan, you see, to outwit them so that they would not know what was what."

"Will they find the scaling ladder, do you think? Then, they will know."

"What of it? 'Tis something every castle keeps. They will take no note of it, rest assured. Nothing to connect it to our little game."

She glanced up the river. "The boat should be here soon. I wish it would hurry. To be this close to freedom, and still know they are on our trail, it makes me nervous."

"There is time, yet. And I assured you, they will not be after us so soon. Relax. Ah, there is something I have not yet told you. The boat…it was safer to arrange for it not to come until the morrow."

"The morrow? We must spend the night here, so close to Gastonbury?"

"Rosamund, be at ease. I sent a messenger ahead with a bag of gold and the boat will be here at first light. And in a few moments, we shall take to the trails again."

Rosamund didn't like it. She didn't like any of this. One night away from her long-relished dream of freedom, and her heart was filled with nothing but regret.

Davey was saying, "We still have a ways to travel, but no rush. We have ridden hard, we must give the horses a chance to rest."

"I should feel so much safer if we were under sail. Why could not the boat come up the river today?"

"Lord Lucien keeps up patrols too well, and I wanted to leave plenty of time for the rendezvous in case there were any problems." He seemed disgruntled to have to admit this weakness in his plan. "Rosamund, cease this questioning. I have planned well for all eventualities. Come, sit by me. Warm yourself. There is a chill in the air this morn. Summer is over." He flashed her a triumphant smile. "By winter, we shall be in warmer climes."

She *was* cold, but it was a coldness no fire could cure. She continued to walk her tight circle. "I cannot be reassured, Davey."

"Rosamund." His voice, amazingly, sounded chiding. Even demanding. "It wounds me that you doubt me so."

"I just do not see why we have to linger here when it is so dangerous." But she did understand part of it. It was his triumph, to languish just under their noses, refuse to hurry because his clever plan was so brilliant that they could never figure it out in time.

Rosamund was reminded of the old fable of the tortoise and the hare. She was tempted to say so, but Davey had had enough of her challenges. He snapped, "'Tis all taken care of, now sit yourself down and not another word about it!"

She saw his arrogance and realized in a flash of

clarity that she had made a dreadful mistake in trusting him. On the heels of this revelation, she heard the hoofbeats.

Davey shot to his feet. "Who is that?" he barked accusingly, as if it were her fault. As if she would know who it was who approached.

But she did.

Oh, she did—she knew who it was, as if a part of her that was inexplicably connected to that Viking could sense his increasing nearness as his great destrier ate up the ground with every long-reaching stride.

"I only hear one. Do you only hear one?" Davey's anxiety was infectious. Her joy receded. Her heart began to hammer. "I think 'tis only one man, Rosamund. Stay there."

Frozen, she watched him steal into the forest. Was he abandoning her?

She whipped around when the sound of snapping bracken pierced her confusion.

Agravar appeared, breaking through the foliage like an apparition. He reared the destrier to a halt and slid off its back in one fluid motion. He went perfectly still, standing with his legs braced wide, arms loose at his sides, pinning her with those brilliant eyes of blue.

Something filled her up. Inside, a bittersweet emotion flooded through her, drowning her apprehensions, overshadowing every thought.

She had thought never to see him again.

She walked toward him, her legs seeming to move of their own volition. Forgetting Davey, forgetting everything that was insane around her, she kept going, step after step. His eyes held hers fast and they were wild, as wild as the thing inside her that she could no longer keep under control.

Chapter Sixteen

Agravar was stunned when she flung herself into his arms.

He had expected her to run, he had expected her to rile, to curse him, damn him. What he had not expected was to see the look of naked agony on her face as if she had been awaiting him. Wanting him for the longest time and he had finally come.

Ah, God, she was alive.

She fit beautifully up against his body, snug, with all the right parts meshing. Her soft breasts against his chest, her hips against his thigh, her long legs all along his. His arms pulled her tighter. He wanted to take her into himself, possess her, feel her—with such a fierceness it left his mighty body trembling.

He placed a large hand over her head as she lay her cheek against his shoulder, his fingers pushing into her hair. Nuzzling her neck, her scent assaulted him. As always it made his head swim and his body hard. He looked up, seeking distance from its drugging effects, and breathed in deep, clean air to clear his head.

Leaning back, she peered at him curiously. Taking

his face in her hands, her eyes searched his features. There were tears brimming in her eyes. "I'm sorry," she murmured, and then she kissed him.

Her mouth was soft, supple. He was too taken aback at first to answer the timid demand, but then his need seized him and he slanted his mouth across hers. Opening her, he tasted gently, sliding his tongue between her lips, over her teeth, then deeper, boldly thrusting. She reacted with shock at first; she most likely hadn't known about this new, intimate kind of kiss. But as his tongue twined around hers, she melted again in his arms, and answered with a dawning passion that flooded his head with intoxicating vigor.

Some part of his brain that still functioned sent out a sluggish warning. He knew, remotely, inconsequentially, how strange it was that she would be here with him after fleeing, and that part clamored for answers. He acknowledged its weak prodding, designated it for a time in the future. Now was for sensation, the sweet foolish drug that stole away all sensibility. He could not get enough. This was Rosamund, he kept thinking, here at last in his arms. His. His at last, if only for a little while.

Their lips parted. She looked up at him, dazed, heavy lidded. He slid his fingers over her cheeks, brushing away the lingering wetness.

He didn't understand why her eyes widened, or why she took a step away from him. "Rosamund?" he asked, his hands outstretched. He thought the look of horror on her face was for the fact that they had just kissed so crazily, and now, in her typically unpredictable and incomprehensible way, she regretted it. Then she did something that unnerved him further.

She held out her hands for him and screamed, "Nay!"

He was standing there dumbfounded when the blow landed on his head. There was pain, and a deep, abiding flash of disappointment. Then there was nothing.

"Did you have to hit him so hard?" Rosamund shrieked, falling on her knees to Agravar's side.

"Of course, I had to hit him that hard, he's a giant Viking!" Davey circled the downed man, the heavy branch at the ready lest the Viking prove not completely subdued.

Rosamund rolled Agravar onto his back, smoothing the tangled strands from where they weaved into his lashes. He looked pale, so pale. Her hand trembled as it touched the back of his scalp where a huge welt had arisen. Her hand came back bloodied.

"Oh, dear God."

"Don't be a ninny," Davey snapped. "I didn't kill him. He is only unconscious, and for but a little while. Get the rope from my saddle. We must tie him before he awakens."

She shot him a resentful, doubtful look. Davey narrowed his eyes. "Go, or do you wish to be taken back to Lord Robert? What will he do to you now, do you think? Surely he will not be pleased at your having fled him."

Her mouth went dry.

He continued, "You could beg his forgiveness, I suppose, but would it weigh on your conscience at all that I will hang?"

Scrambling to her feet, she went to do what he told her.

"Stop weeping," Davey demanded when she returned and handed him the line of hemp. "Here, help me. He is too heavy."

Together they managed to get Agravar's ankles bound together. Lashing his thick wrists behind his back proved more challenging. His arms were heavy, his shoulders overlaid with muscle so that it took all Davey's might to hold the Viking's hands behind his back while Rosamund quickly tied the ropes. Davey checked her knot, securing it. She winced at Agravar's face being pressed into the dirt while they yanked and pulled at his massive form. "Be gentle," she admonished. Davey threw her a mutinous glance and jerked the hemp tight.

"Now help me drag him into the woods," Davey said when they were done.

Rosamund took one side, Davey the other. It was several tries before they even managed to budge their burden.

Rosamund straightened, chest heaving. "We cannot do it, he is too large."

"Come, try again," Davey urged.

They did, making slow progress toward the copse. It sickened Rosamund to see how Agravar's head lolled, his hair dragging. She thought of his wound and fretted he was being hurt anew. She worried whether he would ever wake again, then wondered with dread what would happen if he did.

She felt like a betrayer. She *was* a betrayer.

Davey paused, looking around them as he pushed a damp lock of hair out of his eyes. "We can leave him here. I shall tie him to the trunk of this tree."

"Nay," Rosamund protested. "He will be utterly defenseless."

Davey spun on her. "Would you rather dump him into the water? We can take him back down to the river's edge and do it."

Having had enough of the man's imperiousness, she drew herself up and took a stern tone. "He shall not be left out in the open where any passing beast will have him at their will. Your mercilessness is appalling, Davey. I never intended to bring harm to anyone. We thought it out carefully for that purpose."

"Then what do you wish to do with him? Think you to bring him with us?" He sneered. "That would suit you, I'll wager."

"Of course not. Let me think." She pulled at her gown as she walked away a bit. It clung to her, her body wet with perspiration from her exertions, the cool turn in the weather notwithstanding.

Whirling, she said, "Did we not see a ruin on our way here? 'Twas an abbey or something. We can take him there. 'Twill provide a shelter for him."

"What? Ridiculous. That is in the wrong direction. We cannot head back to Gastonbury."

She cocked her hands on her hips and jutted up her chin. "I'll not go another step if he is left thusly, Davey. Forget not I am your mistress and I shall make it a command if I have to. We will take him to safety or we will not go on."

"Rosamund, think of the time we will lose."

"What is this? Only moments before he arrived, you assured me that we had plenty."

"To a point, aye, but with this delay…"

"Then you will have to make it turn out for the better, Davey, but I shall not waver. We head to the ruins. I shall not leave him to perish."

His lips pulled back from his teeth in an ugly grimace. "Is your heat for the Viking so great you would risk this for his sake?"

Her voice was cold. "You will not speak to me in that manner. Now bring him. Together, we must do it."

Sullenly he grabbed Agravar's arm. With no attention to the prone man's comfort, he yanked, dragging him along the forest floor.

"Gently, Davey, gently."

First there was pain. The physical kind, outside him, all over his body, and inside him, in his brain. His head throbbed.

Then there was touch. Soft pressure at his forehead, soothing, caressing.

Agravar slitted his eyes open and there were soft brown orbs staring back at him. Her lips trembled into the slightest of smiles, but her eyes stayed sad. "Hello."

He frowned. "What happened? Where are we?"

She jerked her gaze away, suddenly reluctant. "You were struck."

"Who—?" He made to stand but several things stopped him. Pain, for one thing. It flared anew, nearly taking him back into the void. The realization that his hands were bound was another. His ankles as well.

Her hands came to his chest and eased him back. "Rest, Agravar."

He looked around them. They were in some sort of a ruin, an old church, it looked like. A large one. Sections of walls, crumbling arches, empty window holes devoid of its glass were lined up on either side.

Huge chunks of stone were strewn willy-nilly, as if some gigantic child had been playing and left his toys untidied. Grass grew around them, attesting to the mythical creature's long absence. "What is this place?" he asked. "Rosamund, untie me. What are you about?"

"I cannot. Please, just relax. I promise no harm will come to you."

"You kissed me!" he accused, his memory returning. "Then someone knocked me on the noggin."

"'Twas dreadful, I know."

His look was wry. "The kiss?"

"Nay! My man striking you."

"The devil with the plumed hat. He was your man all along, was he not?"

"Aye. His name is Davey."

"Is he a priest? I thought I saw a tonsure before I blacked out."

"Nay. He was posturing as one."

"Oh. I understand now. He was the one at Gastonbury. The one you were always running off to meet. Is he your lover?"

"Nay!"

He found relief in her denial. "He hit me." It was a bit difficult to focus, but he could do so if he concentrated. However, the effort made him feel queasy. "It is time for answers," he demanded weakly.

"Be at ease." Her delicate hands brushed down his chest, soothing him. It felt erotic. It wasn't, it was sweet and tender, but anything this woman did would seem erotic to him. Embarrassingly, his body responded. God, this was agony of every kind!

"Davey is helping me to escape."

"Why do you need to escape? Escape what?"

"I am leaving Gastonbury. I am leaving England. I..."

She looked off, her eyes searching the sky for something. Perhaps for some help. Perhaps for Davey. Where had the knave gone to, anyway?

"You shall hate me when you hear it," she said quietly. So demure, so deceptively reserved.

He settled back, nesting the back of his head in the softness of some leaves. She must have fashioned him a little pillow. The thoughtfulness touched him. "Tell me," he croaked. "Put an end to all of my wondering."

She took a long time to begin. "I do not wish to marry Robert. This you know."

"But I cannot fathom why."

"I know he is kind, I know he is gentle and good, and...how can I tell you how it is? There are no words. I wish to belong to no man. I have seen things, Agravar, that have made me afraid. My mother..." Halting her garbled confession, she drew in a shaky breath.

"I shall start at the beginning, and then perhaps you will understand. My mother married Cyrus of Hallscroft when I was three. My father had been slain in a border raid in the Welsh marches, and we were forced to return to my mother's home. My grandfather made the second match for my mother without knowing much about Cyrus, but I do not believe it would have made much difference if he had. Once, years after she was married, she ran away and made her way back to him. She told them about Cyrus, about what 'twas like for her. He brought her back to Hallscroft. He told her a wife's place was with her husband, no matter what.''

Words to ease her came to his lips, but he choked them back. He listened.

''You met Father Leon. He was the least of the trials at Hallscroft. Hateful sermons on the corruption of Eve, dire predictions of Jezebel and Delilah and the whore of Babylon. I had the stories in my head to divert me.''

''What?''

''Oh…'tis another matter altogether. Suffice it to understand that the poisons Father Leon spewed— they were only words. Cyrus encouraged Leon, approved of his ways. I was put under his supervision.''

Agravar ground his teeth to think of it. The action caused his head to feel as if a woodsman's ax had split it asunder.

His vision blurred, readjusted. ''Rosamund, untie me.''

She winced, obviously wanting to. ''Nay, I cannot.''

''I shall not harm you. I swear it.'' He wanted to touch her. ''Just free my hands. Please.''

She hesitated. Finally she shook her head.

Grimacing against the ache in his head, he sighed. ''Very well. Let me hear the rest then.''

She was silent so long, he thought he had ruined the moment with his demands, but she eventually spoke again. ''Father Leon was not the worst of it, as I have said. 'Twas my mother—what I saw happen to her. I watched it, Agravar. Day after day as she…withered. Cyrus's cruelty was so horrible.

''She was kept as a prisoner—nay, worse. She had no more independence than one of the hounds that were trained to sit at their master's feet. He governed every action, every move. She was not allowed out of her solar without permission. Sometimes she would beg to go for a walk in the gardens. Weeks would pass until finally her wish was granted. And Cyrus, with his smooth lies and falseness, would act as if it were the epitome of beneficence that he allowed it. When in the hall, she had to attend him. She would have to wait in silence for her husband's bidding, and when he called, she was to answer without question. The smallest infraction, the slightest delay, was not tolerated.''

She swallowed hard. She still hadn't looked at him.

"Once, when she was with child, we were at supper. She…she needed to use the garderobes. This was a frequent occurrence because of her condition. She asked to be pardoned to attend to her needs. Cyrus was in a foul mood. He refused, forcing her to remain and attend him until he saw fit to excuse her. As her discomfort grew, she began to weep. This made him furious. He ignored her. The hour waned. She…she was humiliated when she could no longer… He…was the first time he ever struck her in front of others.''

Her chin quivered and she blinked rapidly, fixing her gaze on some far-off point, not seeing it anyway, for all her thoughts were focused within.

"He killed her soon after that. I often wonder if the horror of that last time did not spark some rebellion in her. Did she provoke him too far, so far that he finally lost control of himself?''

"Dear God, Rosamund, 'tis a nightmare you describe. Did no one know he was a murderer?''

"'Twas judged an accident. He pushed her from the battlements where she used to sneak off to walk sometimes. I remember how she used to climb the tower stairs with her cloak around her, with such a look of anticipation it used to make my heart ache. I think 'twas the only time she had peace. I'm glad 'twas there she had her last hours on earth. It was her happiest place."

"Ah, Rosamund, I am so sorry." Bracing himself against the taunting fuzziness in his head, he pulled hard at the ropes at his wrists. He thought he felt them loosening. He desperately wanted his hands free, for the need to reach out to her was fairly choking him, but his strength ebbed abruptly and he had to stop.

Dashing away the tears, she seemed to recollect herself. "So you see, I could never marry. I cannot marry any man, and be like she was."

He said, "Surely you know not all men are like Cyrus."

"How is one to know? No one looking at our family from the outside could have known the truth. Cyrus was crafty. So much of what he did was in private, and when my mother's bruises showed, he always had an excuse ready. His men admired him and thought, if they ever did give the matter any consideration, that their lord was merely meting out just punishment, just as many husbands do to wayward wives."

"That was what you meant, then, when you said you were an expert in evil."

She nodded.

"Surely there were good men at Hallscroft, who might have guessed at the truth. Men who could have helped if had they known. I cannot believe the entire castle was so misguided, or depraved.''

''Oh, aye, I daresay there were. Good men who ignored their liege's wife's limping, or the purple bruises on her neck where it showed just above the neckline of her dress. No one questioned her long absences from the hall when the damage couldn't be concealed and she had to hide herself away. 'Twas none of their affair, you see, so they lowered their heads when she hobbled by and drank their mead and no one helped us. Nay, Agravar, I have never in my youth known a man to be of a good and kind nature.''

''Someone helped you. This Davey—who is he?''

''A crofter's son who, but for his humble station, would have made a fine knight. He had been friend to my brother, Harold, who I lost in my tenth year. Often, I would hide in the pantry and he and Harold would come and keep me company. He remained my friend after Harold died, always there to help me in so many ways. Often, I would be banished to my room for hours on end, sometimes days, to contemplate my 'lessons,' and Davey would steal manuscripts from the library and sneak them to me under my food tray because he knew I liked to read. A few times, he lied for me. 'Twas much for him to risk. He was my only protector, my friend. If Cyrus had ever known of it—'' she shuddered ''—I dare not think of what he might have done to us.''

A cold fist closed over his throat. ''Did Cyrus raise his hands to you?''

''Beyond the normal beatings given a child, nay,'' she answered. She sniffed, drawing herself up as she shook off the worst of her melancholy. ''He was obsessed with my mother, you see. She was *his*. I was nothing of consequence. A tool to get to her, sometimes, but beyond that, nothing. After she died, he kept up my instruction in *proper behavior* under Father Leon, but until he thought to make an alliance with Robert, I do not think he ever gave me much thought.''

''Perhaps a blessing.'' He felt weaker. He felt he was fading. He struggled to remain alert.

She looked down at him, her hair falling on either side of her, pooling on his shoulders. It seemed to curtain them in a secret place, just the two of them alone. Her long, graceful fingers fiddled absently with his tunic. The action was nearly affectionate. ''I often dreamed of killing him. I wish I could have. I wish I had.''

''Nay, you do not want that.''

''How can you know, Agravar?''

''Oh, Rosamund, have you never wondered why we seemed drawn to each other? What is this bond we share? You feel it, too, that I know. We have had it between us from the first. 'Tis the attraction of like souls. Yours and mine. We are a kind. We understand each other.''

Her honey-brown eyes were clouded. ''How can you understand anything? Oh, I realize you comprehend it, but understanding…'tis different. 'Tis deeper. That I have no hope of. Not from you, nor from anyone else.''

''And yet you have it. You would detest pity, so I'll not offer such a paltry thing. But I can know what burdens your heart bears, for I have shared similar ones in my time. *I know*, Rosamund. The suffering you describe tears me asunder, for I know what it is to feel it.''

"Then you will know why I must leave. I shall never vow to obey a man, and should it be sin, I shall gladly pay my debt to the Lord. No roasting in purgatory could serve up as much suffering as a husband. I want no man.''

"You want me," he said with a sudden burst of knowing.

Her head fell forward, chin to chest, and all at once she began to weep. Quickly she scrabbled to her feet and walked away.

He wanted her back. He would have called her, but the weakness was coming again, and this time it wouldn't let him go. She stood on the edge of the copse, her back to him.

He needed her.

His world was shrinking, the pain growing larger and larger. His own words were faint and faraway.

"I'm afraid I have to sleep now. I do not know what undid me more—" he chuckled "—your kiss or the blow."

His dry laughter echoed as he faded into the depths of darkness.

Chapter Seventeen

His words stayed with her, dogging her, leaping up to nip at her conscience.

You want me.

Oh, aye, she wanted him. But what good was it?

Sighing, she raised her eyes and scanned the woods. Where was Davey? He should have returned by now. When she had refused to leave Agravar until she was assured he would recover, he had ridden to the rendezvous spot to leave a message for the boat he expected, informing them of the delay and arranging another time. It had been midmorning when he left, and now the sun was drifting along on the waning side of its zenith. She had no talent to tell the hour by it, but would suppose it was two or three hours after noon.

Sometimes she stole looks over at Agravar's sleeping form. She had taken the blanket from her horse to cover him, even though it was warm enough here where the sun slanted down in yellow bars between the remnants of the cathedral walls. Still, if it didn't bring him comfort, it made her feel better to see him tucked up more cozily than just strewn carelessly onto the ground.

He was such a beautiful man. In sleep, his features in repose, he was perfect. It made her heart ache a little to look at him.

After a while, she went to the far corner of the ruin and sat to await Davey.

When he awoke again, he was in the same spot, in the same position. There was a blanket over him. It smelled of hay and horse sweat and it was making him impossibly hot.

Looking above him, he saw that there were shattered remnants of stone arches reaching aimlessly toward the thin blue of the sky. He hadn't noticed before how the place looked like a carcass, bare ribs cradling him in the cavity where once the heart had resided.

Rosamund? Where had she gone? Had she left already?

Turning his head, he saw her. She was sitting a ways off, where the nave would have been in this derelict cathedral.

"Weren't you going to leave England?" he said dryly.

Her head came up at the sound of his voice and she was at his side in an instant, a skin of water in her hand. "Here, drink," she prodded.

He did so and felt better. His head still ached, but his thoughts were clear. His limbs were stiff from their immobility and the bindings cut painfully into his flesh. "Where is your man?" he asked. "How long have I been sleeping?"

"Only a few hours. Davey is down the river a

ways. We were to make a rendezvous, but the delay meant he had to go to his friend to arrange—'' She cut off abruptly, perhaps considering that it was not wise to tell him so much.

His laugh was humorless. ''I was merely curious. I am hardly in a position to stop you.''

''I shall never underestimate the mighty Viking Agravar,'' she said, and nearly smiled.

''You imbue me with powers I do not have, I assure you.'' Slowly he began to work his wrists together, remembering just now that before he lost consciousness, he had thought he felt them loosening. He was right. There was enough give for him to twist his wrists into a different position. His fingers curled inward, probing for the knot.

''Does your head pain you?'' she asked, threading her hands through his hair. She had touched him frequently enough that it shouldn't cause these frissons of pleasure to jolt through him like this.

''It will be all right,'' he said, jerking away. Not that he didn't like it—he did. But it was nearly too much. And he couldn't stand being helpless. ''Where shall you go, Rosamund?'' She hesitated and he laughed. ''I am not going to come after you and fetch you back, considering my present circumstances.''

''I am leaving England.''

''So you have said.'' He found the knot. His fingers explored it, located the ends and began to pluck at it. All while he endeavored to keep the rest of his body as still as possible. ''Shall you go north? South?''

''To the continent,'' she said, then pressed her lips together.

''You do not have to do this.''

"Nay?" She gave him a look that seemed to say she found him daft. "What alternatives do you propose?"

"You have friends, you know. People who will help you."

"I think that people like to think themselves good, but when the test of their charity comes, they find excuses to avoid mixing in other's affairs."

"Think you Lady Veronica to be that sort?"

That snagged her. Her breath caught in a ragged gasp, and her face closed, a signal their conversation was over.

Of course, Agravar pressed on. "And what of Alayna? I have known the lady a long time and she has proved no more timid than her mother. These people would never betray you, Rosamund. Go to them and let them help you."

"What would they do? There is nothing unlawful in my being given in marriage to Robert. There is nothing even immoral. Cyrus may do with me what he will. Do you think he will lament and give me my freedom? I assure you, you are mistaken if that is your hope." She notched up her chin and asked again, "Who could stop him, Agravar?"

"I would fight for you."

"Nay." She sat quietly. "*I* shall fight for me. I will depend on no one, and I will go to a place where I can live in peace. And there no one will hurt me again."

"How can that be when your disquiet is within yourself?" he challenged.

"You speak nonsense," she scoffed, but she was disconcerted.

"Do I? Sometimes, Rosamund, even after our tormentors are gone, we do not have the sense to let go of what has passed.''

She gave him a strange look. From behind her, the sound of someone approaching went unheeded. He kept her attention. "Free me, Rosamund. Allow me to help you. I promise, we shall think of something together. Davey is but a boy. I will—"

"Would you aid me in escaping, Agravar?" she challenged abruptly. "Can you promise me that?"

"Fleeing is not the answer. But I say again, I will fight for you."

"In the end, the law is against us, and so we would lose. Can you not see, mine is the only way?"

She looked so alone and tragic, standing there with the filtered sunlight behind her, her body stiff and straight, her hair like a luxurious ribbon of golden silk. Her man, Davey, had arrived. He came to her, leaning his head into hers and speaking in low tones. She answered in kind. Agravar could not hear what it was they said to each other.

Davey looked over Rosamund's shoulder at Agravar. There was undisguised hostility in his face.

Agravar's hand slipped, jerking his shoulder. He stilled his movements. Waiting, he held his breath to see if that blasted boy had noticed. After a moment, he began to work the bindings again.

There was something terribly vile about what they had done to Agravar. Hitting him, trussing him up like that and leaving him in the ruins—everything within Rosamund rebelled against it. She knew he would recover. His wound had stopped bleeding and he was quite alert. He hadn't even needed to sleep too much since waking this last time. Still, a protective feeling asserted itself, and it was only with a great deal of effort that she refused it and forced herself to follow Davey's instruction.

They were to meet the boat in a few hours, and the journey would take them almost that long. It was time to go.

Kneeling beside Agravar, she said, "I shall send a message to Gastonbury as soon as we are ready to sail. I shall find someone to take it to Lord Lucien, and he shall come for you."

He shook his head. His blond hair was lank, dark with dirt and dried blood. "You should not risk it. Lucien will find me soon enough."

"You are injured and need tending."

"This? 'Tis but a scratch. You should have seen the gash in my head the time we routed the poachers from Deaston Manor."

His crooked smile made him all the more appealing, all the more impossible to leave. "I am so sorry for all of the trouble I have caused you," she said sincerely.

"You should be." His eyes were soft and his lips quivered against a smile. "God be with you, Rosamund."

"Rosamund!" Davey called, impatience giving his voice an edge. "Come."

Agravar raised a tawny brow but said nothing.

"Thank you," Rosamund said.

"For what?" he asked.

For what. For everything. For all he had done, all he had given her. All that he was.

"Rosamund!"

She called, "I am coming shortly. Do not shout at me, Davey." Turning back to Agravar, she merely looked one last time. He should resent her, even hate her for all her deceit and for this, for what she was doing to him right now. Yet, his face was abnormally impassive, almost sad.

"Fare thee well." She rose swiftly and went to Davey.

Davey was irritated when she told him her plan, snarling, "I do not know why you will take this risk, Rosamund."

"Not another word," she commanded, and this time his mouth snapped shut. "I send word to Gastonbury before we leave, else I do not sail."

He slit his eyes but said nothing more. They mounted their horses. Davey said, "I need to see if there is any sign of patrols in the area. I should do it now while we are close. We do not want to be surprised while on the trails."

"Should I wait here for you?"

"Nay. Here, let me help you mount. I'll take you as far as the river path. It is closely sheltered by the cliff face on the one side, the water on the other. No one can come upon you in surprise. You can follow it down to where the river meets the Trent. Wait for me there. I shall not take long."

"Very well," she said, and they set off.

She was acutely aware of Agravar, and her guilt troubled her. She would send word, she promised herself. Davey said there was a village not far from where the Trent and Dove came together. She would find someone there.

I promise, she thought silently as she rode away, never looking back.

Chapter Eighteen

The rope was almost undone.

In the sky, the sun began to swell and sink toward the horizon as if its bloated weight could no longer be suspended. It darkened, casting shadows about him as Agravar worked to free himself.

How far could they have gone? he wondered. At least he had gotten Rosamund to tell him enough to know that they were headed downriver. He would know where to head, then. His hands wrenched as he lost patience, jerking savagely against the bloodied rope. Stopping, he calmed himself, stilled his hands and began again, this time with a supreme effort of control. The knot loosened further. If he could just snake the end through...

The crisp sound of footsteps on dry leaves halted him. He cocked his head, listening. Whoever it was was making no effort to conceal their approach.

"Lucien?" he said. The sound of his voice was like a violation of the quiet. It died down, leaving only the soft noises of the forest and those steady, approaching steps.

"Who comes?" he called again.

Davey walked out of the forest. Swaggered, rather. He was smirking. He was holding a short sword loosely in one hand.

Ah. Of course.

Agravar watched as the younger man approached, and understood perfectly. He began to yank more furiously at his bindings, clenching his jaw against the pain as the rope tore into flesh and muscle.

"Do not bother struggling," Davey said calmly. "I tied those ropes very tight."

Not as tight as you think, you self-satisfied little bastard.

"Does Rosamund know you are here?" Agravar asked, his tone conversational.

"Rosamund," Davey answered, "does not know what is best for her."

"She will dislike it that you have disobeyed her."

"We are men of the world, are we not, Agravar? We know what must be done."

"I heard you were a crofter's son. A man of the world, is it now?" He was stalling. He kept his eye trained on Davey as that one sauntered back around, like a dog circling its weakened prey.

"A crofter's son by birth. An adventurer by choice. Not all men can bear the station fate has assigned them. Character does count for something, wouldn't you think?"

Playing along, Agravar mused, "I would be the first to agree with that sentiment as the circumstances regarding my own birth are particularly…humbling. So 'tis adventure you choose, eh, Davey. But 'tis for Rosamund you fight. Are you in love with her?"

He was but a boy, yet when his eyes narrowed

craftily, it aged him. Agravar thought perhaps he had dismissed this one too easily.

"I do not know why my lady finds sympathy in her heart for you, but her tender feelings will be her undoing. 'Tis up to me, her protector, to shield her from threats, even threats she does not wish to see." He raised his sword.

"Let us dispense with all this nonsense about 'protection' and such. 'Tis not for Rosamund that you do murder now, Davey, but for yourself. You want her. And she wants me."

That got him. He took an impulsive step forward, then halted, bringing himself under control. "'Tis true you've been a thorn in my side. I could have had her safely to Italy by now. Or France, if she wished."

"But she doesn't really wish to go with you. She wants to stay. You know that. She wants to stay with me."

Davey's sneer was ugly. "Ha, but you cannot have her. If she stays, she belongs to Robert. You silly nobles count a betrothal as good as a marriage done, so *she can never be yours.*"

Steady, Agravar cautioned himself. Steady. Smoothly he said, "True enough. But she shall never be yours, either, my friend."

That did it. Davey snarled fiercely, drawing back the sword. Agravar waited, holding out for the last moment. He had wanted Davey off guard, crazed, angry. Out of control. The boy was all of that, charging with his eyes bulging and his teeth bared, putting all his force into the blow.

The sword came down and Agravar surged slightly to one side, just as he had done with Lucien on the practice field. The blow meant to kill missed its mark. Still, with his hands tied and his mobility hampered by his feet being bound, Agravar had not been able to completely get out of the way. The sword sank up to the hilt into his side.

Davey stared down at the sight of his sword protruding from a man's flesh, the quickly spreading stain of blood glimmering slick and crimson in the light. He seemed aghast by what he had done, but Agravar knew that he had only seconds before the boy recovered his senses and finished the job.

Closing his mind to the pain of it, he wrenched his hands to the side and passed the ropes under the tip of the blade protruding from his back.

He was free.

His hands came up in two matched arcs to land simultaneous blows to either side of Davey's head, stunning him. His eyes flew open and he shot bolt upright.

Agravar grabbed the sword in his side and yanked it out with a scream to ward off the pain. He looked down to his ankles and began to wedge the blade into the bindings.

A foot connected with his chin, sending him sprawling onto his back. Davey lunged for the sword, but Agravar's hand closed over it, angling it at the last moment. Davey jumped back, clutching his shoulder. His eyes were full of accusation, as if he could not believe Agravar had drawn blood.

Agravar began to sit up. There was menace in his eyes. Davey scrabbled backward, frightened now. Agravar could almost read his thoughts. He was alone with the Viking, who was now armed and almost unbound. And he had no weapon.

Davey turned and ran. Agravar sawed frantically at the ropes at his ankles, kicking them free and scrambling to his feet.

The world tilted, first to one side, then to the other. Agravar cursed, placing a hand over his side and pressing down hard. He only managed a few steps before the dizziness came again, this time bringing him to his knees.

Impossible. The blade had passed clean through the meat of his side. How could it be it was hindering him this much?

He turned his attention to the wound, working to tear open his tunic to take a look. His head felt light, as if it were made of nothing more than air.

There was a lot of blood. Something must have been nicked inside. Not fatal, perhaps. At least not right away.

His legs buckled and he collapsed to his knees. Then his strength drained out of him and he fell onto his back, gazing at those macabre broken arches as the twilight shadows began to descend. Where was that blanket? he wondered. He was suddenly cold.

Rosamund had dreamed of being free all of her life, of leaving England, living on the continent. She never thought there would be a sadness with it. Then again, she could never have imagined a man like Agravar.

Best not to think about that, she admonished herself.

''They should be along presently,'' Davey said.

He had arrived back from his patrol with the curt message that no one was about and they should most likely remain undetected. That was all he had said, which was unusual. Davey was a talkative fellow, and she had seen before how he rather liked to preen and brag on his great prowess.

"I am hungry," she said. "Did you bring anything to eat?"

He shook his head. Actually, he looked a bit pale. "I thought we'd be aboard ship by now, so I did not bother."

"'Tis no matter. I shall wait. It shan't be long now."

There was a long silence. Davey rose and walked to the river. Rosamund's eyes followed him.

The last of the sunlight was stretched out over the water. Before long, it would be dark. "Will they come, do you think, if it grows too late?"

"I sent word to fetch us in the morning if they could not make it this day. It depends whether they can slip safely upriver. Secrecy is crucial."

"Perhaps we should prepare for the night, then," she said.

Davey considered this, then nodded. "Fetch your horse blanket. You can use that to lie upon."

She didn't tell him that she had given it to Agravar. She merely went to a spruce tree and sat on the thick moss that clustered about its roots.

There was another day, not so long ago, when she had reclined on a soft bed of moss, with Agravar's laughter floating pleasantly in the air.

She closed her eyes and hoped to sleep.

Darkness fell, and sleep did come, but it was fitful and full of terrifying images. When dawn broke, she was on her feet and at the river's edge, scanning for the first sign of the ship.

It took nearly an hour, but she spotted it. It was far-off, sailing upriver from the Trent.

"Davey," she said, coming to his side and shaking him. "Davey, the ship has come. Rise, 'tis here."

He was sluggish. She gave him a couple of jostles, then rose to watch the boat arrive. Something on her hands felt strange—sticky. She looked, then looked again. Blood?

Blood. She smeared it between her thumb and fingers, frowning. Where had it come from? Turning, she looked at Davey, who was just sitting up. He was scrubbing his eyes groggily. He winced, turning his attention to his shoulder, peeling back a ripped flap of his shirt to reveal a patch of rich, fresh blood.

"Davey, are you hurt?" she said, going to his side. "What happened?"

She froze. It was his look that told her, the guilty glance that touched her, then skittered away as if he had no courage.

"I got it riding." His voice lacked conviction. It was almost wheedling. "A branch whipped me as I went by. 'Tis nothing."

He stood, holding a hand over his wound.

"Where is your sword?" she asked in a flat voice. He had carried a short sword tucked in his belt since they had left Gastonbury. She saw now that it was gone.

"I...I must have lost it."

Her voice lowered, and sharpened to a keen edge. "What did you do? Davey. Oh, God, Davey tell me. *Tell me what you did.*" She sobbed as fear gripped her. "Did you kill him?"

"What about me?" he shot. "Look at what he did to me? Do you not even care?"

"You killed him! Oh, my God." She ran for the horses.

He raced after her. "I did it for you. He was about to come after us. He had gotten himself free and he would have stopped you, Rosamund."

"Do not call me that!" she cried, trotting the mare to a high rock so she could mount. "You are not to call me by my name again. I am your mistress, and you have aggrandized yourself, Davey. Move out of my way. Nay! Do not dare to touch me."

"Where are you going? Are you mad—the ship is here! You cannot leave."

"I am going to him."

"Nay! Rosamund! Do not leave." He grew angry. "If you are taken back to Gastonbury, I shall not help you. I have done everything for you, and this is how you reward me? I swear, if you go, that is the last I shall risk for you. I swear it!"

She leveled a glare at him. "Hold the ship. If he…" She swallowed. "If he is dead, I shall come back, but if he is alive, I shall do what I must to save his life. But hold that ship for as long as you can."

If he had any more words of protest, she didn't give him a chance to speak them. She kicked her horse into a run and raced back to the cathedral ruin.

Chapter Nineteen

Agravar's laughter sounded hollow in the belly of the church, bouncing about in soft echoes before it took flight and died on the breeze. It was not funny, not in the least, and yet the laughter rolled out of him until he was mortified to feel the sting of tears in his eyes.

He felt strange. He was awake, somewhat. He couldn't feel his body all that well. His head seemed to float. It was fever, he knew. He had lost a fair amount of blood and the wound hadn't been cleaned. Blood fever. A bad sign.

Rosamund.

They were a pair, the two of them. He had always felt it. Part of each other. How dreadfully unfortunate to have discovered that only to have her clobber him and leave him for dead. It was just too absurd.

The laughter bubbled up again, shaking him. In the thin darkness of earliest morn, the shadows shifted eerily. Or perhaps his mind was fading. He felt he could float, yet he could not move his limbs for their heaviness was beyond his waning strength.

"Mother?" he called as a figure formed before

him. She paid no heed. Plain, proud, stiffly erect, she walked by him without looking his way. He was glad. He wouldn't have liked to have seen the hatred in her eyes. It was always there, ever since he could remember.

This was all too confusing. Closing his eyes, he sought sleep. A dream snatched him up, like an owl taking an unlucky field mouse into its talons. His father's longhouse—he was in his father's longhouse. The men were drinking, laughing loudly, singing bawdy songs. Lucien was there. They had just came back from a raid and were celebrating. Lucien was his father's slave, a warrior slave whose life was lived under the yoke of a master possessed of unmatched cruelty.

Lucien's eyes burned straight into Agravar's over his cup as he took a long, long draft of ale. There was a message in those eyes, and Agravar understood.

Tonight they would kill Hendron.

Lucien gave the signal and rose, walking slowly to the master of the hall. Agravar followed. Hendron was a bleary-eyed man with a red bulbous nose from too many nights like this, his barrel chest spattered with days' worth of food.

"Father," Agravar said.

Hendron looked to him, his avaricious eyes gleaming in the firelight. There was a woman with him, leaning in close so that her breasts nearly spilled out of her clothing. She never took her eyes off her thane. Greedy wench, she took her role as his whore very seriously. Agravar immediately saw why. A large ruby lay against the milky-white of her skin, nestled neatly between her generous breasts.

Lucien grabbed her and heaved her to the side. Agravar moved, slipping an arm under his father's neck and pulling him back. Defenseless, his eyes had bulged as Lucien placed his blade tip to Hendron's heart.

Behind them, the raucous melee of the crowd sputtered to a halt.

Thus it was silent when Lucien said, "Give me my freedom."

Hendron looked at the blade, then to Lucien, and last to his son. "I'll have the both of you flayed alive. And for your insolence this day I'll feast on your entrails while you yet live. You will beg for death."

No one moved. Hendron's men watched with interest, but no one interfered. No one would interfere with Lucien.

Agravar let go of his father. He had the urge to wipe off his hands. He felt defiled, but it went deeper than the greasy feeling on his palms.

Lucien said again, "Release me and you will live."

"You best kill me, useless dog, but you won't. You haven't the stomach for it. All the English are spineless, just like you. Like little piglets ripe for the wolf to devour. And *I am the wolf*."

Lucien buried his blade in Hendron's throat. Agravar had watched it dispassionately before turning to put his sword up beside his friend as they faced the other men of the hall.

Some fought, though more out of a desire to take a hold of Hendron's leadership for themselves, or thoughts of the bulging coffers abounding in the storerooms, than love for their felled thane. Agravar slipped and slid in the pooling blood of his father as he fought. He and Lucien made short work of those that rose up until no one was left to oppose them.

Lucien was free. But Agravar was not. He could never be free of the crime his father had committed. He *was* the crime.

Hendron was dead, and it didn't matter.

Agravar was confused. Was it happening again? He saw it, smelled it. But it had taken place a long time ago, hadn't it? How could it seem so real?

He opened his eyes, fighting the pull of the dream. Or the memory, whatever it was. He saw her again, his mother, a stark study in living pain. But it couldn't be his mother, for she was bending over him. His mother had never even looked at him. Not like this. He closed his eyes and turned away.

Other spirits visited him. Alayna, Veronica, Will, Lucien, Robert, even Davey. He asked them to help him. He pleaded with them.

He dreamed again, this time that it was Rosamund beside him, touching his brow, murmuring soft words close to his ear, so close he could feel her breath fan across his skin. His eyelids fluttered open, almost afraid to look, for he knew she was merely a figment of wayward memory.

But she was there. There was light all around her and it fell on her golden hair. He thought fleetingly that she looked ethereal in that light, like an angel, and that maybe he had died. It would be a shame if he had, he considered. He didn't wish to die.

Then she leaned forward and pressed a kiss to his brow. "I am here. Fret no more. I shall tend you. Rest and be at ease, Agravar, for I am with you."

He laughed again, this time without irony or regret. Her arms felt wonderful wrapped around him, the slight pressure of her head laid on his chest filled him with happiness.

If he was dreaming again, it was wondrous, and he didn't care to wake.

Her first worry was the fever. Her perfunctory knowledge of healing had taught her how to tend them, and she began by stripping off everything, from his boots to his shirt, all the way down to his linen undergarments. Putting out of her mind the masculine form she was unveiling, she ran to the river and stripped off her surcoat and soaked it in the water. Back at his side, she bathed him with it, wringing the heavy cloth out, over and over, until every last drop was gotten. Then back to the river again.

This she did until noon. He began to shiver. She let him clutch the foul-smelling blanket around his shoulders. His eyes gazed at her, dazed.

"I am sorry," he said, and there were tears brimming there.

"Agravar, hush."

"Mother, please…"

She eased him back, and when he had subsided again into a fitful sleep, she examined the damage to his wrists. Then she probed the wound in his side.

It was festering. It needed to be opened and bled, then cauterized.

If she could have calculated a way to get him onto his horse and back to Gastonbury, she would have done it, even if it meant giving herself up. But there was not going to be any help. She was going to have to do it herself. The blood fever was not lessening. He would die unless she did what had to be done.

Pulling the dagger from the front of his belt, she saw it would do well for her task. She'd need a fire, to heat the steel. She set to work gathering a pile of kindling, then scouting out rocks suitable to use for flint.

Her hands shook, but she got the fire going well enough. Tending it carefully, she worked it to a goodly blaze.

Knife in hand, she turned to Agravar. Taking several deep breaths, she laid the edge against the mottled surface of the entrance wound. "Forgive me," she whispered, closed her eyes, and cut.

He roared, coming out of his stupor to rear up to a sitting position and glare at his tormentor. Rosamund considered that perhaps she should have retied his arms at least. In his deranged state, he could kill her without even knowing what he was doing.

His action helped tear open the crusted wound. Fresh blood flowed, which was good. Murmuring comforting words in his ear, she settled him back again, wringing out the sopping cloth she had soaked in the river. He fell back asleep, his body agleam with sweat.

When the water was gone, she ran to wet it again. Over and over again, she made the short trip, cursing her lack of even a drinking skin to aid her. Finally she was satisfied that the wound was clean, and she took the glowing steel blade out of the flames.

Her vision wavered threateningly. This was going to be no good unless she could focus. Deep breaths, she told herself. Deep breaths.

In the end, she let out a wailing little cry and cringed as she pressed the white-hot implement into the spoiling flesh. His scream rose up and mingled with hers, but he didn't fight, as if he somehow knew in his befogged brain that it was for his good. She sobbed as she counted to five, not knowing at all if that were enough time, or maybe too much.

The smell was putrid. Leaping to her feet, she fled, stumbling a short ways away to retch and retch until her body lay weak and quivering on the ground. Dragging herself back to his side, she gently covered the wound. She leaned over his naked chest and kissed his still-hot flesh, then lay her head down upon it and wept.

Later she thought the fever was less.

Famished, she foraged for what she could find in the woods. She knew how to locate and identify tubers and herbs. She found a few things that were edible and shoved them into her mouth, grimacing against the taste, until the edge was off her hunger. Gazing at Agravar, she wondered what she should do for him. He would weaken if not fed. She had nothing with which to brew a broth, which she could dribble into his mouth and he would take strength from the meat.

His need for food gave her tremendous vexation. She thought of the animals in the forest, wondered if she could hunt them.

The idea was ridiculous. She did not know the first thing about trapping and killing an animal. The only solution to the problem of finding Agravar some nutrition was to get help.

Going to his side, she smoothed her palm on his forehead. Yes, he was definitely cooler. His wound looked well, no streaks reaching like fingers of poison to his heart. "Do not dare awaken while I am gone," she scolded softly.

He slumbered on, his mighty chest rising and falling evenly, unlabored. It gave her ease as she went forth into the woods.

She returned a few hours later with a cook pot and kettle, some flint, dried apples and salted meat, all wrapped in a sturdy blanket. Checking on Agravar, she saw he still slept. She filled the kettle with water and fished out an armful of good-sized rocks from the riverbed.

Back at their makeshift camp, she hummed happily as she set the rocks up over the fire and set the filled cook pot on it, sticking in some of the beef to boil. She had no idea if this was an effective method of making broth, but it seemed plausible. It was, in fact, all she had, so she gave up the worry and set about other chores to make them comfortable.

After assessing Agravar's wounds, she coaxed some water between his lips. He coughed and sputtered and after he had gotten the idea to swallow, she tried some of the weak broth, which hadn't, after all, been so successful in becoming anything like she had hoped. It had, however, softened up the dried meat enough for her to break off tiny pieces and feed it to him slowly, washing it down with the broth water. Feeling better for her efforts, she reflected that action was always preferable to inaction, even when said action advanced their comforts so meagerly. Somehow, it felt like all the difference in the world.

As dusk set, she settled in next to Agravar, stroking his face and murmuring soft words of reassurance. She doubted he could hear her, but she kept at it. The encouragement was for her own benefit.

Tiring, she lay her head down beside his. She wondered about the occupants of the cottage she had plundered, and what they would think when they found their home had been raided. No doubt they would be more puzzled than angry. Rosamund hadn't taken much—only what she and Agravar would need to make it through the next few days. There were many more valuable items she had left behind. They would think her an odd thief, indeed.

Content, optimistic, at peace, she snuggled close beside Agravar, breathing his scent and falling asleep. And she was content for a while, until the dark tendrils of uncertainty clasped her in its cold, cold fingers.

Chapter Twenty

A woman was weeping.

Agravar opened his eyes and gazed at the sky. Morning. He blinked, taking in the crumpled walls, the stonework fingers clawing at the dawn. Where was he?

The sound of weeping came from beside him.

Mother? He had seen his mother weep before. Sometimes she would cover her face and sob quietly. She had never spoken to him. She had never touched him. Could this be his mother by his side, touching him now?

He reached to the head laid against his shoulder and lifted a tendril of her hair. Soft. Holding it up, he saw it was dark gold.

"Rosamund," he whispered.

She lifted her face to him and smiled, then laughed. "Agravar. Thank God."

He stared in wonder. It *was* her. Reaching for her, he murmured her name again. His hand closed over the back of her head and he brought her down to him to be kissed. She made a small noise. He thought it must be contentment, for she kissed him back.

Her hands splayed on his chest, moving restlessly. He twisted, bringing her down to lie across him. A sharp pain in his side warned him against the action, but he ignored it. It was nothing, forgotten the moment it receded.

Sliding his hand down her back, he rode the curve of her hip, to the top of her thigh. Breaking the kiss, she lay in the crook of his arm.

"I am dreaming," he said huskily.

She smiled at him. "Nay, 'tis not a dream. It cannot be. My dreams are never this wonderful."

"True. Then I must be awake. That means you are real. 'Tis even better."

"Thank God, you are well. Do you know you would have broken my heart if anything had happened to you?"

"I knew no such thing. Mayhap you would have counted yourself well rid of me."

"Never," she said fiercely, kissing him again. "I love you, you dreadful man." Her lips brushed along his stubbled cheek, laying tiny kisses in the corners of his mouth. "You dogged my every step, watched me until I thought I would scream, you pestered and followed and questioned and generally made me wish to have you boiled in oil."

He drew back, staring with amused shock. "'Tis the strangest declaration of love I have ever heard."

"Mayhap. But 'tis all of it true."

"Aye, 'tis. I did it because you had me in your grasp from the moment you wielded my broken sword at me. I could not put you from my mind, and if 'twas one of us who bedeviled the other, 'twas I who was put upon by you."

"You? Nay."

"Aye. Hopelessly besotted, I was. Do not pretend you did not know it."

"I swear!"

He ran his fingers down the curve of her neck, savoring the lazy way her eyes drifted closed. "You were always a wretched liar."

"A fine knight you are. You kiss me, then insult me."

"'Tis only fair play after your example. You kiss me, then strike me on the head."

"'Twas not I!"

"Your man did it, then—the same thing. Where is Davey, by the by?"

"I left him down by the lee."

He grew serious. "You missed your ship."

"I came back to…" She shrugged. "'Twas my fault Davey did what he did. I had to come back. If you had perished, I would have gone insane, I think."

"Lucien will find me, in time," Agravar warned gently. "When they have routed out the village and the woods, they will come this way. In fact, I am surprised he has not come already. 'Tis odd, now that I think of it. I wonder what could have delayed him. The fact that I did not join him right off would have alerted him."

"I am not concerned about the Lord of Gastonbury, nor the Lord of Berendsfore for that matter. 'Tis only the man I have before me I have a care for."

"I had never thought to hear those words from any woman, least of all you." He nuzzled her ear. "But I had hoped."

"Then you do love me?"

"Have I not been saying so?"

"Actually, nay." She erupted in wild giggles as his tongue traced the outline of her ear. The increased pressure of her hands on his shoulders told him she liked it. "You never actually said it."

He stared at her, hard, and there was a fierce sincerity in his voice. "I do love you, Rosamund. With all my heart, I love you to madness and beyond."

She grinned and joy shone from her eyes. "You have the tongue of a troubadour when you set your brain to it."

"Do I? How amazing—I never knew I had a talented tongue. Allow me to show you its other uses." Capturing her face, he brought it to him to be kissed.

Wrapping her arms around his neck, she pressed up against him, nearly stealing his breath away. He broke the kiss and slid his mouth along the delicate line of her jaw to the hollow just below her earlobe. She gave a short, crisp gasp and he answered with a throaty chuckle of pleasure. Taking the tip of his tongue, he gently ran it up the curve of her ear, touching lightly, breathing softly. At his shoulders, her fingers curled convulsively into the fabric of his tunic.

He took her chin between his thumb and forefinger and turned her face to his. Her gaze was hot, like honey warmed slowly on a fire. Her hands tangled in his hair as her eyes touched on his every feature.

"I am yours, Agravar," she promised with solemnity. "Every bit of me belongs to you. I hardly understand it, but 'tis not something that can be subject to reason, I think. I just know deep in my soul that you are part of me, and were before we even met."

She kissed him lightly, then deeply, then lightly

again as if her emotions of tenderness and passion were all tangled up together.

"Does it sound too much like a jongleur's song, do you think?" she asked. The insecurity in her voice made it tremble a bit. "Do you think me silvered of tongue? Or worse—hysterical? Overemotional?"

"Nay, Rosamund. Ah, my precious love, you have no idea what it is to me to hear you speak like this." He smiled as she turned her face into his palm and placed a kiss on the callused flesh. "I never thought 'twas for me, Rosamund. I've waited for a sweet touch…" He broke off, ducking his head. "No matter."

"Tell me. Please."

"Now is not the time for that sort of musing, not when I have you. Right here, in my arms, if that miracle can be true, so let us not dwell on the bittersweet regrets of the past. Just now, Rosamund. Let us take this moment—no past nor future to dog us. You are mine, so you say, and so I will have that lovely thought for now."

"Aye, I am yours, and 'tis forever." She looked at him with wide, solemn eyes. "Forever in my heart. I swear it."

"And my heart as well. I am yours, Rosamund, as true and fast as anything I've ever held dear." He kissed her with passion, the demands of his flesh not fully in check.

He wanted her. So badly his whole body shook with the restraint it took to keep his hands from sliding down to the plump roundness of her breast, or from lifting her hem to test the length of her legs, the texture of their skin and the delicious curves hidden underneath the heavy folds of her skirts. But he would not dishonor her. As much as it burned inside his breast, in every limb and in the molten pit of heaviness in his groin, he refused to submit to desire.

"Come here," he told her, and pulled her against his side, just as she had been when he awakened. She lay down, contented. A soft sigh fanned across his cheek. Her fingers traced the seams of his shirt.

"Are you feeling well?" she asked.

"Do I seem ill?" he countered with a tight laugh. The movement of her fingers set his teeth on edge and challenged his good intentions.

She nudged him playfully. "I meant your wound."

His wound? Half of him could have been cut away and he would not have been aware of it. Other, more insistent, pangs were making themselves felt. "It pains me not."

"You must take care," she scolded. "I'll not have you risk its healing. 'Twas in bad enough condition when I arrived and I toiled long and hard to set it aright. God, I set to trembling when I think about it even now. 'Twas dreadful."

He laughed again, tenderness fusing with his smoldering arousal. "I like your fussing. 'Twould make me soft if I allowed it."

"I doubt it very much."

He lay his head back and focused on the brightening sky. It was clear, cloudless and vivid azure. Her hands were moving absently, rousing him to unbearable heights with their innocent wanderings.

He squinted, thinking of the particular mace he was having the armorer cast according to his specifications, the new chain mail he had only just purchased, and how well it was crafted. He thought of how his broadsword felt in his hands, heavy and familiar.

Anything but the stiffened part of him that was growing more difficult to ignore with each passing moment. Blast, each movement of hers, no matter how small, how innocent, sent jolts of reaction through him.

She didn't know what she was doing, he told himself reasonably. She was but a maid. There was no way for her to realize the effect she was having on him.

Then she shifted her leg, adjusting herself tighter against his side, and her thigh brushed up against the swollen length of him.

Her eyes widened and caught his gaze.

He grimaced and sighed. "Rosamund, you must understand that men...being close like this with a woman you love—it brings on a lust in a man. I am only human, after all, though I would not—"

"Your body...it is like that because of me?"

He was stunned by her curiosity. His only ability to move was two short nods.

"Hmm," she said, and it was as light as a sigh. "There is something inside me, too, Agravar, that feels tight and exciting...ah, but I know not how to explain it. Only that 'tis something to do with you. Only you."

His voice was nearly a croak. "We should not speak of such things."

"I *want* to know. Agravar," she said carefully, "when you touch me, I feel...a longing." She frowned, puzzling over the exact right words. "Or perhaps 'tis more of a need. Is it like that—?"

"Rosamund, please." He took her gently by the

shoulders and set her aside. Sitting up, he bit down hard against the pain in his side.

He got to his feet, then stumbled under the stiffness, the hurt of his wound. Beside him, she stayed seated, her legs curled around her. She appeared so fresh and young and innocent, and that made everything worse.

"Is there food?" he asked gruffly. "I am nigh starved."

"But—" She broke off. "There is food over there." She rose and walked past him, body rigid. "I shall get it for you."

He felt immediate regret, but concentrated on his first, faltering steps. When he looked at her again, she was staring at him with her expression veiled. "Do not rip the wound open." Her voice was flat.

Oh, Rosamund.

But he said, "I've received worse than this."

"Of course." Inclining her head, as if bowing to his superior knowledge in these matters, she turned and began to rummage among the items piled by the fire.

He limped over to her side. He did not bend down, though. Experienced or not, she was right about his not testing his endurance too far. The mending wound was still too new for his usual activity level. He doubted he could mount his destrier, for example.

It would not trouble him if he made love to her, he thought suddenly.

He shook the thought off, as if it were a cobweb caught in his hair. "Where did you get all this?"

She was still wounded. Refusing to look at him, she answered, "I stole it from a crofter."

He grunted, impressed. "Let us hope he does not

come hunting for the thief with a longbow and a quiver full of arrows.''

She whirled on him, retorting sharply, ''And should we have starved instead? It seems I can do nothing to please you.'' With that she stomped off a few paces, then stopped, her back still to him, and crossed her arms over her chest as she faced the trees.

She was in a snit, he realized, and grinned like a fool. A well-deserved one, he could admit, but he liked it all the same. It was so…normal. Lucien and Alayna had fought since the first moment they set eyes on each other, and so Agravar thought of this present spat with Rosamund as a kind of affirmation that this—what they felt, what they were to each other—was real.

And she was waiting for him to come to her and make peace. It was evident in the fact that she had retreated only a small distance away, and her stance spoke not only of her ire, but also her need to be comforted.

In confirmation of his hypothesis, she cast a quick, annoyed glance over her shoulder.

He had hurt her. By protecting her, by trying to act honorably, he had been clumsy and upset her. She didn't understand how it was with him, with any man. God, he placed honor above all things, but even he had his limits.

He recalled her words. *When you touch me, I feel…a longing. A need.*

Foolish, inexperienced virgin. There was not a doubt she had no clue what it was she was inviting with those evocative words. How could he take advantage of her like that? It was against everything he held himself to be.

Unlike his father, he did not prey on the weak, the inexperienced, the vulnerable.

With a sigh, he squared his shoulders. He supposed he had to make it up to her as best he could.

Chapter Twenty-One

She heard him come up behind her. "Rosamund?" he said softly. "I did not intend to make you unhappy."

She lifted one shoulder carelessly. "No matter. 'Tis I who needs must apologize to you. 'Tis plain I...erred. I would appreciate it if we did not mention it again."

"Oh, nay, sweet," he said, placing his hands on her arms. "You did nothing wrong. 'Tis only that—well, as a maid you would naturally be unaware of certain things—"

"Please, just go away. If you do not want me, I shall accept it without further complaint." Her words were spoken bravely, but she was terrified that at any moment she would burst into tears.

"My God, woman, is that what you think?" He turned her around to face him and, when she wouldn't look at him, tugged her chin up until her lashes lifted and she was staring into his eyes. "I love you. You are in my soul, you ridiculous creature, and you can rest assured my whole self wants you with a single-minded obsession that is near stripping me of my sanity. But Rosamund, you are but a maid, an innocent. You know not what that means.''

"Do you know something?'' she asked, tilting her head to one side. Disarmingly girlish, it ill prepared him for her next words. "I am sick to death of you thinking for me. I may be a maid, but I am not an imbecile.''

It shocked him. "You cannot have thought this through.'' He gave his head a definitive shake. "To act on an impulse—''

"Oh, stop it!''

He cut off, startled.

She said, "I love you and you love me, but we both know that in the end we shall have nothing from one another. But now, today, we do have *this* time.''

He refused to meet her eye. She tried to twist out of his grasp, but instead her breasts brushed against his chest. She heard his short, hissing intake of breath, and she stopped.

Slowly she turned her body back into his once again. Her hips molded against the rock-hard muscle of his thigh.

The tips of her breasts were suffused with a strange ache. Then she touched her body to his and the contact sent threads of pleasure into the pit of her belly.

"Rosamund. I have nothing to offer you.'' His voice sounded choked. His hands shifted to her shoulders as if he would put her away from him, but he did not. "'Tis not lack of wanting that keeps me away.''

"Why do you seek to protect me from something I have no wish to be protected from?''

He shook his head. "If we go beyond the wanting,

have you not thought of the consequences? What will your husband say when you go to your wedding bed no longer virginal?'' His face transformed slightly, hardening in imperceptible degrees. ''What if there would be a child? If we should make a child together, Rosamund, it would be your disgrace. And the babe…you would hate it and I would have no right to see it. 'Twould near kill me to have that be so.''

''How could I not love anything of yours? I would treasure a part of you to keep with me always, Agravar. You must know that no other babe would be more loved, more welcomed, more cherished.''

He refused to be swayed. ''You would be in ruins. Your reputation would be dishonored forever.''

''When I was a child, I was treated as the most vile creature God had created. I was female, and in Father Leon's mind, I *was* evil, even before I took my first steps or opened my mouth. I was berated, tutored on the sins of Eve and all the harlots in the Old Testament and their ignominious fates were paraded before me. I was told I was no different from any of them.''

''Do not speak of it,'' he said quickly.

''Oh, I will speak of it, and you will listen, even if it hurts you to hear it, because this is part of me, whom you claim to love.''

''God, I have unleashed a monster. Go ahead, then, and speak your peace.''

''No matter what I said, no matter what I did, I was told I was bad. Evil. I was punished. And do you know what I think, Agravar? I think it was a terrible waste not to have had the fun of the wrong-doing if I must live with the consequences of it.''

Spreading her hands out before her, she continued,

"What punishment would be unbearable if I know that 'twas worth it? If in failing to remain chaste, in making one choice for my heart, it condemns me to a future as dismal as my past, 'twill be no hardship, because I will finally have had something of my own in the bargain. And that is worth everything. *Everything*."

She stood before him, no longer timid, no longer rejected. Magnificent, she shone in her defiance, and in his eyes she saw the admiring reflection of that spirit. This was her at her best—at last unafraid. And, she found to her amazement, she approved of herself like this.

With relish, she declared, "I am not afraid of what you describe—a husband's rage, the disapproval of others. I think I am afraid of nothing any longer. Because of you, I am strong."

His voice, when he spoke, was filled with emotion. "But I have given you nothing."

"You have given me everything. I have so much time to make up for. No more hiding. No more shuddering in fear and living in my head, telling stories to distract myself from my dismal life. I shall not beg you, Agravar, but I have had quite enough sheltering."

He caught her all of a sudden, taking the breath out of her as she was enveloped in his arms. He kissed her soundly until she could hardly breathe.

"Have a care not to become a tyrant," he warned. "You may find getting your way has its attractions."

"I am finding that is so already."

"You are fearsome, do you know that?"

She wrapped her arms about his neck. "I think I

shall endeavor to make it so that you do not mind so much.''

He had no reply for that, only a slow smile. Then he grew serious as he played with a tendril of her hair. ''I would do nothing to harm you.''

''I know it.''

''I shall ask you one last time…are you certain, Rosamund? There is no going back.'' But his eyes were dark, the lids heavy and his teeth were set edge to edge.

''I want you to love me. I want to belong to you.''

''Then come, beautiful Rosamund,'' he said, taking her hand. With slow backward steps, he led her over to the ground where she had made him a comfortable bed out of the blanket and a soft padding of leaves. ''Lie with me,'' he commanded gently, pulling her down with him.

Chapter Twenty-Two

She found she was trembling, but she thought it was from anticipation rather than doubt. His hands were large and strong, as one cradled her head, the other gripped her hip. He pulled her to him.

"What do I do?" she asked.

His eyes were fastened on her lips. His hands brushed over them, outlining their shape. "Give me your mouth," he replied roughly, then dipped his head to claim the prize.

She settled into the crook of his arm as his tongue slid over hers. She liked this new way of kissing. She had never thought that a man could invade her like this, and that it would feel so delicious. Timidly at first, then more boldly, she answered with her own delicate parries until she heard a small, low sound come from deep in his chest.

His hand came over one breast. It felt hot. She gasped at the contact, and he froze as if uncertain. She didn't want him to stop. Something instinctual prodded her to arch into his palm. He made that sound again and moved his hand, grazing the tip of her breast. It was the slightest of touches, but it caused shimmers of delight to pulse into her body.

She craved more, but she didn't know what it was she needed.

Spreading his hand over her collar, he paused. Rosamund opened her eyes to see his head bent over. The sound of his breathing, the fall and rise of his shoulders betrayed the veneer of control he exercised as he moved his hand little by little so that the tips of his fingers just dipped under the neckline of her gown.

The feel of his touch on her naked skin spread a languorous feeling through her. Slowly, he went lower, slipping his hand over a shoulder to bare it. Then he kissed her there, and it felt like the touch of fire.

He shifted her in his arms and worked the other side. Obeying his will, she slipped both of her arms free, waiting breathlessly for those strong, callused fingers to close over her exposed breasts, wanting to feel that shimmer again.

He moved so carefully, taking her dress to her waist while his mouth occupied hers, leaving her panting and desperate. His tongue began to move in gentle flicks at the corners of her mouth, then at her ear. Down the column of her throat. Toward her breasts, he went on to where the flesh began to swell, the tips hard and aching for his attention.

"Please," she begged.

Tangling her hands in his hair, she waited. Then his tongue touched her *there* and everything else dissolved.

"You are so beautiful," he murmured, his breath raising gooseflesh over her skin.

"Touch me," she gasped, wanting more.

"Shameless," he muttered with a wry chuckle as he attended the taut peak.

Trapped, Rosamund savored every delicious touch of his lips, every darting thrust of his tongue. The pleasure flooded through her whole body, pooling in a lake of fire low in her belly.

When he pulled away, it felt as if a part of herself had been ripped away. Rising to shuck his clothing, his eyes never left hers. He was not smiling now, not making any jests. The heat of his stare was as potent as the stirring caress of his mouth. Coming to her knees, she helped him off with his leggings. Her hands shook as his body was revealed. He seemed like some god out of Norse legend and she felt a surge of triumph well up within her.

He was *hers*. Not her husband, but in her heart. It was an exhilarating feeling.

Lying back, she ran her hands over her hips and slid her dress down, then kicked it off so that she was as naked as he. Then she held her hand up to him. He took it and reclined gingerly, favoring his side a little.

"Is your wound troubling you?" she asked.

"Nay." He shot her a quick grin. "Now quiet yourself. You shall not distract me." Rolling over her, he braced himself on his elbows on either side of her head.

She had a fleeting impulse to protest his testing his newly recovered strength this far, but the feel of his skin touching hers was too wonderful. She wriggled against him and he thrust his hips in response, his hardened manhood a ridge of heat against her thigh.

"I want inside you, Rosamund."

Hardly able to believe her courage, she slipped her hand down his side and over the flat of his stomach until her fingertips brushed against that part of him.

His eyes squeezed shut and he gritted his teeth. "Ah, *Rosamund*."

Bolder, she felt wonderingly at the velvet length of him. "It feels warm."

"That is because I am on fire."

"Does it hurt?"

A short, choked laugh. "Nay. 'Tis bliss and torture, but not the painful kind."

She liked this power. She stroked again and watched his reaction with fascination.

Catching her hand, he pulled her away. "Do not test me too far, or we shall have a rather disappointing end."

"What do you mean?"

"I mean I can only take so much before…never mind. When you know more, you will understand."

"Show me," she said. "I want to understand. I want to know what pleases you."

"What pleases me, my lady," he said through gritted teeth as he reared back, "is to please you."

"Where are you—oh!"

His mouth closed once again over her breast. This time, he suckled in short, tight contractions that left her writhing and dazed, so that when his fingers slipped into the folds between her thighs, she bucked in shock.

"I merely touch you," he said soothingly. She settled back in degrees. "There," he whispered into her ear. "You are ready to ease my way. Do you feel how wet you are?"

"How—? What has happened?"

"This is how a woman makes ready for her man's entrance."

"Will you come into me now?" *Please,* she wanted to add.

"Not yet. Let me show you what I can while my willpower holds out. There are pleasures a woman finds that I would give you."

Her mouth opened to ask what he meant when his thumb found her. She hissed in a sharp breath and nearly came up to a sitting position.

"Nay, lie back," Agravar told her gently. "See, I but stroke you. It feels good, aye?"

She couldn't answer. She could only bite down on her bottom lip and nod jerkily.

He made tiny circles, tiny exquisitely maddening circles, with the pad of his thumb. Every bit of her was focused on the spot he caressed, soaring with dawning wonder as a strange sort of magical tension began to grow.

Sometimes he whispered encouragement at her ear. Sometimes his mouth lingered at her breasts, teasing while his hand stroked her between her thighs until she began to rock her hips under his rhythmic touch. She found herself yearning, reaching, straining toward some primitive place her body somehow knew.

"Aye, love. Come," Agravar said to her. "Come for me, Rosamund."

"What?" She battled for thought. What had he said? Come with him where? "I do not know—"

"Feel it. Just feel it within you."

"Aye," she breathed, and she did feel it. Throwing her head back, she gave herself over to the sudden surge of sensation. All at once it was upon her, cresting with excruciating rapture that rained through her body in small, delectable darts of pleasure.

He held her tight against him, murmuring words she couldn't comprehend. Yet the sound of his voice added to the tremors, creating sizzling little thrills of feeling up and down her spine. She thought he spoke words of love, words of possession.

He kissed her, this time not gently at all. This time with a demand that was nearly harsh. She reveled in his roughness, and when he nudged her legs apart, she slid her knees up to the sides of his hips.

He came into her in one motion.

The pain was expected. She had been told of this by Father Leon, rather gloatingly, in fact. She bit back her cry and buried her face in Agravar's shoulder.

Kissing her neck, he stilled, nuzzling her ear until she relaxed. ''Now you are mine,'' he whispered.

The thought erased her injury. She pulled back to meet his eye.

He began to move again, small thrusts to get her used to him, to the act itself. Taking possession of her mouth once more, he devoured her soft cries as the discomfort eased and pleasure blossomed again. His strokes lengthened, gained power.

Sweat glistened on his brow, over his strong shoulders as they flexed with his movements. This she found fascinating, unable to keep herself from touching, tasting him as he had done to her. Her tongue tested the saltiness of his skin, and flickered over the corded muscles of his neck to trace the outline of his ear.

He gripped her tighter, his rhythm increasing. Moving harder, deeper, he suddenly stiffened. A hoarse cry tore from his throat and he curled into her, against her, surging over and over to bury himself deep within.

Clasping him close, she raptured in the feel of his body clenching and shifting as it rocked with his fulfillment.

Eventually he slowed. A short, final shudder and he was still.

Lifting his head, his blue eyes glowed and he said simply, "Mine."

She touched a damp strand of his hair where it clung to his brow and answered, "Always."

Then he lay his head down next to hers.

Chapter Twenty-Three

Rosamund refused to weep. She bit her lips, she swallowed hard, she fought and she fought, but the tears slipped down her cheeks all the same, heedless of her embarrassment.

She didn't want Agravar to see. He wouldn't understand. Damnation, even she didn't understand. She wept for so many things—for the joy she had found in their mating, in the sadness she felt for their parting soon to come, for…everything.

Blessedly, he was still not up to his full capacity from his injury. He fell into a light doze, giving her time to collect herself.

She studied him at her leisure, touching reverently the smooth softness of warm, lightly furred skin over sinew and muscle. His body, so different, so appealing, was beautiful to her. From the heat in his gaze when he had looked at her, he apparently felt a similar sort of awe at her. How wondrous to be seen through his eyes.

Odd. She had never thought herself special. Then again, with Cyrus and Father Leon warning her of the sin of vanity, she had never dared take pride in her appearance. She looked down at herself and saw her body, naked but for the thick arm flung over it from the slumbering Viking. She smiled and touched lightly. Agravar stirred but slept on.

She was slim, and shapely. Full, firm breasts with small dusky peaks, a flat stomach with hipbones that protruded slightly. Narrow hips but rounded, and limbs that she had been teased about at the age of eleven for being too gangly. There was more curve to them now, but they were still lean and long.

Ah, well, Agravar seemed to like her form. In her mind's eye, she could recall his expression as he had run his hands over her, as if savoring every bit. It had been glorious to feel that way.

Why in the name of heaven was this a sin? One would imagine a loving God would delight in his creatures finding such bliss. Surely, His great design of how men and women fit together so beautifully, His bestowing the capacity for such tremendous pleasure, meant He intended for this kind of mating. Father Leon would call it the work of the devil, but it felt blessed. In her heart, it felt like the most blessed thing she could ever imagine.

Settling back, she took in a deep, cleansing breath. Her tears were gone. In their place was a deep, calm sense of peace. Contentment, she realized.

Until her stomach rumbled. To her surprise, she realized she was hungry. Mindful of the need to restore Agravar's health, she slid out from under his arm.

He didn't wake. Checking his side, she saw it was knitting together nicely. Grateful their lovemaking had not disturbed its healing, she slipped into her dress before going to find what was left of the food she had stolen.

"What is this?" his groggy voice sounded from behind her. "Are you so anxious to be away from me now that you have gotten what you wanted? 'Tis most unpleasant waking without you here by my side."

She straightened and struck an impudent pose with one hand on her hip. "I was seeing to my beloved's pleasure. Since one appetite has been quenched, I was merely looking toward the other."

He raised up his head and propped it on his fist. "Who said it was quenched?"

Rosamund froze. "Oh." She smiled. "Oh?"

He held his other hand out to her and she dropped the parcel of food. She had just taken the first step when the sound of a horse approaching rumbled through the trees.

She froze. Davey? Lucien?

Her salvation in one, her condemnation in the other.

Agravar shot to his feet, doubling over with a hard grimace and clutching his side. "Damn," he growled. "Rosamund, come here and help me."

Her body moved even while her mind refused to work. She picked up his clothes and handed them to him. Tossing aside the tunic, he grasped the leggings and began shoving his legs in, grunting against the protests of his injury. He barked, "Get my sword. Damn me for not wearing mail." Straightening, he pulled the waist ties tight and reached for the sword she struggled to unsheathe from its scabbard.

Agravar went pale as he tried to take hold of the weapon. He dropped it, his hand coming to his side.

Rosamund retrieved the heavy thing. He took it up again, clamping his jaw down tight against the pain. Brushing aside her efforts to help him, he commanded, ''Get behind me.''

The familiar weight of the broadsword was too much. Agravar's hand trembled as he raised it. The pain in his wound seared him, but he refused to acknowledge it.

Leveling his gaze at the trees, he crouched down. He could feel Rosamund's slender hands resting on the bare skin of his back. Reaching around, he put his hand on her bottom and pulled her up tight against him. ''Stay close,'' he muttered.

The man who rode in through the parting curtain of greenery made Agravar tense and Rosamund sigh in relief.

''Davey!'' she exclaimed. When she would have scooted out from behind him, Agravar's free hand shoved her back.

He raised his sword. ''Get out.''

Looking at the Viking with wide, wary eyes, Davey spoke. ''I came for Rosamund. I have no wish to harm you. Rosamund, listen to me—the ship is here. 'Tis waiting.''

''Get out,'' Agravar repeated.

''Let her go,'' Davey said with force. He wasn't as arrogant as he had been, but neither did he cower. ''She wants to be free. If you…if you love her, then give her the only thing that matters. Release her.''

Agravar felt as if a blow had landed squarely in his gut.

Davey continued, ''Hand her to me. I will take her

away. To safety." He shifted his gaze to Rosamund. "To freedom."

It was falling away. All of the delicious closeness, the sense of oneness, the sublime union that had gone beyond the communion of their bodies. He felt Rosamund stiffen and he knew the boy was right.

Davey darted a look into the trees. "They have started looking for you. The Lady Alayna went to childbed, and Lord Lucien was called to her side. This is why he did not come sooner, but he is back and combing these woods with his men."

Rosamund said quickly, "Is my lady well?"

"How the devil should I know?" Davey snapped.

The little cur was not so changed after all, Agravar noted.

Davey said, "Come, my lady. We must go now, else we have lost the chance. With Lucien's men on the watch, the boat may have no choice but to strand us."

Agravar lowered his sword and turned to Rosamund. "Go," he said.

She looked back at him, her face a tortured mirror of his own heart. "Nay. I no longer want to."

"If you stay, you will be given to Robert. I can do nothing for you here."

Her eyes closed as if she could shut out the truth. They flew open again, a new light in their honey depths. "Come away with me. *Please,* Agravar. *Come with me.*"

"You know I cannot. I have pledged myself to be exactly what my father was not, to hold honor above all things. If I betrayed that, Rosamund...please try to understand." He forced himself to look at her. "I would be nothing if not the man I hold myself to be.''

"I know," she said, her gaze dropping. Her lashes were thick and dark against the paleness of her cheek. The sight of that demure gesture brought on a surge of tenderness. "I have no right," she continued, "to ask it of you."

"You have every right to ask anything. Ah, Rosamund, if I could, I would give you anything you ask for."

"I would have you be no different." Fat, shiny tears spilled onto her cheeks and her breath hitched in as her body crumpled forward. He caught her and held her, wondering if he was crushing her and then not caring because it still wasn't tight enough.

"Go," he said again. "If Lucien comes, it will be the end of your dream. Go."

He released her and she backed away, crying too hard to do anything but stand there, helpless. He took her by the hand and led her to Davey's horse. It was his own palm that cradled her bare foot as Davey pulled her up behind him.

"Wait," he said. Rummaging around, he found one of her shoes. "Where is the other?"

"It doesn't matter," Davey exclaimed with impatience. "Hurry!"

Agravar gave the young man a blistering stare as he handed him the shoe. "Take care of her. Allow no harm to come to her."

"I shall protect her," Davey said coldly. He made to pull the horse around, but Agravar reached up to grab the reins, stopping him.

"If any ill befalls her, I shall hunt you down myself and wear your hide as a cloak."

The lad's throat convulsed. He jerked his hands free and turned the horse around. Agravar watched as his heels dug into the beast's side and the animal reared, then shot off through the trees, disappearing in an instant.

Agravar took a step forward, his arm outstretched as if in this last moment he had changed his mind. The receding sound of hoofbeats fell to silence and he dropped his hand to his side.

Agravar dressed. Dusting off his tunic, he put it on. The side was in shreds, but he did the best he could with it. It didn't matter, it was merely a diversion. Then he rummaged through the bundles Rosamund had left. He ate everything. He was ravenous.

He waited. If Davey was to be believed—and this was, admittedly, doubtful—then Lucien should be arriving fairly soon.

As it turned out, the boy was correct. A group of riders could be heard in the forest. Agravar tilted his head back and let out a long, chilling shout. It was his war cry. Lucien would know it. Except today it sounded mournful, not vengeful at all.

How much time had passed since Rosamund left with Davey? Were they on the ship already?

It was but a few moments later when Lucien and Robert broke through the trees and reined their horses to a halt before him. Their full complement of men flooded through the thinnest parts of the forest around the ruins.

Agravar slowly got to his feet. Lucien dismounted, his relief apparent on his face. "Agravar!"

"My lady, is she well?" Agravar asked.

Lucien nodded. "She is fine. Fine." His grin broadened. "And we have another son."

Agravar found a degree of tension ease out of him. He hadn't realized that since Davey's announcement that Alayna had been brought to childbed, he had been on edge. "Congratulations, my friend. It does my heart good to know all is well with you."

Lucien's eyes peered at Agravar sharply. "'Tis good you are well. I feared…" He stopped, the tick of his that showed whenever he was annoyed throbbing at his temple. "And Rosamund? You never found her?"

"Nay. I fell under the hands of some thieves. They took my horse and left me for dead."

"But we found the horse. It is back home and well tended."

Agravar nodded, as if relieved. Strange that even the recovery of his valuable destrier made no impression on him. "What good fortune."

"You did battle. What happened?"

Agravar was somewhat taken aback. Lucien explained, "That wound in your side?"

"Aye. The little trick I tried on you. As it turns out, it does not work nearly as well as I had hoped."

"But 'tis been cauterized."

Agravar glanced down at the livid flesh with a dismissive shrug. "I tended it myself. After all the times I've been cut open, I should know what to do."

Lucien nodded, a bit bemused. "Very good. I…I was worried about you, old friend. When you didn't return, I thought the worst."

Agravar brushed past him. He felt like hell for his deception. "Lord Robert, I regret I was unable to retrieve your betrothed."

"'Tis not your failure," Robert said. "We can only hope she is well and will be returned to us in due time. I am pleased that you are restored to your friends who love you so well."

"My thanks," Agravar replied. Whirling, he said to Lucien, "Let us to Gastonbury. I need a mount."

"Gregory!" Lucien called. "Ride with Philip. Give my captain your horse."

Going to where he had lain, on that scratchy blanket and pathetic pile of leaves she had lovingly gathered for him, where they had made love together and melded their hearts in a union that would have to last the rest of their lives, he gathered his boots and his sword. He was about to turn back when he spied something half-hidden under the edge of the blanket.

Her shoe.

"Agravar? Are you coming?"

"A moment," he answered, snatching the slender leather slipper into his fist, concealing it under the blanket, which he tucked into the crook of his arm.

It was difficult to mount. The steed was not so large as his own horse, but the effort still cost him. Lucien looked on with concern. "When we return to Gastonbury, we must have Eurice tend you."

Agravar nodded and followed the procession out of the ruins.

Chapter Twenty-Four

Seven months later, and he could still smell her. If he closed his eyes and thought of her, his head was filled with her scent.

Memories were like shades creeping around him all the time. It did no good to keep busy, for no matter how long he was occupied, the moment he fell to rest she would whisper across his mind. When he shut his eyes at night, he would see her—her mouth pursed just so, or slightly open as she gasped in passion. The way she threw her head back when reaching the pinnacle of pleasure, with her golden hair all around her.

After five months, he thought to appease his lust on another. One of the three blond women—her name was Ermengarde—seemed a logical choice. She would certainly be willing, he knew. Agravar had stood in the hall and stared at her for a good hour before she took the lead and sauntered over to him. The moment she opened her mouth to speak, however, he realized it would be no good, and he walked out of the hall. It had been bitter cold that night. He spent the long hours until morning touring the ramparts, fighting the misery, finally deciding he had to get on with things.

After that, he was a bit better. He simply refused to indulge in the sensual fantasy that had kept him company those first months after she left. If any image came to his brain, he shifted his attention. After such discipline, he found he could bear it much better.

But he still could conjure the memory of their lovemaking if he wished. He'd try it, once in a while, like probing a sore tooth with a tongue. He *knew* it would hurt, but just couldn't seem to help himself.

And so, now and then, he'd shut out the world and remember.

Robert and Lucien were playing chess. Off in a corner, Lady Veronica worked at her embroidery. Alayna lay on the floor beside the new babe, named Luke, who was pulling himself about by his meaty fists. Leanna toddled, gently prodding young Luke with trinkets and toys.

Poor Aric was sulking. Having gotten a sound spanking that day for terrorizing the dovecote and setting half the fowl to flight, he was nursing his wounded pride and a slightly sore posterior. The act had put his father in a bad mood, as well. Lucien loved the boy and hated having to discipline him, but he would never allow these tender feelings to interfere with his duty.

Robert rubbed his chin. "You have me, I think."

"'Tis not check yet." Lucien's voice was flat, almost a growl.

"Only a move or two away."

Agravar stood by the hearth, watching the dance of the flames within it.

Robert sat back and pretended to stretch, then glanced over at the women. A small, secretive smile trembled at the corner of Lady Veronica's mouth.

Robert turned back to the game. "The night is mild. Inviting. Why do we not call the game and take some time to enjoy the air?" He twisted toward the women. "Would either of you ladies care to take a turn on the ramparts on such a fine night as this?"

Veronica laid down her sewing. "Honestly, my eyes are tired. This light is poor. Ah, I am weary in any case of this tedious work. What did you say, Robert? A stroll? Well, 'twould be just the thing, I think."

"Finish the game," Lucien growled. "I hate not seeing things through."

Alayna laughed lightly, coming to lay gentle hands on her husband's shoulders. "You hate not having your moment of triumph. Lucien, really, where are your manners? Lord Robert is our guest and he wishes a reprieve."

Lucien made a harrumph that displayed his opinion of polite banality. Alayna stroked his chin and it seemed to soothe him. He shrugged. "Very well, I suppose."

The door opened with a bang. A soldier came in, casting his gaze about frantically. "Captain!" he said, spotting Agravar. "There are travelers at the gate. They say they are from—"

He was cut off by the arrival of another soldier. "My lord, my lady, I must—"

And then he was interrupted, as well. A third soldier rushed in and shouted, "They are coming!"

In the confusion, Lucien had sprung to his feet. Agravar's sword hand came to rest on his hilt, and the two men instinctively positioned themselves side by side, a gauntlet against any danger.

Then a man walked into the room and Agravar felt his entire world suddenly spin off-kilter. A ghost, a memory. Impossible.

It was Davey.

All he could think of was that Rosamund was dead. He moved, wanting the scrawny man's neck in his hands.

There must have been murder in his eye, for Davey stammered and stared in terror as Agravar came at him.

"Nay," a female voice said, and it stopped him in his tracks.

He didn't dare look, didn't dare believe what he had heard. *Thought* he had heard. How many times had her voice come to him in his mind in the time since she had been gone?

But then Veronica cried, "Rosamund!" and flew past Agravar, and he knew it was no trick of his brain. He slid his gaze from the mingling of resentment and fear that played on Davey's face to the door.

Rosamund was there.

Veronica held her, hugging her, but Rosamund's clear brown eyes looked over her shoulder and straight at Agravar.

Something strange happened to his legs. They would not move. When they did, he got two steps closer when a hand closed over his shoulder.

He looked to find Lucien beside him. "'Tis not your place," he said softly.

Robert strode past, going to Rosamund and waiting until Veronica set her aside to brush away her tears. He took Rosamund's hands and said formally, "My dear, I am delighted to have you safely returned."

"Thank you," she answered calmly.

Alayna embraced her next, and the two of them laughed with joy at their reunion. A small body brushed past Agravar's thigh and he saw Aric rushing up to fling himself into Rosamund's arms.

Agravar took a step toward her. Lucien's grip tightened.

Agravar jerked forward, breaking out of his grasp. Rosamund watched him approach with stony composure.

"Welcome back, my lady," he said evenly.

Her answering smile was genuine, full of secrets that only he would know. "Thank you, Agravar. 'Tis most grateful I am to be returned to Gastonbury. Where I belong."

His throat tightened. Robert frowned, and Agravar could almost hear his puzzlement at her reference. She was not destined to belong at Gastonbury.

Veronica took Rosamund in hand. "My dear, I am sure we all have a hundred questions. But for now we shall simply give thanks to the Lord that you are safely restored to us."

Rosamund was brought to the dais with Veronica's protective arm around her. On her other side was Robert. Alayna was close behind, with Aric skipping by her side. Lucien gave Agravar a meaningful look and followed his wife and son, scooping up his daughter on the way and leaving the babe in the care of his nurse.

Agravar shifted his gaze to Davey, who stared back with eyes blazing with resentment.

"I wish I had been allowed to go with the search party," Aric fretted, his wooden sword dangling in his small hand. "I *know* I would have found the bandits that took you."

Rosamund laughed as tears pricked her eyes. It was the first wave of emotion since she had entered these doors and seen all the people she had dreamed of for seven months.

She hadn't even wept when she saw *him*.

Grabbing the boy, she clasped him close in a quick hug. To her surprise, he didn't struggle.

"Come," Alayna commanded. "You must wish to rest."

"Aye," Rosamund agreed, grateful for the opportunity to duck out of her obligations.

There would be, in time, many questions she would have to answer. Thinking about it brought a flutter of trepidation. Then she remembered the look on Agravar's face and knew she had made the right decision in returning.

She had a new plan. And it *was* going to work. But for now, she would take her respite while she could.

The training field was lit with countless torches. Lucien thrust Agravar's sword into his hand.

"I remember what 'tis like." His tone held as much kindness as was possible for him. "Come, swing the sword. You will find 'twill do you good."

Agravar felt numb. His fingers had no feeling.

Lucien swatted him with the flat side of his sword.

Startled, Agravar looked at him. "Come, you womanly knave," Lucien taunted, "and let us see how soft your bewitched heart has made you."

"How did you know?" Agravar rasped.

Lucien scoffed and rolled his eyes. "I do not care how many wounds you've had sewn together, or how many you've stitched yourself. Pressing burning steel to festering flesh—that one I would not believe of the very devil. She was with you."

"You knew all along?"

Lucien swatted him again. This time it hurt.

"Come, then, you addle-brained idiot. Swing the damned sword!"

He struck again and Agravar's limp fingers closed like steel around the worn hilt as he raised the weapon as familiar to him as his own hand. He brought it down with such force that Lucien buckled, going down on one knee. Lucien merely laughed and drew back for another go.

Agravar fought. Lucien had been right. He did feel better.

Chapter Twenty-Five

Veronica trod gently. While they were in her chamber, attending Rosamund's bath with Hilde rushing about making great clucking noises and weeping, Veronica suggested that Robert would want an explanation. Rosamund pretended not to hear.

Alayna, who was more direct, sat down beside her once she had emerged from the water and was having her hair brushed, and asked outright. The door was open as the servants lugged the big tub down the steps. A draft came in, pricking Rosamund's skin into gooseflesh. She was immediately wrapped tightly in a plush dressing gown.

All eyes were on her, waiting. Rosamund bowed her head and took in a long, bracing breath. "I know Lord Robert has the right to know what happened to me. And your curiosity, I know it comes out of love and not malice, but 'tis a matter I would rather not speak of unless absolutely necessary."

A masculine voice cut in. "If 'tis painful to you, then we shall not mention it." Robert was standing in the doorway. He entered. "Pardon me for coming upon you in your chamber, but I wished to speak with the Lady Veronica, to inquire as to your good condition, and found the doorway open.''

Veronica stood and folded her hands in front of her. Rosamund noted the gesture. Why was Veronica so nervous?

"Enter, my lord," Veronica said, "for we are done with our chores."

"I will take but a moment of your time. You look well, Rosamund. Beautiful as always."

"My thanks at your kindness, my lord," Rosamund murmured.

"There is something I wish to be known. Your trials at the hands of the miscreants who took you from here are of no consequence. The important thing is that you are here with us again. I imagine 'tis painful for you to speak of, thus I forbid any inquiries."

Rosamund met his eyes. They looked on her kindly and she felt a pang of remorse for how she had betrayed this good man. She said nothing.

He continued. "If you choose to impart your confidences to someone, that is your affair, Rosamund, but neither I, nor anyone else, shall demand any explanations. And…" He seemed to falter in this. His gaze flickered to the side of the room where Veronica stood rigidly. "There is no question that our betrothal contract is still honored. I fully intend to put it into effect as soon as can be arranged. Then I can take you home with me, and you can begin a new life away from these painful memories."

Before Rosamund could reply, he turned with stiff precision and exited the room.

"There, how splendid Lord Robert is to see your

discomfort and care for you in this way," Hilde exclaimed.

Alayna stroked Rosamund's shoulder and added softly, "He is a most kind man."

"Aye," Rosamund agreed.

Seeing him again, with the haze of panic removed from her vision, she saw a noble-featured man who was quite pleasant to look upon. A bearing that was almost regal and gentle manner that made him instantly likable. He was a good man, a kind man. But she didn't want him.

What he had just done was indeed quite noteworthy. No doubt, all at Gastonbury assumed she had been raped by her captors. This would have been grounds to nullify the betrothal. Many men would not want a sullied bride and if Robert had wished to put her aside, it would not have reflected badly on him at all.

It was, in fact, what she had been counting on to absolve her from her obligation to the betrothal. Robert's announcement swept away that hope.

She felt her shoulders sag. With Robert's magnanimous pardon, nothing had been altered since she had fled.

Ah, nay—everything had changed! She was now more determined than ever to be free. She wanted Agravar. She had risked everything to come here and fight for a future with him.

Hilde was saying something. Rosamund vaguely registered the praise the portly maid was gushing for the lord of Berendsfore. Alayna was on Rosamund's other side, gently prodding her to finish her toilette.

It seemed strange, Rosamund noted as she finished

binding her hair, that Veronica was remote. Almost sad.

Agravar sat in the hall, hunched over his cup and staring at a pile of rushes on the floor. He had a million questions and no way for answers.

Namely, why had she come back?

How frustrating that he had no right to demand to know. He had to sit here, as if she were nothing to him. God, that pierced him to the core. The falsehood, the pretending—that was the worst of it.

He tested the ale and grimaced. It was tepid and sour. The shock to his tongue convinced him he had sat here long enough.

Pushing away from the table, he observed that the place was filling up with people. The servants were setting up the trestles. It must be near supper. Had he been brooding all day?

Looking for a purpose, he went to the stables, but his horse was well tended, so he wandered to the lists. No one was about, which was to be expected at mealtimes. In the outer wards, a few merchants and yeomen were hurrying to get their business done in the castle so they could exit the barbican before the portcullis was lowered and make it home to their humble suppers and waiting families. A typical day. Yet it seemed so vastly empty.

When he walked past a row of houses, a woman caught his eye. She immediately leaned back against the wall so that her breasts jutted out and she gave him a sly kind of smile.

She looked familiar, he thought distractedly, then remembered she was one of those dratted blondes who dogged him with their blatant invitations and cunning looks.

He climbed to the ramparts and watched the sun disappear into the western trees. With its departure, the air grew cooler.

He would not go back to the hall. Rosamund—if indeed she had come down to the meal and not taken food in her room—would be seated with Robert. So he stayed on the ramparts until darkness had descended in full.

A guard passed him on his nightly rounds. "Chilly out, Captain," he commented, stopping to chat.

"Aye," Agravar answered distractedly. He didn't say anything more, didn't even turn around. The guard's friendly smile turned into a perplexed expression, then a shrug as he continued on his way.

Agravar climbed down the stairs and headed for his chamber.

Just outside his door, a figure stepped from the shadows and into the illuminated pool cast by one of the torchlights. He froze. *Rosamund.*

"What are you doing here?" he demanded, surprise making his voice gruff.

She smiled, and the bottom dropped out of his heart. "I had to." Holding up her left hand, he saw she held a shoe. He recognized it immediately. He still had the other, the only keepsake he possessed. It was in a secret place in his chamber so that even the servants who swept and dusted would never see it.

Dangling the slipper from one finger, she said, "What was I to do with this? 'Tis no good without its mate."

He moved. She came to him and he crushed her

against him, burying his face in the elegant curve of her neck, breathing her scent.

"My God, I never thought I'd feel you again in my arms." He grabbed fistfuls of her hair and tugged gently. Her head fell back. She was laughing giddily. "Jesu, woman, how I've missed you."

"And I you, you wretched Viking." She was nearly breathless, smiling while unshed tears glistened in her eyes. "You haunted my every thought. Why, all the while as I was prowling the crumbling forums of Italy, I kept seeing you. You went to a sorceress and had her bewitch me, admit it. All to drive me back here."

He laughed, too. "If you caught sight of my face when you came through the door, you would know I had no inkling you would ever set foot inside these walls again."

"I assure you I had eyes for no other face but yours. I waited far too long to see it." She leaned in closer. "To see you and to kiss you. Would you have me wait longer?"

"Your invitation is too pretty." He began to dip his head, then stopped and cast a look about him. "Nay, not here. We might be spotted. Come here, into my chamber."

They stepped inside, and once the door was shut behind them, he grasped her arm and swung her into an embrace. "Now, allow me to make amends," he murmured, and his lips came down over hers.

Hot sensation, a consuming hunger, grew greater as the kiss deepened. She opened her mouth readily to him, reducing his legs to water with the sweet, timid touch of her tongue. Bolder than she, he delved into her mouth like a ravenous man. His hands slid up and down her back, molding her shape, pulling her more tightly to him.

As he feathered light kisses across her forehead, she said, "Every night without fail, I dreamed of being here with you again."

"I had to banish you from my thoughts." She made a small sound. He explained. "There are differences between men and women, Rosamund. My thoughts, when they are of a certain woman with hair the color of the golden sun just before it sets and eyes deep and dark as raw honey, are rather...noticeable. 'Twould be unseemly if I were constantly walking about the castle in such a state."

He smiled and she bit her lips. Through the meager moonlight, he could see small, white teeth clinging to the plump flesh, and he had an overwhelming urge to feel the contrast of hard and soft with his tongue.

Instead, he took a taper and went just outside his door to catch it afire on the wall sconce, then returned to light the torches mounted on either side of his small window. "Do we need a fire?"

Standing with her arms wrapped around her, she shook her head. "I do not think I shall be cold."

He grinned. "Come, sit with me," he said, leading her to the bed, the only place to sit in the small chamber.

Giving him a baleful glance, she hung back. "You are not so clever as you would like to think, Agravar, if you plot to catch me with that feeble ruse."

"Rest easy, for I am ready for answers first."

Coming to his side, she sat close. Very close.

Agravar drew in a deep breath and observed, "'Tis the first time I ever told you to do something and you did it."

"Surely not the first. I give everything you say to me great weight."

"I remember telling you to untie me and you refused."

She demurred. "Well, there were circumstances…"

"Which were?"

"You were fouling up my plans."

"Thus you felt compelled to whack me on the head and truss me up like a stuffed goose." His hand in her hair was tender, nearly reverent.

"Are we on that again? I told you, 'twas Davey who gave you the whack."

He smiled softly. "I see you do not deny the trussing."

"Aye. I helped," she admitted grudgingly. "But I was very gentle. *And* I returned to you and nursed you to health."

He leaned back. His arm went behind her and she angled into it. He said, "'Twas the least you could do."

"As I recall," she replied, "there was more to it than that. I believe I paid the debt in full."

"Aye, 'tis true. In full and more." Her heat along his side was torture, like a drop of water to a parched man.

His voice lowered. "Tell me, Rosamund. After all you did to be free, *why* did you return?"

"I had to come back. You see, I am very like my shoe."

"Your shoe?"

"No good without its mate, remember? Nothing was any good without you."

"Just for me?" he asked.

"I love Gastonbury. I love the people. But in the end I knew I had traded one misery for another. I would never be content without you. I love you. I thought I had been quite clear on that matter when last we were met."

He bowed his head, absorbing words. It felt glorious and strange at the same time. He, who had never had anyone, save Lucien, care a whit about him. "I cannot think Davey was very happy to bring you back."

"Davey grew…difficult, but I was not about to answer to him as if he were Cyrus. When I insisted to be brought back to England, he reluctantly agreed, but said 'twould be the last service he ever did for me. He would not speak to me during the entire journey home. He promised he would see me safely through the gates. You will probably find him already gone."

"And what of Robert? Did you know he would be here, ready to claim you again?"

Her shoulders sagged as she sighed. "I admit, 'twas a shock to see him when I arrived, but I knew I would face him soon enough." The convulsive way she swallowed belied her worry. "He…he is a very kind man, a good man. I realize I need have no fear of him. So many gifts you gave me, Agravar. I know now that every man is not like Cyrus, because of what you taught me. I will speak to Robert. 'Tis my hope he will have no desire for an unwilling bride. I shall tell him the truth, that is all." She stopped, tilted her head to the side and added, "Perhaps not the *entire* truth."

"Come here," he said roughly, and pulled her to

him to be kissed. She came willingly. Her momentum tipped them gently back onto the bed.

Pulling back, he looked at her closely. "You are certain you can do this—speak to Robert?"

"Aye. I must be honest with him. 'Tis what the Lord says will set us free, after all. Truth." Her lashes lifted and their eyes locked. "And then I shall have to go about trying to find myself a husband. Do you know of anyone who would be willing?"

His hands slid down over her hips. "How would you fare as the wife of a bastard Viking with no property and a tragic allegiance to a dour, sour-faced lord who you happen to dislike?"

"You do not have to make it sound so…unsavory."

His chest felt as if his heart might burst right out of it. "Did I? How clumsy of me. Especially when 'tis what I wish you to do." His voice was hard and hoarse. "Rosamund. You are my life. Do you understand what I am telling you? I am nothing without you."

"Then be something with me. Be my love," she murmured.

"Aye. Always." His gaze fastened on her lips as she drew closer. He couldn't stop himself. His body burned. She moved her slender frame over his. Whether or not she was aware of the fact that her breasts brushed against his chest, or that her hips were flat against his belly, he didn't know. But he was aware of all of it and more. Of the way her hair fell over them, cocooning them in dark gold. Of the soft pressure of her caressing fingers on his neck, touching his ear, tracing the line of his jaw to his chin. Of the delicious feel of her mouth over his.

"I came back to you, Agravar. Only for you."
Taking his face in her hands, she stared hard into his
eyes. "I said it once, and it has remained unchanged—I belong to you."

His hands would not be still. He wanted to take
all of her in, the feel of her, each taste, each texture.
And she was his—*his*. Had she not just said so?

She pushed at his shoulders, so he moved aside
and allowed her to stand beside the bed. Just about
to ask her intention, his breath caught as her hands
lifted to the shoulders of her gown and slowly began
to peel it off.

He rose up on his side to watch, his body growing
unbearably tight. She removed her gown, then her
shift. Stepping forward, she made to come back to
his bed.

Holding out his hand to stop her, he let his gaze
wander, taking in every inch. Where his eyes
touched, his hand followed lightly, almost casually.
Her skin glowed in the light. Her nipples were already tight, and her abdomen rippled when he passed
his hand over it. Between her legs, the soft curls
guarding her folds beckoned.

"Move over, you Viking beast," she said. Kneeling beside him on the bed, she took up the pointed
ties of his shirt. Impatient, he tugged the thing off
and cast it aside.

"'Tis still not fair," she commented, her fingers
tugging at the waistband of his leggings.

"You have become insufferably bossy."

She bit her lips to keep from smiling. "Why thank
you. And I owe it all to you. Now undress."

"I would not dream of denying you."

When he had discarded the remainder of his

clothes, she pushed him back. Her hands went to his side to inspect the healed wound.

"It knitted clumsily. You have a scar."

"There are many others to keep it company. If you ordered me naked just to look at them, I shall be sorely disappointed."

She laughed, and to his utter shock, stretched out full on him. "This is how I dreamed of being with you." She breathed across his chest, raising gooseflesh and tiny, exquisite tremors. Her skin was hot against his.

Hitching in a shaky breath, he managed to say, "I see you gave the matter a great deal of thought."

"Did you never think of me, as well, Agravar?"

"From time to time. When boredom arose."

Her small fist pounded his great chest once.

"Allow me to elaborate. I was bored much of the time."

She angled a coy glance at him. "Is that so?"

"In fact, all the time."

"Hmm."

"Why are you not kissing me?"

"A deplorable oversight," she agreed.

"Shut up," he said with a sultry grin, cupped the back of her head and brought her head down hard so that her mouth was crushed up against his.

That languorous feeling swept over him again. "I have waited too long for you," he murmured. "Later we shall take our time, but I must have you now."

She seemed drugged, nodding and whispering, "Aye."

Reaching down, he pulled her knees on either side of his hips. She braced her hands on his shoulders. He placed a palm on the small of her back and shoved her upward until a taut nipple was within reach. He touched his tongue to it, then suckled until he heard her cries of pleasure. Running his hands down her hips, he cupped her bottom, lifting her.

His manhood was hard, swollen with straining desire, but he slipped inside easily. Above him, she arched.

His hands on her hips taught her the rhythm. She moved silkily over him and he settled back as his pleasure began to mount.

She was so lovely. Then she glanced down at him and their eyes locked. Her hands twined in his. Thrusting his hips upward, he let his body speak the passions that filled his heart. He was taken over by pure need now, riding it out with her. She arched and writhed with her own pleasure and he thought his body would burst into flames.

He saw the moment she climaxed and it spilled him over into that delirious oblivion as well. She stiffened and let out a tiny shout. Her teeth caught the meager light as her lips drew back. With long, smooth strokes, he crested the shattering sensation until it crashed around him, exploding and shimmering in waves that pounded him at first, then gentled until they were only tremors washing down his limbs.

Gradually he came back to himself. Rosamund had curled onto his chest and he gathered her in his arms, kissing her hair, the curve of her ears—anywhere his lips could reach.

"You see what I told you," she said, still a bit out of breath. "Nothing else is any good if we are not together. And we are so good together."

"You talk too much."

"Well, I have been silent and docile all my life. I am finally able to talk and I want to talk."

He sighed. "Very well then, talk."

There was a small silence. "That was all I had to say."

He chuckled and gave her a squeeze. "I love you."

"Hmm. I shall never tire of hearing that. Promise me when we are old and our grandchildren are running about, you will still tell me."

Smoothing the hair back from her face, he peered at her. "Rosamund...you know I want you. I would take you to wife without another thought—but there is Robert."

"I already told you, Agravar. I plan to speak with him. I had thought...I had thought he would not be interested in me after my 'abduction' because he would assume my virtue had been compromised." She giggled and touched a finger along the line of his chin. "Which it was. Only not exactly as he would think. I had thought he would wish to release me."

"Robert would consider that dishonorable. He is nothing if not an honorable man."

"Aye, I see that now. But surely, being so, he will not wish to force the marriage if I do not wish it. 'Tis not as if he has any affection for me. He has barely spoken a dozen words to me. He is always busy with Lucien or Veronica—he far prefers them. And I cannot imagine the fortune or advantages I bring him are singular. Cyrus has no special influence and my dowry is not large. I was merely a mediocre choice for him. He will be reasonable."

"When will you speak to him?"

"I must wait for the right time. I will not deceive you, Agravar, my brave words go only so far. There is still fear. But 'tis a fear I can overcome. I will not shrink from it as I did before."

He kissed her brow, then rested his forehead against it. "Do it as soon as you can. I can barely stand the wait as it is. And if you need me—"

"Oh, I do need you. But as for this matter, I must do it alone."

Chapter Twenty-Six

She left just after dawn. It was foolish to have waited so long, but they had talked for hours. She told him of her travels, the things she had seen, the different way of life on the Continent. They had made love again, and then dozed. When she had awakened, she could not possibly have left him without giving him a farewell kiss. This had roused him and they had simply lost track of the world after that. Now, as she tiptoed along the corridors, she took great care not to be seen by any of the early-rising servants.

In her chamber, she quickly tumbled up the furs as if she had slept in them. She had no desire to go back to bed; she was too euphoric. When Hilde came in an hour later, she was already washed and dressed and impatiently tapping her foot on the rushes.

"My, what has you roused so early?" Hilde asked.

"I could not sleep."

The servant stopped. "Nightmares?"

Rosamund remembered she was supposedly to have just returned from a harrowing abduction. "Just much to think about."

"I should say so," Hilde huffed. "We have to prepare for Berendsfore. With him as your lord and such a place to reside, and as the mistress, no less! La! So much to think about. I am surprised you are not floating about."

Rosamund suppressed a groan. "I am going to the solar until 'tis time to break the fast." She fled the room, and the woman's disturbing words.

Lady Veronica was alone in the large chamber, seated by the window embrasure. She looked up as Rosamund entered. "Good morn. You are roused early."

Rosamund merely shrugged. "Is Alayna not awake yet?"

"She is with the children."

"Ah." Rosamund sat and began to pick at a card of wool.

"Rosamund..." Veronica drew in a deep breath and let it out. "I have been meaning to speak to you—"

The door opened and Alayna came in with Leanna in her arms. "Good morn," she beamed cheerily. "You two have rivaled the cock's crow this day!"

Rosamund raised her eyes to meet Veronica's. The older woman seemed to hesitate, then turned away. "Excuse me. I have something else I must see to."

Later that day Rosamund was pulled into an alcove, a huge hand over her mouth to keep her from screaming.

"If you stay quiet, I promise I will kiss you," a masculine voice said into her ear. The hand dropped away.

She whirled. "Agravar! What are you doing?"

"I needed you near me."

He stopped her retort with a long kiss.

Pulling away, he asked, "Have you spoken yet to Robert?"

"I have not seen him. Do you know where he is?"

"Nay, but I've been busy with Lucien all morn. The squires who have trained here are getting ready to receive their spurs and be knighted." His hands slid up and down her back. His look told her he wanted to do more. "Do it soon."

"I shall do it first chance, I promise." She twined her arms about his neck. "Stop pestering me."

"Only if you will do the same."

"I have done nothing to plague you!"

"Aye, woman, you do. With every breath, I am besieged with wanting you. 'Tis pitiful, what you've reduced me to."

"'Tis your own fault, none of mine."

"Aye, 'tis. You are the one with the laughing eyes and this soft hair, and…" His hand slid down to her waist, spreading out so that his first two fingertips touched the underside of her breast.

Laughing, she pulled away. "Sir, you are debauched!"

"Hmm," he replied, coming after her. The sound of someone approaching stopped him.

He straightened. "I believe you should speak to Lady Alayna," he said loudly as a servant passed. "She would know what you should do."

When the servant was gone, Agravar lunged, but Rosamund skittered out of his grasp. "You may not! What if we are seen?"

"Tell Robert and it will not matter."

"I *will* speak to him, but you must give me time. I shall do it when I feel 'tis the right time."

He stopped his teasing and sighed. "I know 'tis wrong to rush you."

"You are sweet to rush me," she corrected. "I like knowing you are so impatient."

"I endeavor to please," he said mockingly, and offered a courtly bow.

"You look ridiculous. You are much too big for such groveling. Now off with you."

He grinned at her. "You really have changed."

"Do you disapprove?"

His gaze swept up from her toes to level off at her eyes. "I assure you, my lady, I heartily approve."

"Someone else is coming. I will speak to you soon."

"Come to my chamber tonight," he whispered, grabbing her close for a quick kiss.

"I shall not. Let me go. Someone is coming."

"Promise."

"Agravar!"

"Promise."

"Aye. I shall come."

He released her just in time. Another servant came into the hallway. Upon seeing them, he stopped. "Captain, I was looking for you. My lord and lady seek you."

Agravar frowned. "Thank you."

"In the master's solar," the man said. His eyes flickered to Rosamund. He nodded an acknowledgment, his face full of speculation.

"Thank you, Captain," Rosamund said with formality. "I shall take your advice under consideration. Good day."

* * *

When Agravar went to the master's solar, he found only Alayna there.

"Is Lucien about?" he asked as he entered.

Alayna looked a bit distressed. "Nay. I have asked Lucien to allow me to speak to you alone. Agravar, we have had some news that may be rather difficult for you. You may wish to brace yourself."

Agravar clenched his jaw. Was this something to do with Rosamund? "I assure you, Alayna, I am braced."

She held out a small scroll. "This arrived just now. This morning. There…is news. From Tannyhill Manor. Agravar…I know this is very complicated." She sighed. "Your mother is dead."

Of all the possible disasters that flew through his thoughts in the last moments, this was nothing he had imagined. The death of his mother—a woman with who he had never exchanged the smallest pleasantry, who had never held him in the slightest affection—this should not be shattering news.

And yet he felt something brittle inside him start to crumble. He looked about him. "I think I should like to sit down."

Alayna laid her hand on his arm and led him to a stool. "I am so sorry, Agravar. There was no easy way to tell you."

"Thank you, but there is no need to feel badly. 'Tis not the same as the deep devotion you share with your mother." And yet there was this searing sensation inside him, as if a fire scorched his innards.

Her soft hand remained on his shoulder. "I understand a little. Lucien never told me exactly, but a mention here and there and, well, I surmised that she had a difficult time accepting you.''

Nodding, he rose and walked a few steps to stare out the window, not really seeing anything but the parade of images from his past. ''She really meant nothing to me.''

''Agravar, sometimes the things we feel do not make sense. Your mother was still the woman who gave you life and for all of her failings, she did mean something to you.''

''How strange.'' His voice held a hint of astonishment. ''You are correct, of course. I had never realized it before.''

'''Tis right you should mourn her.''

He turned to her and took her hands in his. ''Thank you for your gentleness, Alayna.''

Her eyes grew moist. ''Surely you must know how much you are loved. By so many.''

Swallowing hard, he answered, ''Aye. I feel very lucky to have all of you.'' It was true. But he was also thinking of Rosamund.

With his mother dead, it was like a sign. The past was gone. And he now possessed what he had always desired. For the first time, he felt abundance had come to him.

Rosamund may have always dreamed of freedom, but he…he had craved love. And now he had it all around him. Still, the sadness did not abate. But he could accept it.

''I will tell Lucien he can come in, now.'' Alayna shook her head and laughed. '''Twas not exactly truth when I said I *asked* him if I could be the one to impart the news. I ordered the clod-headed brute out. I can only imagine the delicacy he would have lent to the subject.''

Agravar didn't tell her that her husband was surprisingly astute in some matters and had, on past occasions, displayed a sensitivity that had been uncanny. He only smiled and squeezed her hand.

Chapter Twenty-Seven

Rosamund came to him that night. He took her into his arms and loved her with slow, teasing caresses. It wasn't until after they lay quietly in each other's arms that he told her of his mother. He was surprised he had so many words. Struggling to purge all the confused emotions that crowded in his heart, he found his voice, and discovered the way to open his soul and share it with the only other person on earth with whom he could.

"When she walked by me, she always was so pale. She looked like a ghost, I used to think. It frightened me when I was a boy, but as I grew, I used to watch her. I suppose she fascinated me. I always wanted her to notice me. Just to look at me."

"How wretched," Rosamund said, and her arms tightened protectively around him.

He gave a harsh laugh and stared up at the ceiling. "She gave me nothing but my life, but I did love her. And I was sorry she despised me."

"Not you." Her slim hand rested on the defined musculature over his breast. "In your heart, you are the most loving of men. She never knew you, never knew the goodness inside you."

"You only say that because you love me."

"I do love you, but I am no liar," she said with a jaunty jerk of her eyebrows. "Who else but a man such as you could rescue me *three* times. Four, if you count how you've saved me from my fears."

He smiled. The pain in him still throbbed, but softer now, easier. With Rosamund, everything was easier.

Rosamund was well aware that she had promised Agravar she would speak to Robert at the first opportunity, but the man was never about. In a stroke of acute irony, he left orders for Agravar—as that one had proved so capable in keeping Rosamund from danger in the past—to watch over his betrothed in his absence.

It was simple, therefore, with this tacit permission, to forget the unpleasant task and push it indefinitely into the future. Rosamund's natural interest in the healing arts gave them the perfect excuse to wander off into the woods—ostensibly to gather herbs—and afforded them uninterrupted hours away from any observing eyes.

Invariably, they would talk and dawdle, dream and make love, then hurriedly fill Rosamund's basket with whatever they could find so that when they returned at dusk, they had a boon of bedraggled weeds, crushed wildflowers and wild herbs. Anyone who might have noticed the questionable collection would have thought Rosamund's talents in the healing arts quite wanting.

It happened one such evening, as they passed

through the barbican, one of Agravar's men called him over. Rosamund continued on, smiling dreamily at the sultry pleasure of the day that still clung to her. Glancing down at her basket, she laughed. They had been very naughty today, and the haphazard assortment of flora they had quickly gathered, including Agravar's inexpert contributions, looked particularly incriminating.

"Rosamund! Rosamund!" Aric called to her as he ran to her. "Where is Agravar? My father wants him!"

"He stopped at the guardhouse," she said, tousling the boy's dark curls.

The boy fell into step beside her. "Guess what? Luke smiled today. It was disgusting. Wet and drooly, but Mother said he was adorable."

"Your tiny brother *is* adorable."

"Father did not see it. If he did, he would agree with me, I know. And he's always grabbing my hair in his fists and yanking hard."

"Your father?" she teased as she idly picked through the herbs, tossing aside the most obvious mistakes. They entered the upper bailey.

"Nay! Luke!"

Behind her, someone called a warning. She stepped to the side, bringing Aric with her. A troop of soldiers passed them.

"Strange," she mused. "'Tis awfully late for visitors to be arriving."

"The lookouts spotted them from across the southern meadow. Father was looking for Agravar to tell him."

"That must be why Agravar was detained at the gate. They would have come in just behind us."

It was then she noticed their colors. Green, purple and gold. She stopped dead in her tracks.

Her eyes flew over the faces of the men. Then she saw him, riding toward the rear on his splendid charger, dressed in finery that would have looked absurd on any other man. Cyrus of Hallscroft had come to Gastonbury.

Aric exclaimed in alarm when she crumpled onto the hard earth.

When she opened her eyes, she was in her own bed. She blinked, coming into awareness of the fact she was not under the covers and still dressed in her dusty gown.

The rustle of someone moving beside her brought no alarm. She assumed it would be Alayna or Veronica. When she turned her head, however, her heart froze.

Cyrus leaned forward. "Aye, you impudent little snake, I am here. And we are alone. I sent the others away."

Scrambling up, she swung her legs down. She was stopped by his barked command. "Stay exactly where you are."

"Go away. I will scream."

"Then I will say you were hysterical and I had to slap some sense into you. If that does not work, I will close my fist and try it that way." He said this dispassionately, as if describing nothing more consequential than the arrangement of furniture.

"They will not believe you. They will—"

"You think you have won yourself champions here, do you? Oh, aye, Davey told me all about it." His nostrils flared and his lips curled back, baring his teeth. He was not an ugly man, but to her, every feature brought on a deep flush of revulsion.

He said, "Davey told me everything. How you loved Gastonbury and how you changed. And about the Viking. Aye, you little whore, he told me all about the Viking and your sinful ways."

Rosamund felt as if she were choking. "I cannot believe Davey betrayed me."

"He was but a weak-minded man made senseless by the wiles of the female serpent."

"Why would he turn on me?"

Cyrus pressed his face closer. Rosamund was finding it difficult to breathe. "I asked myself the same question, Rosamund. When he tried to insist on secrecy, his almost desperate need not to have anyone know he had come to me with his little problem, I knew. Aye, and you do, too. It was how you ensnared him in the first place."

"I never did anything but offer friendship."

"Liar. He fancied himself in love with you. Do not act as if you did not know it. A woman is aware when her powers are at work."

"Davey was but a boy whose loyalty to my brother—"

"His loyalty, need I remind you, should have rested with *me!* Instead, the idiot helped you escape. Then, he thought to use me. Ah, what a fatal mistake. He knew I would come to Gastonbury and bring you under heel. Hoping I would take the Viking out of the situation, it would leave you defenseless once again—ripe for him to return to your side. A neat plan. I actually admired it. Of course, on a lesser man than myself, it might have worked."

Rosamund spoke slowly. "What did you mean— 'fatal mistake'?"

"He is dead, you twit. Why do you ask these questions when you know the answers? As if I would let him live after all he had done."

"You killed him…nay! I…" She pressed her hand over her eyes.

"And 'tis all your fault. Your whoring ways brought about the boy's death."

Her head shot up. "You killed him. You are the one who is evil. You killed my mother."

He seemed genuinely surprised. "Nay, I did not. What lies have you spread about me?"

"I need not lie when the truth serves me well enough."

"You grew impudent while you were away. Leon had told me this. Leon told me much, but Davey told me more. Did you really think I would allow you to marry a Viking bastard with no family or money? What advantage does that bring me? Now you have ruined yourself! I swear to you—you will be punished. And I have the perfect means to do it."

She made to leap to her feet, but when he lifted his hand to her, she stopped in midmotion. Fear trickled into her muscles, driving away her impulse to flee.

"Sit down, Jezebel, and listen to your master. 'Tis still I who has that duty, until Robert takes you to wife." His fingers closed painfully over her upper arm. "And he will take you to wife. I have already spoken to him. You have been very clever. I believe he *was* wavering. I had to put much pressure on him to agree."

"He t-told me he would honor the betrothal."

"Aye. But he is reluctant."

Rosamund closed her eyes at the missed opportunity. If her courage had been stronger, she might have settled the matter with Robert before Cyrus arrived.

"I reminded him," Cyrus continued, "that any breach of our contract would be viewed as an act of grave insult. Robert places much importance on such matters, as you know. The man's overdeveloped sense of honor is useful to my purpose."

"You are vile."

His hand shot out and her cheek exploded with pain. "I taught you better, little whore. Just because you have a man plowing between your legs does not give you the right to speak to me in such a manner. You can forget your Viking. He will not help you."

Her jaw ached. She worked it tentatively to test the damage.

His eyes narrowed. "Robert has agreed to marry you, but only if you are willing. He claimed you have seemed less than enthusiastic at the prospect of the union, although what the devil that matters I cannot fathom. Thus, he will keep to our bargain if you show yourself to be more amenable to him."

"Why must I marry Robert? What is it to you?"

"Your marriage will bring me power. Did you not learn your lessons from the priest? You have only one purpose, and that is to further my interests. Then you belong to Robert, and will be of whatever use he deems. Some men are foolish, indulgent. He seems to be one of these. It vexes me, your luck in this matter."

Her chin came up. Where the courage came from to defy him, she didn't know. "You cannot force me.

I am no longer the girl I was. I refuse to take Robert. I shall tell him so."

He smiled slowly, as if he had been waiting for this. "If you disobey me, Rosamund, then I shall kill him."

Panic seized her insides, draining away all her rebellion. "Why would you kill Robert?"

"Kill Robert? An interesting thought, especially when I see it causes you anxiety. But I was not referring to Robert. I meant *him*. The Viking."

She went utterly still. She didn't even breathe for a full minute.

There were words of denial, of challenge, that sprang to her mind, but she didn't bother to say them. There was no doubt in her mind that Cyrus did mean to do what he said.

He had killed Davey, and Davey was but a poor besotted boy. He had killed her mother, when her mother was gone with child.

She fought against the pull of fear. "You cannot best him. And…and I will tell Lucien…I will tell him what you have threatened."

He spread his hands before his and sighed. "Then you widen the circle of death, my dear. You do not wish to make Lucien my enemy. The man has *children*. And a wife, I hear, whom he allows unbelievable freedoms. They would be ridiculously easy to access."

She swallowed back bile. "Why are you doing this?" she cried.

He blinked arrogantly. "Because '*tis my will*. Now, the wedding is tomorrow morn. I want no more delays. You will come to the chapel and say your vows and if anyone suspects the tears you shed are anything but ones of joy, you shall know regret.''

Agravar stood in the archway to the hall and stared at the man seated at the high table. Cyrus of Hallscroft wore an emerald-green tunic, his thinning hair neatly combed into place and a trimmed beard concealing most of his face. His eyes were small and half-veiled with puffy eyelids.

"Stop glaring," Lucien said beside him.

"My God, Lucien, the man is a monster—how could you let him in your house?"

"Rest easy," Lucien said in a low voice. "As I have been given no cause to order him from my home, there is little I can do."

Agravar ground his teeth. "After what he did to Rosamund?"

"He did nothing to her while under my roof. Alayna told me Rosamund fainted when she saw him, and he insisted on staying with her until she awakened. There is nothing sinister in that."

Fury exploded into Agravar's brain. "My God, you let him alone with her?" Surging forward, his face was twisted into a snarl, his mighty fists clenched tight. Lucien shoved him back. "Disgrace me, and I will have your own men put you in a cell until your head cools."

"You do not know what he did—"

"There is nothing I can do, Agravar. He did not harm her while she was here and Rosamund has not made complaint about him. He has given no offense to me or anyone else. I am bound by my position, Agravar. I am lord here. There is a responsibility in that."

Black eyes locked with blue, both shouting steel-clad determination.

Agravar relented slightly. "Very well. But if he does anything that even hints at a threat to Rosamund, I shall go for him."

"Agreed." Lucien let out his breath, a belated sign of the tension he had masked during their confrontation. "Let us go, then. You know what to do."

Agravar's nod was grim. "I know exactly what to do."

Cyrus was the consummate polite guest. Upon meeting Lucien and Agravar, he bowed in a courtly way and commented on the excellent experience he had had thus far in Lucien's gracious home. He managed to string together several compliments without seeming to fawn.

As he spoke to a stoic Lucien, Agravar remembered Rosamund's description of him, how he had been well liked by his people and unsuspected of his crimes. He had to admit, the man had a kind of oily charisma. Yet, even without Rosamund's having told him, Agravar would have sensed something wrong in Cyrus. It was in the way the man tried too hard.

Lucien was not taken in, either. He remained frostily polite throughout supper and the ensuing entertainments. Alayna was conspicuously reserved, but only to those who knew her well enough to contrast her present demeanor with the warm generosity she usually extended to guests in her hall. Cyrus hardly took notice of her, or Veronica, who sat frowning at her daughter's side.

Rosamund didn't appear. Agravar wondered desperately what had happened to her, but in no seemly way could he avail himself of any information. With this frustration, he excused himself early.

"Captain," Cyrus called, stepping down off the dais to follow. "A word with you."

Agravar hid his surprise.

"Ah, I see you are both younger and more energetic than I," Cyrus huffed, keeping pace as Agravar continued on his way. They stepped into the corridor that led up the stairs to the second-floor sleeping chambers. Cyrus said, "I wonder for what reason you are in such a rush? Could it be my stepdaughter? Do you have a secret assignation arranged with the little whore?"

Agravar stopped. Slowly he turned to face Cyrus. The other man was smiling a bland, steady smile that did not extend beyond the stretching of his lips. "You are surprised. Did she tell you nothing of me— of the ways I have to find these things out?"

With a growl, Agravar launched himself at Cyrus, pinning him against the wall. He pressed his forearm against the other man's Adam's apple.

Cyrus let out a choked wheeze. "If you want to see her dead, go ahead and strangle me."

Agravar faltered. The man had too much confidence. It made him uneasy. Loosening his hold, he allowed Cyrus to breathe a bit better. "Speak," he commanded.

Cyrus's eyes were agleam as he said, "You must think me a great fool to imagine I would put myself into your hands with nothing to guarantee my safety. I've arranged for an army of assassins to mete out my debts after my death. Harm me, and Rosamund will die. Others, too, that you care for. I promise you, barbarian, mine will be a horrible vengeance."

The threat hit Agravar hard. Something about this man, the flat, cold eyes, the thin smile of absolute assurance, reminded him of another he had known. He believed that there existed men—like his own father, like this man—for whom no cruelty or injustice was forbidden, to whom power was all and death a toy to be used for a cause, or mere amusement.

His voice held a note of uncertainty when he replied, "I can keep my people safe."

"Ah, what a ridiculous boast. There are so many ways to kill. Poison, the slip of a knife in a crowd, a stray arrow during a hunt, a small child falls to a tragic end…ah, too many to mention now."

Fear flowered inside Agravar's chest. His lips curled, baring his teeth ferally.

Cyrus chuckled, seeing the response he had elicited. "It need not happen right away. I am a patient man, and I shall have eternity to wait upon my rewards. But you…imagine a whole life waiting for it to happen. And then it does. Imagine, then, knowing you were to blame for the death of one of those people in there whom you claim to love."

Agravar merely glared at him. "You would not…you could not."

"You know little of what I would dare." Cyrus jerked himself free of Agravar's grasp.

"What do you want?"

Brushing at the expensive fabric of his cloak where it had been crushed, Cyrus clucked with admonition. "Rosamund is quite resigned to her fate. You will do nothing to alter that. Nor will you meddle with Robert. Your interference, with either of them, will cost lives dear to you."

"Go to the devil."

"In due time. 'Tis the women in our blood, you know. It makes us weak. Oh, I almost forgot. Davey sent you a message." He grinned. "He wants you to know I am serious. *Deadly* serious. And he should know."

Agravar knew his meaning well enough. "You killed him. My God, man, he was just a boy."

"Boys, babes, women. It matters not. He was in my way." He narrowed his eyes and leaned in toward Agravar. "Do not get in my way, Viking bastard. Or you will know an anguish you cannot even imagine."

Frustrated, Agravar stood helpless. This kind of man he understood all too well.

When Agravar had gone to Denmark to find his sire, he had come to know pure greed and blistering malice. It was something he accepted like a cancerous blight—the existence of these creatures who lived only to destroy. He understood that Cyrus of Hallscroft was exactly like Hendron the Viking. And he was afraid.

Agravar swallowed hard. "Your madness sickens me."

"Aye, well, 'tis not your favor I am seeking." Cyrus laughed, and as he started to walk off, he said over his shoulder, "Do not attend the service. I have no desire to make a mockery of all this. In fact, absent yourself for the day. All will go much more smoothly without you being tempted to do something foolish. And do not see her again. Ever. If you do...well, I might decide a warning would be in order to show you how serious I am about this matter. The only problem I would have in doing it is deciding exactly *who* will die."

Agravar watched Cyrus leave, waiting until he had disappeared out of sight before he drove his fist into the unyielding stone of the wall. The pain didn't touch him.

The mighty Viking Agravar was effectively beaten.

Nay. Not yet.

He raised his head. He would think of something.

Chapter Twenty-Eight

The first thing Agravar did was round up three of his most trusted men. It wasn't until he had them assembled, puzzled and anxious at this strange call to arms, that he realized he could tell them nothing. He dismissed them, ignoring their dismay, and went to the battlements to prowl. It was there he saw the first shades of dawn. Rosamund's wedding day had come.

In the end he did go to the ceremony, staying off to the side in the tiny alcove that led to the vestry. Silently he watched as Rosamund spoke her vows. She looked beautiful, poised and surprisingly composed. Robert, stoic and regal, said his own promises in a low, serious voice and Agravar felt the exquisite torture of witnessing Rosamund's slim hand placed into the graceful palm of the man who was now her husband.

The couple turned to their friends and received their congratulations. Alayna came up immediately to Rosamund, engaging her while Robert walked to where a veiled woman sat in a pew just in front of where Agravar stood in the shadows. It was Veronica, he realized. Although she faced away from him, Agravar could see by the bent of her head and the short dabbing motions she made at her eyes with a square of linen that she was crying.

Robert let his mask slip as he drew up to her. His handsome face crumpled. He lifted a hand to Veronica, then let it drop before it touched her. Veronica bowed low and her shoulders trembled.

Turning about, Robert went back to his bride's side.

God's breath! Agravar thought. *He loves her. He never wanted Rosamund.*

Backing away, he left the hall.

Robert loved Veronica.

Agravar paced the confines of his chamber.

Robert. Robert was the key.

When Robert wed Rosamund, he had thought Cyrus was but a protective guardian, not a ruthless conspirator. Cyrus had trapped him. He had played on the man's sympathy, his honor.

But if Robert knew…if he was to learn what Cyrus had done, surely he would not wish to maintain a marriage made under such devious circumstances, especially if his heart lay elsewhere.

Bound by marriage or not, Robert would never hold a friendship with Cyrus. He would certainly despise him, and instead of bettering his prospects, Cyrus would end up the worse for his deeds.

And then Cyrus would gain nothing. Cyrus would lose.

If Robert knew.

Agravar cursed himself for not thinking of this

sooner. The vows had been spoken. Robert and Rosamund were duly wedded.

But not bedded. Yet.

Of course. He still had time. The union had yet to be consummated. It would be easy to dissolve if Rosamund's virtue remained intact, at least to Robert's knowledge.

Rushing to the door, he swung it open—and ran headlong into two of his own men.

"Caspar, Desmond. What the devil are you doing here? Is something wrong?"

The two men exchanged a guilty look. "Ah, sir," Caspar managed. "Nay. Nothing…ah…wrong. Nay." He looked to Desmond as if for aid.

The other looked terrified. "Aye. I mean nay!"

"Explain," Agravar demanded.

They paused. "You tell him," Caspar said.

Desmond looked horrified. "Nay, you."

"I am the elder. You tell him."

"Desmond!" Agravar shouted.

"Lord Lucien sent us to guard you," Desmond said in a rush. "He told us that you were not to leave your chamber."

"What the devil—?" He tossed his head like an angry bull. "Get the hell out of my way at once."

Desmond swallowed. "Sir." Beside him, an apoleptic Caspar stood firm.

"I am your captain. Stand aside, I say."

"Please, sir. Our lord has commanded we not allow you out of your chamber."

He could have taken them, and they knew it. But it was too humiliating, battling the men he himself had trained. Through gritted teeth, he said, "Fetch your master, then, and let me take this up with him."

They looked at each other. Desmond, the senior, nodded to the younger man and Caspar went off to get Lucien.

When he returned, Caspar told him that they were to take Agravar to Lucien's solar. Agravar couldn't resist a vicious shove, sending them against the opposite wall, before striding up the turret stairs to have it out with his old friend.

He opened the door with a slam that echoed in the large room. Lucien was alone.

"How dare you."

Lucien appeared outwardly calm, but a rapid tick in his temple showed his agitation. "Your blood is hot, Agravar. You are not thinking clearly."

"I must speak to Robert. He must not bed her."

Lucien managed to look sympathetic without shifting a muscle. "'Tis too late. They are abed. 'Tis done, Agravar. Please, believe me, friend, when I tell you—"

"Nay, listen to me!" He took three rapid steps and grabbed Lucien by the collar. Giving him a jolting shake, he demanded, "Cyrus had foiled us all, but there is time. They must not be allowed to—"

"Stop it, Agravar!" Lucien shook him off, stumbling as he regained his balance. "Look at you! Look at what you have come to."

"And what would you have done for Alayna, Lucien? What would you have considered too far to go for her?"

Lucien let out an explosive breath and shook his head. "Nothing." He straightened his tunic and began to pace. Agravar hung his head, squeezing his eyes shut as he tried to concentrate. He had to calm himself, get his thoughts together to convince Lucien.

He felt a tap on his shoulder. He looked up.

Lucien stood directly before him. "I'm sorry, friend," he said, "but this is for your own good."

There was a split second when Agravar was aware of Lucien's fist drawing back, but it was done so quickly he didn't have time to react. He could only breathe a soft "nay!" Then the pain came, but the blackness swiftly followed, pulling him away into the void.

When he awoke, the first thing he saw was Lucien bending over him, his elbows resting on his knees. He had a wine flask in his fist. As soon as Agravar sat up, he shoved it at him.

"Is this supposed to dull my senses until 'tis too late?" he grumbled. He took a swig anyway.

"'Tis already too late. I had Eurice give you a mixture to keep you asleep."

"Ah, God, Lucien, what have you done?" Coming to his feet, he looked wildly about. "What time is it?"

"The bedding is done. 'Tis after midnight."

"What?" Agravar thundered. "Lucien! I should…" He let the sentence trail away and dropped the fist he had raised. "Why could you not have listened to me?"

"There was nothing you could say that would alter the fact that they are wed. Robert…Robert is a good man. He will treat her well."

Agravar nearly went for him. He stopped himself with an effort that left him trembling. He raised a palsied fist in front of him. "How the devil can you say such a thing to me?"

As if realizing the horrible ineffectiveness of his words, Lucien shook his head. "I am sorry, friend. I...I...you know I have no facility with words."

"Damn you," Agravar snarled. He rose and made for the door.

Lucien shot to his feet. "Stay away from her."

Agravar paused, his hand on the knob. His voice lowered, becoming nearly strangled. "I shall. You have given me no choice." He bowed his head. "She is lost to me."

When Agravar entered his chamber, he did not bother lighting the torch. He stood at the small window, looked out at the moon and considered the unmanly act of weeping. He wondered if he could, after so many years. Not since he was a very small boy had he allowed tears. He had wept over his mother often, until he had realized it did no good. And then he had resolved not to permit such weakness again.

He thought now that perhaps it did do good. It solved nothing, true. But it cleansed. He envied women that, the healing of tears.

It was so silent, even his breathing sounded labored. The tears never came. Instead, rage grew in slow degrees. Rage and ineffectual regret. Savagely he ground the heels of his hands to his forehead, savoring the pain. No tears for him, then, but the pain was good. Clean, crisp, neat, tangible. Distracting from the terrible rending of his heart.

He made a sound, a half groan, half sigh, and collapsed against the wall, pressing his cheek against the cool stones. There was a noise behind him, a rustling. As if...

"Agravar?"

He froze. Delirium? Had his mind snapped, was he dreaming?

Her voice came again in the unrelenting darkness. "Agravar, is that you?"

He whirled. "Rosamund?"

His eyes had adjusted now. He saw her sitting in his bed, wearing a linen shift. She was propped in the midst of his furs, rubbing the sleep out of her eyes.

In a flash, he was beside her. Snatching her close, he demanded, "What are you doing? My God, how could you come here?"

Her arms went around his shoulders and she buried her face in his neck, just under his chin where his racing pulse beat crazily. "I left before...before he came. I was...oh, Agravar, I know I bragged how brave I had become, but I could not do it. I could not allow him to touch me, not as you had, not..."

"Shh," he said, closing his eyes. He hated himself for the surge of joy washing through him. She had committed a criminal act of defiance and all he could think of was that she was still his own and no other's. "You did right. Rosamund, you were very brave."

"Nay, I was a coward." She shook her head, her hair brushing the exposed flesh at his throat. "I should have spoken to Robert. If I had told him...but Cyrus— I kept thinking of Cyrus, and I was too frightened."

"My love, I believe Robert would welcome your news with a glad heart." At her incredulous look, he explained, "Robert loves Veronica. I would wager he did not wish to wed you any more than you did him.''

She pulled back, her eyes wide with dismay. ''What?''

''Aye. I saw him go to Veronica after the ceremony, and I witnessed their grief. Later, I realized why you could never find him to tell him your wishes. We were too busy sneaking off to be together to realize *they* were doing the same thing.''

''Robert and Veronica? Then, why would he still want to wed me?''

''Cyrus called upon Robert's honor, telling him you wished the union, and Robert must have felt he had no other choice.''

He felt her shiver. Pulling her close, he stroked down her back, soothing her. ''With me, he used more brutal tactics,'' she said. ''Cyrus threatened to slay you. As if that weren't enough, he said he would kill Alayna, Aric and the babies, and anyone else I loved if I refused.''

''He used the same tack with me. He is effective, if unimaginative.''

''He would do it, Agravar. That is why I had to obey.''

''Aye,'' he answered as his fingers curled distractedly in her curls. ''I had no doubt he would.''

She stiffened. Looking up at him, she closed a trembling hand over her mouth. ''Oh, Lord, Agravar—what have I done? When Cyrus finds that I fled the bridal chamber, what will he do?'' Her voice quavered. ''How could I have not thought of it?''

''Nay, love, listen to me. There is something I realized when I saw Robert and Veronica together. Robert was cleverly maneuvered by Cyrus to believe he had a duty to you. This can be the only reason he went ahead with a marriage he clearly did not want. He can know nothing of what Cyrus has been doing to force our cooperation.''

''Do you suggest we tell him?''

''Aye, we must. Robert is our ally, and a powerful one. Remember that there is no advantage in this marriage for Cyrus without Robert's goodwill. 'Twas this he sought to curry with the alliance between your families.''

''But what will it gain us to bring Robert into it at this time? 'Tis too late. We are wed before God.''

''Robert will want to dissolve the union while he still can so he can marry Veronica.'' Giving her a lopsided grin, his eyes sparkled. ''Although how he could miss your more obvious charms, I cannot fathom.''

She seemed reluctant. ''I do not understand, Agravar, how this brings us out of danger. If the marriage is dissolved, Cyrus would carry out his threats.''

''Aye, but the annulment shall be Robert's doing, and I believe Cyrus would not be so foolish as to try to use his brutish tactics with a man as impressively well connected as Robert. It would be too simple for him to be found out and gain him no advantage.''

Rosamund spoke with dismay as understanding dawned. ''Aye. Aye! Robert is powerful, with influential friends in the highest offices at court. Cyrus cannot threaten him. And he cannot harm us once Robert knows of what he has done. He shall serve as our protection. Oh, Agravar!'' She collapsed back into his arms. He heard tears in her voice. ''Can it be true? Have you truly found a way for us?''

''If Robert does what I suspect he will, then, aye,

we have found our solution, Rosamund. We have only to speak to him. Then I shall marry you, and no one can say naught about it.''

''Robert will help us.'' She dashed away the moisture beading on her lashes. ''I know it. If he loves Veronica and she him, then he will be as happy as we to put this marriage aside.''

''That is what I am counting on,'' he murmured, taking her face in his hands. His thumbs caressed the high ridge of her cheekbones. ''Although I must admit my pride would like it better if I could deal with Cyrus my own way.''

''How can you smite wickedness with a sword? Cyrus's cunning is too low, too base for honorable battle.'' She tossed her head back and laughed. ''Oh, what does it matter? We have found our freedom. At last, Agravar, there shall be nothing to stand between us.''

He looked down at her and a fierce, primitive emotion surged up from his soul. Pure possessiveness. She was here with him, here in his room where the whole of the world was held at bay. Here in this bed, where they had lain before, where they had loved before.

He trapped her gaze with his. Her smile melted. He studied her mouth for a long moment before lowering his head. Touching his lips to hers, he felt himself slipping away. Losing himself in her, as he had done so many times before.

But this was different. Whatever plans they had for the future, the fact remained she was another's wife until released by the church.

It was, in fact, her wedding eve—the night where she should, by rights, be lying in her husband's arms for the first time, sealing the contract of marriage forever.

Still, her hands moved over him, hungry and stirring. Happy to oblige her, he slipped off her shift and bent to her breasts, licking and sucking the plump mounds of flesh the way he knew would inflame her. Her small cries made him hard, impatient.

Far back inside his brain, some vague bleating of his conscience sounded, some vestige of the honor he had sworn himself to amend for his father's base savagery. It warned him that it would be unspeakably indecent to lie with her, touch her in the ways that he had no right to.

The possessive savage in him answered—*she was his.* By right of the heart, if not the law, and the voice was quelled, lost in the glory of her kiss, and the wild abandon of her lovemaking.

It troubled him not the least as he finished undressing her. Nary a twinge interrupted the pleasure he found as he entered her deliciously welcoming body and loved her until they were sated and at rest.

He fell to sleep with only selfish bliss in his thoughts, the niggling little voice that could have saved them having been thoroughly vanquished.

When the pounding woke them, he came cleanly and suddenly out of sleep. Panic exploded before he even sat up.

His first thought was that he had not bolted his door. He swung his legs to the floor.

But it was far too late. The portal opened and Lucien entered his chamber.

"Agravar, wake. You are not going to believe this, but that wretched girl has gone missing again—" Lucien stopped.

Beside him, naked under the furs, Rosamund shrank into his side. Slowly Agravar rose from the bed, positioning his nude body to shield her from view.

Lucien said nothing. He stood perfectly still.

Agravar broke the silence. ''I realize we have, as brothers do, little formality between us. But I believe that in the future, you should knock before entering my chamber.''

''Get her out of here,'' Lucien snapped suddenly. ''Robert is right behind me.''

The warning was futile. Robert stood in the doorway.

Chapter Twenty-Nine

Rosamund slowly reached for the crumpled shift on the floor. Her humiliation was boundless, even with the Viking's massive body shielding her. She slipped the garment on and wrapped herself tightly in one of the furs, tucking her chin into her chest and wishing devoutly to disappear.

Robert broke the silence at last. "I came in search of my wife." His voice held no rancor. Only surprise, and a vague regret she didn't as yet understand. "Lucien suggested you might know something, where she might have gone. I doubt he suspected how correct he would be."

Agravar took a step forward, his hands held out before him. "Let me explain."

Lucien's voice cut in sharply. "For God's sake, Agravar, make it good."

Rosamund was relieved when she saw the Viking retrieve his leggings and pull them on. His nakedness, as well as her own dishabille, made her feel all the more vulnerable.

Agravar turned to face her husband. "I love her.

And she loves me. She did not wish to marry you. 'Twas Cyrus who forced her.''

Robert's gaze slid to Rosamund. "If this is true, why did you not tell me so?''

She slowly extricated herself from the bed and stood before him, forcing her head up and refusing the unrelenting urge to cringe. Her trembling, however, she could not control. It made her voice waver. "'Tis my fault, all of it. I...I was afraid to tell you. I have no excuse for what I did. I was wicked. I was...weak.''

"Rosamund, hush! Do not do this." Agravar stepped in front of her as if to shield her. To Robert, he said, "She is not to blame. 'Twas I who should have known better. I could have set things aright.''

Rosamund shoved him aside and went to stand before her husband. "'Twas deplorable, what I did. You may punish me any way you see fit.''

Robert's look was full of pity as it settled on Rosamund. "Oh, child, you are only unhappy. Is this why there was always such sadness in you, always so remote? Because you love him? Because you feared me? How could you not know I would never, never harm you?''

She hung her head. "I could not see it. I...''

"Answer me. Is it true you love him?''

Somehow, the betrayal of her heart seemed worse than that of her body. Pushing the words past her fear, she whispered, "I do. So much.''

"For God's sake, why did you never tell me?" He shook his head, his face full of misery. "So much could have been avoided had you but spoken of your heart.''

Agravar spoke up. "She was afraid to do it.''

"But why? What did I ever do to inspire her fear?"

Again Agravar answered for her. "It was Cyrus who terrorized her. All throughout her early years, she saw—she lived—unspeakable things, giving her a terrible dread of marriage, and of men. When she had finally resolved to speak with you, Cyrus arrived at Gastonbury. He threatened to kill you, and me." Indicating Lucien, he said, "He would have slain Alayna and the children, and Veronica—all who were dear to Rosamund."

Lucien's eyes flashed instant fire. "What is this? Alayna was in danger, my children were threatened, *and you did not tell me?*"

"Have you forgotten my father, Lucien?" His voice was harsh. "He would slaughter a village on a whim. Boredom was cured by torturing one of his slaves. How many times were you victim to his cruel amusements? They are of a kind, Cyrus and he. Cyrus told me he had assassins ready to carry out the executions after his death. I did what I thought was best to keep you all safe."

Robert placed his index finger under Rosamund's chin, tipping her face up to him. "Did he likewise threaten you to make you wed me?"

She couldn't meet his eye. "He did. I—I am so sorry."

He waited a long time before speaking. "Perhaps there is no excuse for what you have done. But there are reasons. And I can understand love, Rosamund." He closed his eyes and dropped his hand. "Unfortunately, I am bound by my honor to do what I must." He drew in a deep breath and turned to Agravar. "Captain, it gives me no pleasure to do this, but

I challenge you to a battle on the lists, to repay the debt of honor.''

Lucien raked his hand furiously thorough his hair.

Agravar seemed preternaturally calm. ''I will meet your challenge. Yet, I dare ask a boon of you. One favor. If you prevail, you must never take revenge on Rosamund. There is much you need to know, to understand her and the choices she made. 'Twas not her fault. You must forgive her.''

Robert gave a short, humorless laugh. ''I shall grant you this favor, Captain. But let us be realistic. I am an excellent knight, adept at the sword, if I may say so without prejudice. But for heaven's sake, look at the two of us. Look at you. Consider your profession, your size, your strength. I am older, a statesman now. You are a warrior.'' He paused, then added grimly, ''I shall not prevail. My honor dictates that I challenge, and 'twill be met just as duty demands. But I shall not prevail. We both know that.''

Agravar's eyes narrowed. ''We shall see. Men of faith believe that the righteous always triumph through the intercession of God. You are to remember your promise, Robert, should Providence find you the worthiest.''

Terror flared in Rosamund's breast. She realized then that Agravar meant to die.

Rosamund was sitting alone in the solar when Veronica swept in.

The room was empty. Everyone was down on the lists, watching two good men fight a battle neither one had any taste for. All because of her.

Veronica's smartly clicking footsteps drew closer, coming to an end just before Rosamund's bent-over body. Raising her head, Rosamund lifted her eyes to the woman she once called friend. "Is it done?" she asked in wooden tones. "Is Agravar dead?"

Veronica reached out and grabbed Rosamund's arm, yanking her to her feet. "Nay, he is not dead, and he will not be if I can help it." She whirled and pulled her toward the door.

"Please, nay!" Rosamund protested. "I am not going down there. I will not see him die."

"You *are* going." For a petite woman, Veronica's strength was not minimal, but it was more her indomitable will that made it impossible to refuse.

Still Rosamund pulled against her and wailed, "'Tis enough I am the cause of his death."

"Stop being a ninny and listen to me, Rosamund. I need you to have courage. One of those half-wits is going to die and the other's life shall be ruined if we do not do something."

"You shall stop them?" Hope flared, choking her as Rosamund stopped struggling and fell into step beside the older woman.

Veronica strode with grim purpose, never letting go of her grip, down the hallway and out the door into the upper courtyard. She headed for the inner wall, which would lead them down to the lower wards, to the training yard where the deadly challenge was taking place.

Rosamund grew impatient. "Veronica, please tell me—what are you going to do?"

"Exactly the question which has plagued me since I learned of this impossible situation. Then it came to me. I only hope 'tis not too late."

"What? What is it you plan?"

"Not I. I can do nothing. 'Tis *you.* You, Rosamund. You must stop them."

"I? But, Veronica, how can I?"

"Do you not tire of being a victim, child?" Veronica's voice was sharp, but it shook, laden with feeling. "Do you not grow weary of ever being helpless? You must *fight,* Rosamund. For God's sake, fight—with all you have in you. You must, or your love will die and mine will be his murderer. For once in your life, child—fight!"

Rosamund cried, "Fight how? I have no way to fight against them."

"Women have had to survive by their wits since the dawn of creation, for we are smaller, weaker in body. You have the means within you, child. Search yourself. You will find the words."

"I am too afraid!"

Veronica stopped and with a jerk of her elegant arm, she swung Rosamund about to face her. "Then your man will die. 'Tis your choice. Make up your mind."

Chapter Thirty

The crowd gathered at the lists was utterly silent.

Robert slipped on his gauntlets. He picked up his sword and inspected it.

Agravar stood motionless and stared at the nervous movements of his opponent. He was ready.

Over on a dais set up with a brightly colored awning to shield it from the sun, Agravar spied the man whom he wished could fall under his blade. Cyrus was not pleased with what had transpired, especially since Robert had made it abundantly clear that he wished no further alliance between their two houses, his union with Rosamund notwithstanding. Now, the Lord of Hallscroft glared at Agravar with ferocious heat. Agravar read the look. Cyrus wanted vengeance. He wanted blood.

There was a touch of bitterness in giving the bastard his wish.

Swiveling his head to the other side, he saw Lucien standing with a very pale Alayna. Beside them were Pelly and some of the major knights of Gastonbury. His comrades, his friends.

She wasn't here. He was disappointed, but he understood. It was best she stayed away, he supposed, and yet his soul silently keened her name.

"I am ready," Robert called.

Agravar began swinging the broadsword to loosen his arms.

Lucien came to stand at Agravar's side. He swallowed, then said carefully, "You had better fight, damn you. If you throw in your lot, I shall never forgive you."

Agravar stopped and bowed his head, studying the dirt between his feet. "I loved you like a brother. You were my only kin." And then he strode onto the field.

Robert was waiting for him. He raised his sword in salute. Agravar returned the gesture. His muscles tensed as he awaited the signal.

A movement out of the corner of his eye brought his attention to the people lined up on the fringes of the field. Someone was shouting—a woman. He turned just in time to see Rosamund burst out of the crowd.

She stumbled onto the field, her feet tripping her up so that she spilled onto the dust between the two combatants.

Behind her, hanging back a ways, Veronica made a more graceful entry.

The wave of dismay quickly hushed when Rosamund slowly rose to her feet and raised her hands. "I demand you stop this."

As incongruous as it was, Agravar feared he might laugh. She looked ridiculous, this scrap of a girl, warding off two armed knights about to battle.

Quelling the urge, he said, "Rosamund, step aside."

She ignored him. Instead, she turned to Robert. "You would murder him?"

Robert blinked, caught off guard. "I challenged him."

"And you know he will not fight you. He is prepared to die today. I ask you—for whose sake do you murder him? For yours, or mine?"

Robert swallowed hard. "For honor's sake."

Her shoulders drooped. "What a hideous price to pay for something as precious as a man's life."

"Duty demands—"

"What duty, my lord?" she asked wearily. "Christian duty?"

He faltered again. Shaking his head, he tried to dismiss her. "I cannot ignore what happened."

"Why not? It matters not to you. You care nothing for me. You love another. Tell me, my lord—you who are famed for your kindness and fairness, you say you do this for honor's sake. I ask you, then, what would you do for love's sake?"

His eyes narrowed. "I do not understand."

Rosamund took a step toward him. Agravar watched her in awe. She was not ridiculous any longer; she was magnificent. Back straight, head high, she moved steadily, unwavering until she stood just before the point of his sword. With two hands, she grasped the blade of Robert's sword and brought the gleaming steel to rest at her chest.

"For love's sake, Agravar would die for me. For love's sake, I would die for him. So, I ask you, Lord Robert, what would you do for love's sake?"

Turning, she pointed to the left, where Cyrus sat under his pretty awning. Agravar saw the man was leaning forward, his lips curled back from his teeth like a pagan mask of terror.

"His evil has tainted us, all of us. Would you let him spread his poison to all you love? What of those who love you, Robert? Do you let them suffer to please your honor? Look at Veronica, and see in her face what misery your honor has wrought, and then tell me, please, what master does honor serve." With a flick of her chin, she again indicated Cyrus. "Him?"

Veronica came to stand by Robert. "Listen to the girl, Robert, for she makes more sense than you clod-headed males. 'Tis time to talk of amends. This has gone on quite enough and I am weary of it."

There was utter silence. Robert looked first to Veronica, then back at Rosamund. Agravar winced when he saw blood trickling from her palms, down her arms to stain her sleeve. She was grasping the blade so hard it was cutting into her hands, yet she seemed oblivious.

Lucien came into view. He said, in as gentle a voice as Agravar ever heard from him, "Robert, she is right. This serves no purpose. No honor is lost here."

There was a long silence. Agravar's eyes were locked on the crimson stripes snaking down Rosamund's arms. He stayed perfectly still in obeisance of his reason, but his arms throbbed with the need to hold her.

"There is no honor in murder," Robert announced at last. He lowered his sword. "And I am a hypocrite to avenge a wrong that has hurt me not at all. I refuse to be a puppet to evil." He glanced up at Cyrus, then turned his back. "I am done with this."

Taking Rosamund's bloodied hands, Robert closed them in his own. "Agravar, come and take this child. I release her. When the church declares she is free, you shall marry her with my blessing."

Agravar moved, forcing himself to walk, not run, to her side. It seemed to take an eternity. Robert placed her wounded hands in Agravar's and stepped aside.

Rosamund gazed up at him, her brown eyes wide and clear. "I did it," she said with awe.

"You did, my most fearsome lady," Agravar said.

"I was so afraid."

"Never be afraid any longer. All your dangers are past."

She smiled, then. God, how he wanted to kiss her, but he held himself in check. To do so would be a tasteless insult to Robert's generosity.

"Come," Lucien called, "let us away from the battleground, lest I be tempted to treat this crowd to the bloodsport they've been cheated of. I can think of a pretty show I would like to give them." His dark eyes pinned Cyrus in his seat. "You, my lord, may take your leave. My soldiers will escort you to the boundaries of my lands. Be grateful I allow you your life."

"Crow all you like, de Montregnier, but you will rue the day you made an enemy of me. And you—" he turned to Agravar and Rosamund "—will beg for pity when I am through with you."

Putting Rosamund aside, Agravar's swift strides ate up the ground between him and Cyrus. "A threat heard plainly by one and all is ample cause for a challenge. Perhaps this crowd will get their entertainment this day."

Speaking low, Cyrus spit the words from between gritted teeth. "Are you forgetting my little arrangement? I promise you, my death will bring you no ease. Rather a host of my agents will descend upon you until every last one of my wishes is met. This earth will run red with the blood of Gastonbury."

Agravar looked droll. "My father was a man such as you. He was a Viking, a veritable warmonger among a race renowned for that occupation. He was very vile, very cruel, *and* very rich. We killed him, Lucien and I. I held him and Lucien sliced him in two."

To Agravar's satisfaction, Cyrus looked disconcerted. "What? Why do you tell me this?"

"We took his gold. Mountains of it, chests filled with jewels and coins and valuables beyond imagining. Cyrus—I am a very wealthy man."

Placing his booted foot on the board next to where Cyrus was seated, Agravar leaned in close. "I shall use every last piece of gold to buy off your minions. Far and wide will I spread the news that any assassin in your employ will find double his purse by coming to me in peace. Now I ask you, what man, no matter how twisted, would rather risk capture and execution for half the money he will win by becoming my friend?"

Cyrus's mouth worked, but no sound came out.

"It is brilliant, is it not? I must say so myself, even though my modesty, as all can attest, is one of my greatest virtues." He couldn't keep the gloating triumph from ringing in his voice. "I only regret my wit is not one as well. It took me far too long to realize such a simple solution."

Agravar stood and said in a sharp, clear voice, "I

call you out to a challenge, Cyrus. Right here and now. Grab your armor and meet me on the lists.''

He turned his back and called to his men. ''Ready my destrier. I will fight after all—''

There was a single, sharp pain exactly where Davey's blade had found him. The scars tore and agony took him over.

He went down on his knees, his gaze locked on Rosamund's puzzled face. ''Damn,'' he said. ''Ever since I met you, I have been felled more times than in the entirety of my life before. I think you are unlucky.''

''Agravar?''

He pitched forward.

Rosamund bent over Agravar, her hands swiftly assessing the damage. She was sobbing, screaming for Eurice, the healer, and she was covered in blood—her own and his. It mingled on her hands, making them slick.

A shadow blocked the sun and she started. Looking up, she saw Lucien charging toward her, his sword already raised.

She was confused. Why did Lucien come for her? Did he think she had done this?

Then she saw his blazing glare was fixed on a point just above her head, and she swung her gaze up to find Cyrus looming over her. His eyes were feverish, mad. Sensing the menace, she held her bloodied hands in front of her to ward him off.

Cyrus grabbed her by the hair, dragging her up and throwing her before him as a shield. The cold, sharp edge of steel pressed against her throat. The smell of blood was everywhere.

Alayna's voice sounded, calling a warning to her husband.

Lucien skidded to a stop just in front of Agravar's prone body.

Cyrus laughed, a short, sharp bark. "Step any closer and I shall cut this worthless serpent into shreds." He pushed her forward, advancing on Lucien. "Drop your weapon." Rosamund gasped as pain flared. Lucien's dark gaze flickered down to the knife and she saw the rapid tick at his temple. Heat tickled her skin just under the knife, and she realized Cyrus had cut her.

"Go around him," Cyrus spat in her ear. With Cyrus shoving her forward, she carefully skirted Agravar's prone body. The wound began to sting. The knife slipped, cutting deeper. A cry went up from the onlookers and Lucien twitched in indecision.

Out of the corner of her eye, she noticed a shadow stretching along the ground to her left. A familiar shape—large, broad-shouldered with a massive chest fitted with hard muscle.

She sobbed once, but the increased pressure of the knife stopped her. "Now," Cyrus said to Lucien, "do exactly as I say. The girl comes with me. I want my horse and my men assembled at the gates, and I want it done now."

Robert called out, bringing Cyrus's attention to the right, away from the encroaching shadow. "You cannot think to get away with this," Robert said.

"This girl belongs to me, since you do not want her. I admit my methods are crude, but I am within my rights. We all know a woman needs to be shown a little force now and then."

He stopped and Rosamund felt something wet and hot down her back. The knife fell away. She turned, amazed to find herself soaked in blood and suddenly free.

Across from her was Agravar, scarlet-tipped knife still in his hand. His other clutched his wound. But his eyes were on her.

At her feet, Cyrus's movements stilled. The ground around him darkened, and the darkness spread as life spilled out of him from the neat slice across his throat.

Agravar only spared him the briefest glance. "He was wearing on my nerves." Wiping off the knife on the hem of his tunic, he tossed it to a young knight. "My thanks, Pelly," he called. Grabbing Rosamund, he pulled her away from Cyrus's body and started up toward the keep.

"What are you doing?" she asked, too numb to assimilate the rapid chain of events.

"Well, I am bleeding and you are drenched in blood. I suggest we bathe—separately, I regret—and have our wounds dressed. And I may nap. I am tired. You are exhausting, do you know that? How many times do I have to rescue you?"

Then feeling returned to her limbs, to her soul, flooding her with relief. Around her were her friends, the women with wet faces and smiles, the men stunned but relaxed now that the danger had passed.

She laughed. "I shall do my best to keep them to a minimum in the future."

"See that you do," he replied. "I am getting too old for this."

Epilogue

Rosamund's dream left her at peace for a long, long time. When it came again, it was changed.

She sat up in the night with a gasp.

Beside her, the heavy form of her husband stirred.

"Rosamund?" Agravar asked.

Smoothing her hair back from her face, she answered, "Aye. I am fine."

"Is it the babe?"

"Nay."

He sat up beside her, his arm coming protectively around her shoulders. His free hand slid over the roundness of her belly. "You are not ill? Did you sleep?"

"I slept. I just awoke, that is all."

"Is the sickness back again?"

"Nay, Agravar. That was over months ago."

He stiffened. "The pains have not started yet, have they?"

Relaxing against the support he offered, she laughed. "Nay, nothing is amiss. Go back to sleep."

"Do you need some drink?"

"Very well," she conceded, knowing he would

not rest until he had done something that—at least in his own estimation—eased her discomfort.

His hair was wild from sleep. She watched him rise from the bed, his body flexing with tempered power. She could see every detail of his masculine form by the moonlight coming in through the open windows, and she gazed appreciatively as he went to the table by the empty hearth and poured her a glass of mulled wine.

It was late summer again. Six seasons had passed since their first meeting, and yet she could not still her heart when she looked at him.

On his way back to her, he tripped and the cup flew out of his hand. It landed on the rushes with a hollow sound and a splash, followed by Agravar's succinct curse.

Rosamund bit her cheeks. She knew quite well what ill had befallen her husband.

Agravar bent and picked up a small wooden sword. "This is the last time this happens," he growled.

"I agree." She tried very hard to look serious.

"He is careless with his toys."

"Aye. 'Tis true."

"I could have been crippled."

"Nay, not the mighty Agravar."

This appeased him. He grumbled something and fetched the cup, refilled it and brought it to her side. Taking it from him, she had to sip it under his watchful eye. She began to giggle.

"What is funny?" he asked.

"Nothing."

"Tell me."

"You. Look at you, hovering over me. You are silly for protecting me so much."

"I cannot help it," he defended. "When Lucien worried over Alayna, I thought him addled. Yet, I cannot keep myself from doing the same thing. Worry vexes my brain."

Reaching out a hand, she placed a slender palm against his cheek. "'Tis the third child. You should be well used to this by now."

He sighed. "The third one…'tis the most difficult of all. The first is too exciting, the second, you are still dazed, but by the third the possibilities of danger start to occur to you and you could go insane with it."

"Then it is settled."

He was puzzled. "Settled? What is settled?"

"This must be our last child. After the birth, then we must not lie together for—"

"If you think to tease me, I tell you that you are being too cruel." He grinned and stretched himself out on the bed. Taking in the fertile curves of her breast and belly, he murmured, "You know I cannot keep my hands off you."

"How can you look at me that way? I am bloated and misshapen."

"You are beautiful to me."

She fell silent, a quiet pleasure glowing in her chest. Agravar made a pile of pillows and insisted she recline.

"Try to return to sleep," he said, his voice betraying his own increasing grogginess.

"Agravar?"

"Hmm?"

"I had the dream again."

"Hmm."

"But 'twas different. This time, I heard her."

He raised his head. "Your mother?"

"Aye. Each time before when I was with child, while I carried our sons inside me, I worried that the dream would come to haunt me again. Seeing myself as she had been when she died, I thought was sure to bring it on again. It never happened, of course. I nearly forgot about it. I thought 'twould never return. But tonight it did."

He studied her for a moment. "You do not seem distressed."

"I am not. She said goodbye."

"I do not understand."

"The dream is a memory. It really happened. When I was a child, she came to my room. She bent over me, thinking I was asleep, and she whispered into my ear. All these years I could not remember what it was she said. It was an indistinct sound, blurred because, I believe, I could not accept the truth."

"And what is the truth, Rosamund?" He was watching her so closely, with worry etched on his handsome face.

She had to touch him. It never failed to thrill her, that this man was hers. Hers to touch, hers to love.

"She told me goodbye because she knew she would die that night. I always thought Cyrus killed her, but I think she went up to the ramparts by herself."

His eyebrows hiked up. "You think she jumped of her own will?"

"Do not sound horrified. And aye, I do. I know she did. I think I knew all along."

"Oh, my love, I am sorry."

"And yet 'tis not so horrible now to know it. She was unhappy, and she found her own way to freedom. But she had been driven to it. Cyrus did that, and he was responsible, as surely as if he had done the deed himself."

She thought for a moment, then continued, "In a way, 'tis almost all right. The sadness has faded. I mourned her for a long time and I think my dream protected me when I was too vulnerable to accept the truth. But now I have great happiness—" she smiled and Agravar pulled her close "—and am safe. And I have the oddest, most firm notion that the past cannot touch me any longer."

His finger touched the short thin line still visible at her neck. "There are the scars."

"Aye. They are there. But they trouble me not."

"That is my brave, fearsome lady." He kissed her brow and they lapsed into silence.

After a while, she began to giggle. He pulled back and gave her a wary look. "I fear this extreme moodiness is troubling. I recall how Alayna was so emotional in her last days of confinement with her third child, and I wonder if 'tis a common condition."

"Nay, 'tis not madness. I was thinking of our wedding day."

"And what precisely did you find funny in that?" Tightening his hold, he brought his lips to her ear and rumbled, "Surely not that night. I recall it well. Do you?"

She shivered and smiled. "Aye. But since you are possessed of such great modesty, as you have often told me, I know you are seeking no praise for that wondrous occasion.''

He growled and nuzzled her neck.

"What I thought was funny," she continued, chuckling and pulling away, "was the horrible wailing and gnashing of teeth that abounded in the chapel that day."

"Rosamund," he warned. "I have asked you not to mention those three women."

"Oh, husband, have a care not to become as serious as your lord." She held up her hands and rushed to add, "Whom I have come to appreciate as a good man. I know he is only fearsome in his looks, but that he has a very kind heart. 'Tis just that he is so...very...serious."

"I swear, I am ever in amazement at the workings of your mind. Pray tell what those three pudding-heads have to do with our conversation? Or Lucien, for that matter."

"Well, I was thinking of my mother and how the past is over and my life so different now."

"Different in a good way."

"Oh, most assuredly. And so thinking of such good and happiness brought you to mind, of course."

"Of course."

"And then for some reason, my mind harkened back to those poor girls who did not succeed in ensnaring the mighty Viking Agravar—"

"I wish you would cease calling me that."

"—and I remembered how they cried and sobbed and carried on all throughout the wedding ceremony."

He looked at her and grinned. "As I say, your brain is most facile."

"'Tis about time you noticed it. Your eyes seem perpetually apt to sink to a lower point of focus."

"Am I to blame if your breasts are magnificent?"

"Really, you are impossible."

They laughed and fell silent. After a while, they slept, still entwined in each other's arms.

That morning, Rosamund woke to the first pains of childbirth. They proceeded quickly and by midafternoon, she gave birth to their third child. A daughter.

They named her Isabella, after Rosamund's mother.

Their two boys, Brice and Ranulf, came to visit their sister, whom their father bore proudly to them for their inspection.

Brice, who was five, peered doubtfully at her and said, "She has not any teeth."

Ranulf, a bright four-year-old, added, "She's red and wrinkly."

Agravar looked over their blond heads to gaze in exasperation at their mother.

Rosamund held her hands out for her sons and they came hesitatingly to her side.

"'Tis all right," she said gently, and swept them to her. After a hearty hug, Brice turned around and squinted at the bundled babe his father had laid in the cradle. "I do not suppose she is all that bad," he said grudgingly.

Ranulf sidled up to gaze down at the tiny creature. "She's got no hair."

Brice nudged him. "Ow!" Ranulf cried, whirling angrily. Interpreting his brother's glance, he slumped his shoulders and said, "I guess she's pretty."

"Thank you, boys, for your kind approval of your

sister," Agravar said. His voice remained even, but the corners of his eyes crinkled.

His gaze darted to Rosamund. She was doing her best to look unamused. "You know, boys," she said, "your sister is going to need you two to look after her."

This brought both their heads up.

Agravar stepped in. "'Tis true. She is just a tiny thing, and when a girl grows up, she depends on her brothers for protection."

Their little chests puffed out.

Agravar hunkered down and looked both of them deeply in the eye. "By the time she is your age, why you will be pages and know all manner of knightly things, especially in chivalric matters. Your mother and I will be depending quite heavily on you to help Isabella."

Ranulf wrinkled his nose. "Isabella? What kind of na—"

He was cut off by Brice's elbow in his ribs. The elder leveled his large brown eyes at Agravar. "Aye, Father."

"You boys may go and play," Rosamund said. "Brice, your father has the sword you left in our chamber."

Agravar handed him the toy. "And if you leave it lying about again, you shall not get it back."

"Yes, father," he answered absently. "Thank you for finding it. I shall need it today. We are going to battle, you know."

"Battle, eh? With whom?"

"'Tis Aric, Luke, and us against the boys from the stables."

The two boys raced out, in high spirits.

"Do not hurt anyone," Rosamund called.

"Bloodthirsty little devils," Agravar muttered.

He turned and looked at his wife. Her eyes locked with his.

The sound of their laughter filled the room. They laughed until tears swelled in their eyes and their new daughter stirred and began whimpering.

They were forced to quiet their merriment, but continued to chuckle and giggle long after the babe was safely nuzzled against Rosamund's breast.

* * * * *

Take a romp through
Merrie Olde England
with four adventurous tales
from Harlequin Historicals.

In July 2000 look for

MALCOLM'S HONOR
by **Jillian Hart**
(England, 1280s)

LADY OF LYONSBRIDGE
by **Ana Seymour**
(England, 1190s)

In August 2000 look for

THE SEA WITCH
by **Ruth Langan**
(England, 1600s)

PRINCE OF HEARTS
by **Katy Cooper**
(England, 1520s)

**Harlequin Historicals
The way the past *should* have been!**

HARLEQUIN®
*M*akes any time special ™

The threat hit Agravar hard. Something about this man, the flat, cold eyes, the thin smile of absolute assurance, reminded him of another he had known. He believed that there existed men—like his own father, like this man—for whom no cruelty or injustice was forbidden, to whom power was all and death a toy to be used for a cause, or mere amusement.

His voice held a note of uncertainty when he replied, "I can keep my people safe."

"Ah, what a ridiculous boast. There are so many ways to kill. Poison, the slip of a knife in a crowd, a stray arrow during a hunt, a small child falls to a tragic end…ah, too many to mention now."

Fear flowered inside Agravar's chest. His lips curled, baring his teeth ferally.

Cyrus chuckled, seeing the response he had elicited. "It need not happen right away. I am a patient man, and I shall have eternity to wait upon my rewards. But you…imagine a whole life waiting for it to happen. And then it does. Imagine, then, knowing you were to blame for the death of one of those people in there whom you claim to love."

Agravar merely glared at him. "You would not…you could not."

"You know little of what I would dare." Cyrus jerked himself free of Agravar's grasp.

"What do you want?"

Brushing at the expensive fabric of his cloak where it had been crushed, Cyrus clucked with admonition. "Rosamund is quite resigned to her fate. You will do nothing to alter that. Nor will you meddle with Robert. Your interference, with either of them, will cost lives dear to you."

"Go to the devil."

"In due time. 'Tis the women in our blood, you know. It makes us weak. Oh, I almost forgot. Davey sent you a message." He grinned. "He wants you to know I am serious. *Deadly* serious. And he should know."

Agravar knew his meaning well enough. "You killed him. My God, man, he was just a boy."

"Boys, babes, women. It matters not. He was in my way." He narrowed his eyes and leaned in toward Agravar. "Do not get in my way, Viking bastard. Or you will know an anguish you cannot even imagine."

Frustrated, Agravar stood helpless. This kind of man he understood all too well.

When Agravar had gone to Denmark to find his sire, he had come to know pure greed and blistering malice. It was something he accepted like a cancerous blight—the existence of these creatures who lived only to destroy. He understood that Cyrus of Hallscroft was exactly like Hendron the Viking. And he was afraid.

Agravar swallowed hard. "Your madness sickens me."

"Aye, well, 'tis not your favor I am seeking." Cyrus laughed, and as he started to walk off, he said over his shoulder, "Do not attend the service. I have no desire to make a mockery of all this. In fact, absent yourself for the day. All will go much more smoothly without you being tempted to do something foolish. And do not see her again. Ever. If you do…well, I might decide a warning would be in order to show you how serious I am about this matter. The only problem I would have in doing it is deciding exactly *who* will die."